CHOOSE ME

CHOOSE ME

TESS GERRITSEN
GARY BRAVER

THORNDIKE PRESS
A part of Gale, a Cengage Company

Copyright © 2021 by Tess Gerritsen and Gary Braver.
Thorndike Press, a part of Gale, a Cengage Company.

Thorndike Press® Large Print Basic.
The text of this Large Print edition is unabridged.
Other aspects of the book may vary from the original edition.
Set in 16 pt. Plantin.

LIBRARY OF CONGRESS CIP DATA ON FILE.
CATALOGUING IN PUBLICATION FOR THIS BOOK
IS AVAILABLE FROM THE LIBRARY OF CONGRESS.

ISBN-13: 978-1-4328-8950-0 (hardcover alk. paper)

Published in 2021 by arrangement with Thomas & Mercer.

Printed in Mexico
Print Number: 01   Print Year: 2021

For Kathleen and Jacob

■ ■ ■ ■

AFTER

■ ■ ■ ■

CHAPTER 1
FRANKIE

There are dozens of ways to kill yourself, and in the course of her thirty-two years working for Boston PD, Detective Frances "Frankie" Loomis has probably come across them all. There was the mother of six, overwhelmed by the pandemonium of her household, who locked herself in a bathroom, slashed her wrists, and peacefully drifted unconscious in a bathtub of warm water. There was the bankrupt businessman who fastened his $500 ostrich-leather belt to a doorknob, looped the belt around his neck, and simply sat down, using his own weight to usher him down a painless road to oblivion. There was the over-the-hill actress, despondent over her dwindling prospects for new roles, who swallowed a handful of Dilaudid tablets, donned a pink silk nightgown, and stretched out on her bed, serene as Sleeping Beauty. They chose private, unspectacular exits and were considerate enough to leave behind a minimum of mess for the living to clean up.

Unlike this girl.

The body has already been bagged and removed by the ME, and the sidewalk, splattered with her blood, will eventually be washed clean by the falling rain, but Frankie can still see watery rivulets of it trickling toward the gutter. In the flashing rack lights of the police cruisers, those bloody streaks gleam as black as oil. It is now 5:45 a.m., an hour before sunrise, and she wonders how long the girl was lying here before the alert Lyft driver, passing by on his way home after dropping off his passenger at 3:15 a.m., spotted the body and realized it was not just a bundle of clothes on the sidewalk.

Frankie rises to her feet and peers up through the falling rain at the apartment balcony. It is a five-story drop straight down, clearly high enough to account for the trauma — the shattered teeth, the caved-in face. Gruesome details that probably didn't cross the girl's mind when she climbed over the railing and made her fatal swan dive onto the sidewalk below. Frankie is the mother of twin eighteen-year-old daughters, so she knows firsthand how catastrophically impulsive young people can

10

be. If only this girl had paused long enough to consider the alternatives to suicide. If only she'd thought about what happens to a body when it smashes into concrete and what such an impact does to a pretty face and perfect teeth.

"I think we're done here. Let's just go home," says her partner, MacClellan. He holds a pink umbrella that clearly belongs to his wife, and he is shivering beneath the dripping paisley dome. "My shoes are soaked."

"Has anyone found her cell phone?" she asks.

"Naw."

"Let's go back upstairs and check her apartment."

"Again?"

"Her phone has to be around here somewhere."

"Maybe she didn't have one."

"C'mon, Mac. Every kid her age has a phone practically grafted to their hands."

"Maybe she lost it. Or some asshole passing by here picked it up off the sidewalk after she fell."

Frankie looks down at the fading halo of blood, marking where the girl's head landed. Unlike a human body, a cell phone in a hard case can survive a five-story fall. Perhaps

11

Mac is right. Perhaps a passerby came upon the scene, a passerby whose first impulse wasn't to render aid or call the police but to snatch the victim's valuables. It should not surprise her; three decades as a cop have regularly shaken Frankie's faith in humanity.

She points across the street to a security camera mounted on the building that's facing them. "If someone did make off with her phone, that camera should have picked it up."

"Yeah. Maybe." Mac sneezes, clearly too miserable to care. "I'll pull the video in the morning."

"Let's go back upstairs. See if we missed anything."

"You know what I miss? My bed," Mac whines, but he resignedly follows her around the corner to the apartment building's entrance.

Like the building itself, the elevator is old and it's painfully slow. As it climbs to the fifth floor, both Frankie and Mac are too weary and dispirited to say a word. The cold weather has inflamed Mac's rosacea, and under the harsh elevator lights, his nose and cheeks are neon red. She knows he is sensitive about his condition, so she avoids looking at him and stares straight ahead, counting the floors until the door finally creaks open. A patrolman stands guarding the door to apartment 510, a numbingly boring task at this early hour, and he gives the two detectives a half-hearted wave. Yet another cop who'd rather be home in his own bed.

Inside the dead girl's apartment, Frankie once again searches the living room — but this time more carefully and with a mother's knowing eye. She's become adept at spotting the clues to her own daughters' misbehavior: the wet boots in the closet after they sneaked out one rainy night. The distinct scent of marijuana clinging to a cashmere sweater. The mysterious jump in mileage on the Subaru's odometer. The twins complain she's more like a prison guard than a cop, but that's probably why her girls have survived their turbulent adolescence. Frankie used to believe that if she could keep them both alive until adulthood, then she would have accomplished her job as a parent, but whom was she kidding? A parent's job never really ends. Even if she lives to be a hundred, her sixty-something daughters will still be keeping her awake at night.

It does not take long for Frankie to repeat her circuit of the apartment. It is a cramped unit, sparsely furnished with what look like thrift-store rejects. The sofa has clearly known more than a few owners, and the wood floor bears the scrapes and gouges from countless college-age tenants dragging furniture in and out. On the desk is an empty wineglass and a laptop, which Frankie has already powered on and discovered is password protected. Beside it is the printed draft of an essay for a class at Commonwealth University: "Hell Hath No Fury: Violence and the Scorned Woman."

It was written by the girl who lived here. The girl who is now on her way to a refrigerated drawer in the morgue.

Frankie and Mac have already combed through the girl's purse, and in her wallet they found a Commonwealth student ID card, a Maine driver's license, and eighteen dollars in cash. They know she is twenty-two years old; her hometown is Hobart, Maine; and she is five feet, six inches tall, weighs 122 pounds, and has brown hair and eyes.

Frankie moves into the kitchen, where they earlier found a single serving of Marie Callender's mac and cheese in the microwave, lukewarm but unopened. Frankie finds it strange that the girl heated up a meal that she then never ate. What happened in the interim that made her turn

14

away from her meal, walk out to her balcony, and jump to her death? Bad news? A distressing phone call? On the countertop lies a college textbook with a woman's face on the cover, a woman with hair aflame, her mouth open in an angry roar.

Medea: The Woman behind the Myth.

Frankie knows she should be familiar with the myth of Medea, but her college years are decades behind her, and all she recalls is that it has something to do with vengeance. Inside the textbook, she finds a letter tucked under the flyleaf. It's an acceptance letter to the graduate program in the fall, sent from the Department of English at Commonwealth University.

Yet another detail that puzzles Frankie.

She returns to the balcony door, which is now closed. When the building supervisor first let them into the apartment, this door was wide open, and rain and sleet had blown in. Water still sparkles on the wood floor. She opens the door, steps outside, and stands under the shelter of the overhanging balcony above. Two Boston PD cruisers are parked below, the hypnotic flash of their rack lights reflected in the windows across the street. In another hour it will be daylight, the cruisers will be gone, and the sidewalk will be washed clean by rain. Pedestrians

15

will never know they are walking across the spot where only hours ago a young woman's life flickered out.

Mac joins her on the balcony. "Looks like she was a pretty girl. What a waste," he sighs.

"If she were ugly, it'd still be a waste, Mac."

"Yeah, okay."

"And she was just accepted to grad school. The acceptance letter's on the kitchen counter."

"Shit, really? What the hell goes through a kid's head?"

Frankie looks out at the silvery sheets of rain. "I ask myself that question all the time."

"At least your girls have their heads screwed on right. They'd never do something like this."

No, Frankie cannot imagine it. Suicide is a form of surrender, and her twins are fighters, iron willed and rebellious. She peers down at the street. "God, it's a long drop."

"I'd rather not look, thank you."

"She must have been desperate."

"So you're ready to call it suicide?"

Frankie stares at the street, trying to identify what is bothering her. Why her instincts are whispering: *You missed something. Don't turn away yet.*

16

"Her cell phone," she says. "Where is it?"

There's a knock on the door. They both turn as the patrolman pokes his head into the apartment. "Detective Loomis? Got a neighbor out here. You want to speak to her?"

Standing in the hallway is a young Asian woman who tells them she lives in the apartment next door. Judging by her bathrobe and flip-flops, she's just rolled out of bed, and she keeps glancing at the dead girl's apartment, as if the closed door hides some unimaginable horror.

Frankie pulls out her notepad. "And your name is?"

"Helen Ng. That's spelled *N-G*. I'm a student at Commonwealth. Like her."

"Did you know your neighbor very well?"

"Just in passing. I moved into this building only five months ago." She pauses, looking at the closed door. "God, I can't believe it."

"That she'd take her own life?"

"That it happened right *next door.* When my parents hear about this, they're going to go nuts. Make me move back home with them."

"Where do they live?"

"Just down the road in Quincy. They wanted me to save money and commute to school, but that's not a real college experience. It's not like having your own apartment and —"

"Tell us about your neighbor," Frankie cuts in.

Helen thinks about this and gives a helpless shrug. "I know she's — she was — a senior. Comes from some little town up in Maine. She was pretty quiet, for the most part."

"Did you hear anything unusual last night?"

"No. But I have this cold, so I popped a few Benadryls. I woke up just a little while ago, when I heard the police radio in the hallway." Helen glances again at the apartment. "Did she leave a note or anything? Did she say why she did it?"

"Do *you* know why?"

"Well, she *did* seem depressed a few weeks ago, after she broke up with her boyfriend. But I thought she got over that."

"Who was her boyfriend?"

"His name's Liam. I've seen him here a few times, before they broke up."

"You know his last name?"

"I don't remember, but I know he's from her hometown. He goes to Commonwealth too." Helen pauses. "Have you called her mother? Does she know?"

18

Frankie and Mac exchange looks. This is a call neither one of them wants to make, and Frankie knows exactly how Mac will palm off the task. *You're a woman; you're better at this sort of thing* is his usual excuse. Mac has no children, so he can't imagine, the way Frankie can imagine, the heartbreak of getting such news. He can't imagine how hard these calls are for her to make.

Mac has also been jotting down the information, and he looks up from his notes. "So this ex-boyfriend's name is Liam, he's from Maine, and he attends Commonwealth."

"That's right. He's a senior."

"He shouldn't be too hard to track down." He closes his notebook. "That should do it," Mac says, and Frankie can read the look he gives her. *Boyfriend left her. She was depressed. What more do we need?*

After leaving the death scene, Frankie needs to go home. She needs to take a shower, eat breakfast, and say hello to her twins — if they're even awake yet. But on her way home to Allston, she can't help but make a detour. It's only a few blocks out of her way, and most days she's able to resist the compulsion to see the building again, but this morning her Subaru seems to veer off course of its own accord, and once again

19

she finds herself parked across the street from the brick building in Packard's Corner, staring up at the fourth-floor apartment where the woman still lives.

Frankie knows the woman's name and where she works and how many parking tickets she's racked up. These facts should not really matter to her anymore, but they do. She's shared these details with no one else — not with her colleagues in the homicide unit, not even with her own daughters. No, this knowledge she keeps private, because the fact she even knows about this woman's existence is too damn humiliating.

So Frankie sits alone in her car on this drizzly April morning, watching an apartment building she has no legitimate reason to be watching, except to torment herself. Everyone assumes she's recovered from the tragedy and moved on with her life. Her daughters have graduated from high school with honors, and during this gap year they're both happy and thriving. Her colleagues at Boston PD no longer avoid her gaze or look at her with pity. That pity was the worst part of it — having her fellow cops, right down to the patrol officers, feeling sorry for her. No, her life is back to normal — or has assumed some semblance of it.

Yet here she is, parked once again in Packard's Corner.

A woman emerges from the building, and Frankie jerks to attention. She watches as the woman crosses the street and walks past Frankie's vehicle, obviously unaware she is being watched, but Frankie is certainly aware of *her.* The woman is fair haired, bundled up against the cold in black leggings and a white down jacket that is formfitting enough to reveal a narrow waist and slim hips. Frankie used to have a figure like that, back in the days before the twins arrived. Before middle age and too many hours sitting at her desk and too many meals wolfed down in a rush expanded her hips, ballooned out her thighs.

In the rearview mirror, Frankie watches the woman walk away toward the T station. She thinks about getting out of her car and following her. Thinks about introducing herself and suggesting they have a civilized little chat, woman to woman, perhaps at the coffee shop down the street, but she cannot bring herself to step out of the car. In Frankie's long career as a cop, she's kicked open doors, tracked down killers, and twice stared down the barrel of a gun, yet she cannot bring herself to confront Ms. Lorraine Conover, age forty-six, a sales clerk at Macy's with no criminal record.

The woman walks around the corner and disappears from sight.

Frankie slumps back in her seat, not yet ready to start the engine, not ready to face what other horrors this day will bring.

One dead girl is bad enough.

■ ■ ■ ■

BEFORE:
THREE MONTHS
EARLIER

■ ■ ■ ■

CHAPTER 2
TARYN

No one knew she was there. No one ever would.

At nine thirty in the morning, all the tenants on the second floor should be out of the building. The Abernathys in apartment 2A, who used to be annoyingly friendly with Taryn, by now would have left for their jobs, his in the City of Boston's Auditing Department, hers in the Office of Neighborhood Development. The two engineering grad students who lived in 2B should be somewhere on campus, huddled over their laptops. The blondes in 2C should have shaken off their usual weekend hangovers and stumbled off to classes at Commonwealth.

No one should be home in 2D either. By now, Liam was headed to his econ class on the far side of campus, a fifteen-minute walk away. After econ he had German III, then he'd eat lunch, probably his usual sub sandwich with extra jalapeños in the student union, and then it would be poli-sci. Taryn knew every detail of his schedule, just as she knew every inch of this apartment.

She turned the key, quietly pushed open the door, and stepped inside 2D. It was larger and so much nicer than her own crappy apartment, which smelled like mildew and old pipes. Here, when she took a deep breath, what she smelled was *him.* The velvety steam that still lingered after his morning shower. The citrus notes of his Sauvage aftershave. The yeasty scent of the whole wheat toast he always ate for breakfast. All the smells she missed so much.

Everywhere she looked brought back a happy memory. There was the sofa where they used to spend Saturday nights watching cheesy horror flicks, her head nestled against his shoulder, his arm draped around her. There was the bookshelf where their photo had once been prominently displayed. In that photo, taken the summer they'd both graduated from high school, they were standing on Bald Rock Mountain with their arms around each other, his windblown blond hair lit up like a golden halo in the sunlight. Liam and Taryn, forever. Where was that photo now? Where had he hidden it?

She went into the kitchen and remembered their Sunday-morning pancakes and mimosas mixed with cheap cava because real champagne was too expensive. On the kitchen counter was the stack of yesterday's mail, the envelopes already slit open. She read the note sent by his mother, along with the clipping from their hometown newspaper. Dr. Howard Reilly, Liam's father, had received the town's new Citizen of the Year award. Whoop-de-do. She flipped through the rest of his mail — a rent bill, an envelope of pizza coupons, and a credit card application. At the bottom of the stack was a thick brochure for Stanford Law School. Why was he looking at Stanford? She knew he was applying to law schools, but not once had he ever mentioned going to California. They'd already agreed that after graduation, they would both stay in Boston. That was their pact. It was what they'd always planned.

It was just a brochure. It didn't mean anything.

She opened the refrigerator and surveyed old friends on the shelves: sriracha and Hellmann's mayonnaise and Yoo-hoo. But among these familiar condiments lurked an alien invader: Chobani yogurt, low fat. This should not be here. In all the years she'd known Liam, she'd never seen him eat yogurt. He despised it. The sight of this anomaly was so unnerving it made her wonder if she'd accidentally walked into the wrong apartment and opened the wrong refrigerator. If she'd wandered into a parallel universe where an imposter Liam resided, a Liam who ate yogurt and was planning to move to California.

Unsettled, she went into the bedroom, where, on weekend nights, their cast-off clothes used to lie tangled like lovers on the floor, his shirt flung across her blouse. Here, too, something was not right. His bed was made, the sheets neatly tucked in and squared off in hospital corners, the proper way one made a bed. When had he learned to make hospital corners? When had he ever made his own bed? She always used to do it for him.

She opened his closet and surveyed the shirts lined up on hangers, some of them still draped in plastic from the laundry service. She plucked up a sleeve and pressed her face to the crisp cotton, remembering all the times she used to rest her head against his shoulder. But these freshly laundered shirts smelled only of soap and starch. Anonymous smells.

She closed the closet door and went into the bathroom.

In the toothbrush holder, where hers also used to perch, his toothbrush now stood alone and forlorn, missing its mate. She lifted the lid to the laundry hamper, dug through the dirty clothes, and pulled out a T-shirt. She buried her face in it, and the scent intoxicated her. He had so many other T-shirts; he would never miss this one. She stuffed it into her backpack to keep as her secret Liam fix, something to tide her over while they played out this farce of "taking a break from each other." Surely their separation wouldn't last much longer. They'd been together so long that they'd grown into a single organism, their flesh melded, their lives forever bound. He just needed time to realize how much he missed her.

She stepped out into the hallway and quietly pulled the door shut. Except for stealing his T-shirt, she'd left everything in his apartment exactly as she'd found it. He wouldn't know she'd been here; he never did.

Outside an icy wind swept between the buildings, and she pulled up the hood of her jacket, wound her scarf more tightly. She'd lingered here for far too long; if she didn't hurry, she'd be late for class. But she couldn't help pausing on the sidewalk to take one last look at his apartment.

That was when she noticed the face gazing down at her from the window. It was one of the blondes in 2C. Why wasn't she already on campus, where she was supposed to be? While Taryn had been rummaging through Liam's apartment, this woman was still at home. They stared at each other, and Taryn wondered if the other woman had heard her moving about in the rooms next door. Would she tell Liam about the visit?

Taryn's heart was thudding as she walked away. Maybe the blonde hadn't heard her. Even if she had, she'd have no reason to mention it to Liam. Taryn used to spend every weekend here with him and had been in the building dozens of times before.

No, there was no reason to panic. No reason to think he'd ever know.

She picked up her pace. If she hurried, she could still make it to class on time.

CHAPTER 3
JACK

Her name was Taryn Moore, and she slunk into Professor Jack Dorian's life on the first day of the semester, entering the seminar room dressed in a silver bomber jacket and shiny black tights that lacquered the bottom half of her body. They were already ten minutes into the class, and she murmured an apology as she squeezed her way past the other students crammed into the small room and took the last open seat at the conference table. Jack could not help registering how alluring she was as she slid into her chair, her figure as lithe as a dancer's, her windblown dark hair with reddish highlights. She settled beside a chubby guy in a Red Sox cap, set her notebook on the table, and fixed Jack with a look so direct that for a fleeting moment he nearly forgot what he'd been saying.

There were fifteen in the class, all that could comfortably fit into the English

Department's cramped seminar room. The group was small enough for Jack to soon commit their names to memory.

"And you are?" he asked, glancing down at the list of students enrolled in his Star-Crossed Lovers seminar. It was an admittedly gimmicky name for the course he'd created, exploring the theme of doomed love in literature from antiquity to the present day. What better way to entice jaded college seniors to read *The Aeneid, The Romance of Tristan and Iseult, Medea,* or *Romeo and Juliet* than to wrap it all up in a sexy package of love, lust, and ultimate tragedy? What unlucky circumstances led to the lovers' deaths? What religious, political, and societal forces doomed their romances?

"Taryn Moore," she said.

"Welcome, Taryn," he said, adding a check mark to the name. He found where he'd left off in his notes and continued the lecture, but he was still distracted by the woman at the end of the table. Maybe that was why he avoided looking at her. Even then, on that very first day, some instinct must have warned him to be careful.

Four weeks into the semester, his instincts proved right.

They were discussing the twelfth-century letters of Abelard and Heloise. Abelard was older, a famous philosopher and theologian at Notre Dame. Heloise was his intellectually gifted student. Despite a host of social and religious taboos forbidding their romance, Abelard and Heloise became lovers. Pregnant with Abelard's child, Heloise retreated in scandal to a convent. Her uncle exacted a brutal punishment on her lover: he hired henchmen to castrate the unlucky Abelard, who was later exiled to a monastery. Although forever separated, the lovers kept their romance alive through the letters they wrote to each other, documenting the heartbreak of two star-crossed lovers who were doomed to never again touch.

"Their letters reveal fascinating details about monastic life in the Middle Ages," Jack said to the class. "But it's their tragic love story that makes these letters so poignant and timeless. Tragedy defined them, and their suffering in the name of love rendered them heroic. But do you see their sacrifices as equal? Which of the lovers stands out as more heroic?"

Beth, her expression serious as always, raised her hand. "I thought what made Heloise especially impressive, given the norms for women back then, was her continuing defiance." She looked down at her text. "She writes from the convent that as others are 'wedded to God, I am wedded to a man' and 'I am the slave to Abelard alone.' This was a strong-minded woman who defied the taboos of the time. I'd say *she's* the real hero."

He nodded. "And she never gave up on her love for him."

"She says she'd even follow Abelard into the flames of hell. That's true devotion."

Jason piped up: "I can't even get my girlfriend to follow me to a Bruins game."

The class burst out laughing. Jack was happy to see everyone engaged in lively discussion, unlike those dispiriting days when he had to do all the talking and his students merely stared at him with bored and glassy eyes, like carp in a pond.

Jason continued. "I also liked how Heloise writes about having sexual fantasies while she's in Mass. Man, I can identify with that! Divine litany in Greek churches runs a whole two hours. That's long enough for me to get it on with a dozen girls. In my head, anyway."

More laughter. That was when Taryn caught Jack's eye. She'd been scribbling copious notes, and now she raised her hand.

"Yes, Taryn?" he said.

"I have an issue with this story. And the others you've assigned as well," she said.

"Oh?"

"There seems to be a theme going on here with the stories you've introduced so far. And it's that the men invariably betray the women they claim to love. Heloise gives up everything for love. Yet most scholars celebrate Abelard as the true hero."

He heard passion behind her words, and he nodded for her to continue.

"Abelard even depicts himself as some sort of romantic hero because of his suffering, but I don't see him that way at all. Yes, it's terrible that he was castrated. But while Heloise keeps their flame alive, Abelard eventually renounces all his sexual feelings for her. He voluntarily chooses piety over love, while she *never* surrenders her passion for him."

"Excellent point," he told her, and he meant it. Clearly Taryn had thought about what she'd read, and she dug deeper than the other students, many of whom did only the bare minimum to complete their assignments. Her insights and intellectual enthusiasm made teaching a pleasure. In fact, students like her were why he taught. He wished he had more like her. "You're right, she does hold on to her passion, while he chooses to walk in the footsteps of saints and renounce the pleasures of the flesh."

"That makes him sound so noble," she continued, "but think of what Heloise gave up. Her freedom, her youth. Her own child. Imagine the despair she felt when she writes, 'I was just your whore.' It's as if she realizes he's discarded her and left her to rot in a convent."

"Oh, come on!" Jessica snorted. "She gets stuck in the convent because of social and religious pressures. He didn't make her go there."

Caitlin, her roommate seated next to her, nodded mechanically in agreement. Jack didn't understand why, but the pair always seemed hostile to Taryn, exchanging glances and rolling their eyes whenever she made some insightful remark. Jealousy, perhaps.

"Not true," Taryn responded. She turned to the relevant page in her book. "Heloise writes, 'It was your command only which sent me into these cloisters.' She did it for *him*. She did everything for him. It's obvious to anyone who actually read the material."

Jessica reddened. "I read the letters!"

"I never said you didn't."

"You implied it."

"Look, the letters are densely written. Maybe you just missed their point."

Jessica turned toward Caitlin and whispered, "What a bitch."

"Jessica?" Jack said. "Did I hear you right?"

She looked him straight in the eye and said with an innocent smile: "I didn't say anything." But clearly the others had heard her as well, because they all looked uncomfortable.

"There's no place in this classroom for personal attacks. Is that clear?" he said.

Jessica responded by silently staring straight ahead.

"Jessica?"

"Whatever."

It was time to move past this little tiff. He turned to Taryn. "You said Abelard betrayed Heloise. Care to expand on that?"

"She's given up everything for him. She needs his comfort, his reassurance that he loves her. And what does he do? He tells her to embrace the cross. I think he reveals himself as a heartless jerk, claiming to have suffered more than she did."

Jason said: "Well, he did have his balls cut off."

The laughter was a welcome respite from the tension, but he noticed Jessica didn't join in. She and Caitlin had their heads tilted together, whispering.

He needed to hear new voices, so he

looked at Cody Atwood, who as usual was sitting beside Taryn. He was a shy kid who perennially seemed to hide under his baseball cap, sometimes pulled so low that no one could see his eyes. "What do you think, Cody?" Jack asked.

"I, um . . . I think Taryn's right."

"He always does," Jessica said. She turned to Caitlin and whispered, "Loser."

Jack chose to let it pass, because no one else seemed to have heard the insult.

"I just agree with Taryn that Abelard's kind of a jerk," said Cody. "He's her teacher, and he's twice as old as she is. That makes him even more of a jerk, taking advantage of his student."

"And that's the same dynamic we see echoed in later literary works. Think of Philip Roth's *The Human Stain* and Jonathan Franzen's *The Corrections.* And I'm sure many of you have read *Gone Girl.* These stories all explore how an older teacher might fall in love with a student."

"Just like in *Hot for My Prof,*" Jason said.

"What?"

"Oh, it's just this cheesy YA romance."

Jack smiled. "Funny how I missed that one."

"So is that the real theme of this class, Professor?" Jessica said. "Teachers getting it on with hot students?"

He stared at her for a moment, sensing they'd wandered into dangerous territory. "I'm just pointing out that this is a theme that recurs in literature. These stories illustrate how and why a situation that's forbidden by society can happen. They show us that anyone, even the morally righteous, can be drawn into a disastrous sexual affair."

Jessica smiled, eyes glittering. "*Anyone,* Professor?"

"We're talking about fiction, Jessica."

"Really, what's the big deal if a teacher falls in love with a willing student?" said Jason. "It's not like there's a law against it in the Ten Commandments. *Thou shalt not get it on with hot coeds.*"

"But there *is* a commandment against adultery," Beth pointed out.

"Abelard wasn't married," said Taryn. "Anyway, why are we hung up on this point? We're getting off the subject."

"I agree," Jack said and glanced at the clock. He was relieved to see the hour was nearly over. "Okay, I've got a little announcement, and I think you'll like this. In two weeks, the Museum of Fine Arts opens a special exhibit of illustrations inspired by Heloise and Abelard. They've agreed to give our class a personal tour. Instead of meeting here, we'll have a field trip at the MFA. Be sure to mark your calendars, and I'll also send out an email to remind you. But next week, we meet here as usual. And be ready to discuss *The Aeneid*!"

While students filed out of the room, he gathered his notes and slid them into his briefcase. He didn't notice that Taryn was standing right beside him until she spoke.

"I can't wait for the field trip, Professor Dorian," she said. "I've seen some of the images on the museum's website, and it looks like a beautiful exhibition. Thanks for arranging it."

"Of course. By the way, you did a great job on your Medea paper last week. It's the best paper I've read all semester. In fact, it has the level of sophistication I'd expect of graduate students."

Her face lit up. "Really? You mean that?"

"Yes. It's quite thoughtful and very well crafted."

By reflex she gripped his arm like he was a close friend. "Thank you. You're the best."

He nodded and gave his arm a twitch, and she pulled her hand free.

He suddenly noticed Jessica watching from the doorway, and he did not like the look in her eyes. Nor did he like the obviously sexual gesture she gave to Caitlin as Taryn walked out, one finger thrusting in and out of her fist. Caitlin giggled, and they both left the room.

Jessica's paper had been worse than mediocre, and he'd found it immensely satisfying to scrawl a C-minus on it.

He closed the briefcase with a loud thud, more disturbed by Jessica's obscene gesture than he cared to admit. Only when the classroom had completely emptied did he finally pull on his coat, and he walked out alone into the cold January wind.

CHAPTER 4
JACK

As usual, Maggie was late. She showed up at the restaurant a little after six thirty, looking harried and windblown, but with a big smile on her face as she hustled to their table and gave her father a big hug, then air-kissed Jack.

"So how's God's gift to medicine?" her father, Charlie, said.

Maggie pulled off her jacket, hung it over her chair, and sank into the seat like a deflating weather balloon. "Exhausted. I don't think I sat down once all afternoon. It's this cruddy virus going around. Everyone wants me to prescribe antibiotics, and I have to talk them out of it." She flagged down the waitress for a chardonnay, then took Charlie's hand. "And how's my favorite birthday boy?"

"Feeling a lot more celebratory now that you're here."

"We've been waiting for forty minutes,"

Jack said, trying not to sound sour. He had picked up Charlie on the way to the restaurant and had been watching the clock while they'd sat here making small talk. He was already on his second glass of wine.

"Jack, she's got the best excuse in the world," Charlie said. "All those sick people who need her."

"Thank you, Dad." Maggie flashed her husband a so-there look.

"And you're lucky to have her, boyo," Charlie added. "You ever get sick, you have your own personal doctor in the house."

"Yeah, I am lucky," Jack conceded and took a sip of pinot noir to quell his annoyance. "At least tonight, we'll actually get to eat dinner together."

"Speaking of dinner," Charlie said, rubbing his hands together, "let's get on with the pig-out. I've been looking forward to this meal all year. If there is a God, he doesn't have a cholesterol problem."

Every year, the three of them celebrated Charlie's birthday with what he called their "pig-out," gorging on all the menu options forbidden by his doctor. Dino's Steer House was an old-fashioned steak joint that had been in business for more than half a century, and while other restaurants in town had turned haute cuisine, Dino's had no

43

such pretensions. It still served steaks, burgers, and heart-stopping sides like porky sticks — a mountain of french fries covered with a thick cheese sauce topped with bacon bits and sour cream.

"Happy birthday, Pops," said Maggie, clinking her wineglass against his beer. "And look what I have for you." From her brief-case she removed a package wrapped in shiny red paper with a large golden bow.

"Ah, darlin', you shouldn't have brought me anything," he said, but his eyes sparkled as he took the gift. He struggled to unwrap it without destroying the paper, painstak-ingly slicing the adhesive tape with a steak knife.

"They close at nine thirty," Jack said to Charlie.

With a chuckle, Charlie ripped off the paper in one swoop and beamed at the box partitioned with various roasted artisanal nuts from Fastachi. Charlie loved nuts. He leaned over and hugged Maggie. "You're the best, kiddo. And my doctor says nuts are great for my heart." He gave Jack a wink. "But you can't have any. They're mine, all mine!"

Maggie's phone dinged with a text mes-sage. Jack sighed. She was a primary care physician at Mount Auburn Hospital in

Cambridge, and they never made it through a meal without that damn phone dinging or ringing or buzzing — if she made it home for a meal at all.

The waitress came to take their orders, and even as Maggie asked for a jumbo sirloin cheeseburger, she was scrolling through her text messages.

"And you, sir?" the waitress asked Jack.

"If you order salmon," Charlie said, "you're a disgrace to your Armenian heritage."

Jack ordered the shish kebab.

The waitress turned to Charlie. "And what will you have?"

"My doctor's got me on this blasted five-low diet." And he counted on his fingers. "Low fat, low salt, low sugar, low meat, low taste. So bring me a medium-rare heifer with mozzarella sticks, and a side of melted bacon fat for dipping."

The woman snickered. "I'm afraid heifer's not on the menu."

"Then how 'bout barbecued ribs and porky sticks? Oh, and fried mozzarella for an appetizer. It's my birthday."

"Is it? Well, happy birthday!"

"You wanna guess how old I am?"

The woman screwed up her face, not

wanting to insult him. "I'd say fifty, fifty-five."

"Not even close. I'm thirty-seven."

The waitress's eyebrows shot up. "Thirty-seven?"

"Celsius. You get to be my age, you go metric." He winked as the woman left, still snickering.

Most of the time Charlie's face was hard to read, a fixed and expressionless mask that hid whatever emotions were roiling inside him. It was a face made for interrogations. Before he'd retired seven years before, Charlie had been a detective in the Cambridge PD. Jack often imagined criminals squirming under the glare of those flat blue eyes, set in a face that gave no clues — an inscrutable, emotionless Easter Island blank that could make even a saint confess to murder.

But tonight Charlie was all grins and twinkling eyes as he and Maggie traded their usual father-daughter banter. Watching them together, Jack missed the evenings when he and Maggie used to share their own affectionate banter. The evenings before she'd started dragging herself home exhausted from the clinic, too hollowed out for conversation. It didn't seem that long ago when Maggie and Jack would have dinner around six thirty — dinners prepared together or by whoever got home first. Or they'd go out to a favorite restaurant or on a warm night drive to Kelly's on Revere Beach for lobster rolls. With the exception of special nights like tonight, dinners were takeouts now, or they ate separately — she at the hospital and Jack at the Subway down the street from their home. Maggie's cell phone buzzed again. She frowned at the screen, then tapped the button that sent the call to voice mail.

"Maybe you could turn that off while we eat?" Jack suggested, trying his best not to show his irritation. With a sigh, she slipped her phone into her handbag.

"Happy birthday!" the waitress said, sliding their plates onto the table.

"And what a happy day it is," Charlie said, beaming at the rack of ribs, dark and glistening with apricot glaze, and the bowl of fries piled high with melted cheese and studded with bacon chips.

Maggie eyed the intimidating burger on her plate, oozing with cheese. "I haven't eaten one of these monstrosities since your last birthday, Dad."

Charlie grinned and tucked a napkin into his shirt. "I know this is supposed to be bad for me. So maybe you should call an ambu-

47

lance to wait outside with the motor running. If I go into cardiac arrest, I want that cute little waitress to give me mouth to mouth." He snatched up the steak knife and suddenly paused, wincing.

"You okay, Dad?" Maggie asked.

"Except for this ice pick in my back."

"What do you mean?"

"It feels like someone's stabbing me between the shoulder blades. I hate when that happens."

Maggie set down her drink. "How long have you had this pain?"

"A few weeks." He gave a careless wave. "It comes and goes. Just a nuisance, really."

"Maybe you pulled a muscle at the gym," Jack said. Charlie worked out regularly at Gold's in Arlington Heights and had always been in superb physical shape, bicycling sixty miles or more a week when the weather permitted. Even at seventy, his arms were as thick as hams.

"Have you seen your doctor about it?" Maggie asked.

"He said it's just a muscle strain."

"Did he prescribe anything?"

"Just Tylenol. Maybe I should see a chiropractor."

"God, no," Maggie said. "You know what I think of chiropractors. At your age, you

48

probably have a degenerative disk or two. The last thing you want is someone jerking around your spine. You should get an MRI."

"What'll that show?"

"Maybe a herniated disk pinching a nerve."

"Hmph. I figured it was just from getting older."

"I'll give your doctor a call. See if he can at least get you in for x-rays."

Charlie slapped his chest. "Uh-oh. Old-guy alert! Where's that waitress? I need mouth to mouth stat!"

Maggie sighed. "Good try, Dad."

Even though her phone was tucked inside her purse, they could all hear it ringing. She couldn't help herself; she pulled it out, looked at the caller's number, and immediately rose to her feet.

"Sorry, but I have to take this one." She cupped the phone to her ear and headed outside.

"Those patients of hers should be grateful," Charlie said. "I don't think my doctor even knows me by name. I'm just another seventy-year-old white male."

"Hmm."

Charlie dipped a mozzarella stick in sauce and took a bite. "Now there's a discouraging sound. What's up with you, Jack?"

49

"I didn't say anything."

"But I can hear you thinking. Are you two okay?"

"What do you mean?"

Charlie looked at him with that maddeningly unreadable face. "Jack, I spent my career talking to people who were trying to hide stuff."

Charlie was like a seismograph, sensitive enough to pick up even the slightest tectonic tremor, and his gaze was so intent Jack could almost feel it burrowing into his brain. "It's her job, that's all."

"What about her job?"

"The work is so all-consuming."

"She's dedicated to her patients. She has a booming practice. Of course it keeps her busy."

"I know, and I'm proud of her. But lately it feels like we're just ships passing in the night."

"It's the nature of the beast," Charlie said. "Part of being married to a professional. All doctors should be like her."

How could Jack argue with that? At their wedding, his friends had congratulated him for landing a woman who was not only a looker but also a future physician who'd be bringing home fat paychecks. They didn't know about the insane hours the job required. These days, they scarcely watched TV together.

"Maybe she could cut down her hours a bit."

"I wish she could. But when a patient needs you . . ." Jack's voice trailed off before he finished the sentence: *your husband comes second.*

He saw no sympathy in Charlie's face, and why should he? Maggie was his perfect, brilliant little girl; Jack was the guy who'd stolen her away, a guy who spent his days teaching a course called Star-Crossed Lovers.

Maggie returned to the table and sat down. "Sorry about the interruption."

"Everything okay?" Charlie asked.

"I have a very sick patient. She's only forty-three years old, with three young children. And she's dying."

"Jesus," said Charlie.

"Ovarian cancer is the pits." Maggie took a deep breath and rubbed a hand across her face. "It's been a long day. I'm sorry to put a damper on your birthday."

"Maggie, nothing you do will ever ruin my day. You want to talk about it?"

"Not really. I'd rather talk about happy things."

"You're just like your mother, you know

51

that? Never once a discouraging word, right up until the day she died. You look more like her every day."

Jack watched as father and daughter joined hands on the table, a connection forged long before he'd ever met Maggie. He didn't resent their closeness, but he did envy it. And he wished, not for the first time, that one day he'd know just such a bond with his own child.

If they ever had a child.

When they walked out of the restaurant later that night, a light snow was falling. Jack dropped off Charlie at his house, and by the time he arrived home, the snow had changed to sleet. He found Maggie sitting in the kitchen, looking haggard and far older than her thirty-eight years.

"I'm sorry about your patient," he said and wrapped his arms around her. He meant only to comfort her, but he could feel her stiffen at the embrace.

She pulled away. "Please, Jack," she whispered. "Not now."

"It's only a hug. I'm not asking to make love."

"I'm sorry. I just can't tell anymore."

"And would it be so awful if I did want to make love to my wife? It's been so long since we . . ."

"I'm tired." Already she was moving away from him.

"Maggie, is it me?" he called to her. "I can handle the truth, so just tell me. Is it something I've done or haven't done?" He paused, afraid to ask the question but needing to know. "Is there someone else?"

"What? Oh God, Jack, no. It's nothing like that. All I want to do right now is take a shower and go to sleep." She slipped away and headed up the stairs to their bedroom.

He went into the living room, turned off the lights, and for a few moments sat in the dark, listening to sleet pelt the window. He remembered their wedding day and the vows they'd made to each other. A year later, at her medical school graduation, she'd taken another vow, to care for her patients. Who came first?

He was no longer sure.

That night, lying beside his slumbering wife, he wished he, too, could fall asleep. He considered the bottle of Ativan in his nightstand drawer and was tempted to shake out a pill or two, just to help him through the night. But he'd drunk too much wine at dinner, and the last time he'd mixed Ativan and alcohol, he'd gone for a drive in his pajamas and woken up that morning with no memory of the adventure.

He closed his eyes and yearned for oblivion, but sleep refused to come. So he lay awake, inhaling Maggie's scent of soap and apricot shampoo, remembering how they used to be. *I miss you,* he thought. *I miss us.*

CHAPTER 5
TARYN

The more she looks at him, the more the fire grows . . . her gaze, her whole heart, is riveted on him now . . .

And that was the beginning of the end for tragic Queen Dido, whose fatal mistake was saving the life of a shipwrecked warrior. Taryn regretted ever opening this infuriating book, but Virgil's *The Aeneid* was the week's assigned reading for the Star-Crossed Lovers class. Professor Dorian had warned them that the romance ended in tragedy, so she had been braced for an unhappy ending. She'd known either Aeneas or Queen Dido or both would meet an untimely end.

She hadn't been prepared to be so pissed off about it.

All weekend she'd been thinking about Queen Dido and her lover, Aeneas, the Trojan warrior who'd fought valiantly to defend his city from the attacking Greeks.

Defeated by the enemy, Aeneas was forced to flee as his city, Troy, was sacked, and he and his men sailed away on ships bound for Italy. But the gods were not kind. Their fleet was battered by storms, and his ship was lost. Barely alive, Aeneas and his men washed ashore in Tyre, a land ruled by the beautiful widow Queen Dido.

If only Dido had immediately ordered Aeneas put to the sword. Or had him tossed without pity back into the sea to drown. Had she done so, she might have lived to a serene old age, beloved by her subjects. She could have found happiness with a man who was far more worthy of her love. But no, Dido was too tenderhearted and trusting of these strangers from Troy. She offered them food and shelter and safety. And most reckless of all, she offered Aeneas her heart. Casting aside her dignity, she sacrificed her reputation as a chaste widow-queen, all for the love of a faithless stranger.

A stranger who betrayed and abandoned her.

Aeneas sailed off in pursuit of his own glory, leaving behind his heartbroken lover. In sorrow Dido climbed onto the funeral pyre that she herself had ordered built. There she unsheathed a sword of Trojan steel. Desperate for oblivion, she plunged the blade into her own body.

. . . and all at once the warmth slipped away, the life dissolved in the winds.

From his ship, Aeneas could see the distant glow of Dido's funeral pyre, alight with flames. Surely he knew what that fire signified. He knew that at that moment the flames were consuming the flesh of the woman who loved him, the woman who'd sacrificed everything for him. Did he grieve? Did he turn back the ship in remorse? No, he sailed on in cold pursuit of fortune and glory.

Taryn wanted to rip this book to shreds and flush it down the toilet. Or build a little bonfire in her kitchen sink and watch the pages burn, the way poor Dido burned. But they'd be discussing the story in class tomorrow, so she shoved the book into her backpack. Oh, she would have plenty to say in class about Aeneas. About so-called heroes who betrayed the women who loved them.

That night she dreamed about fire. About a woman standing among the flames, her hair alight, her mouth agape in a shriek. The woman reached out in agony, and Taryn wanted to save her, to drag her from the pyre and beat out the flames, but she was paralyzed. She could only watch as the woman burned, as her body blackened and shriveled to ash.

She jolted awake to the wail of a distant ambulance, and for a moment she lay exhausted, her heart still pounding from the nightmare. Slowly she registered the sound of traffic and the glare of daylight in her window. Then she glanced at the bedside clock and bolted out of bed.

She was late for Professor Dorian's class, but Cody had promised to save a seat for her. She spotted Cody slouched in his usual seat at the far end of the seminar table, his Red Sox baseball cap pulled low over his brow. As she eased quietly into the room, the snap of the door's latch made a few heads turn to look at her. Professor Dorian paused in the middle of his discussion, and she felt his gaze follow her as she made her way around the table to where Cody was sitting. The brief silence magnified the scrape of Cody's chair, the hiss of his down jacket as he pulled it off the empty chair beside him.

"Where were you?" Cody whispered as she sat down. "I was starting to think you weren't coming to class."

"I overslept. What'd I miss?"

"Just some overview stuff. I took notes. I'll give you a copy later."

"Thanks, Cody. You're the best." And she meant it. What would she do without Cody, who was always ready to share his notes and his lunch? She really should try to be nicer to him.

Professor Dorian was still looking at her, but not in an annoyed way. Rather, it was as if she were some weird forest creature who'd wandered into his class and he didn't know what to make of her. Then, as if he'd suddenly remembered where he was, he launched back into the lecture and turned to the chalkboard, where four pairs of names were already scrawled.

Tristan and Isolde
Jason and Medea
Abelard and Heloise
Romeo and Juliet

"So far in this course, we've talked about four pairs of doomed lovers," Professor Dorian said. He turned to face them again, and for a moment she thought he was staring straight at her. "Last week it was Abelard and Heloise. Now it's time to move on to another pair whose story ends in tragedy. And like Jason and Medea, the story of Aeneas and Dido involves betrayal." He wrote the lovers' names on the chalkboard. "By now, you all should have read *The Aeneid*." He looked around to see a few nods, a few noncommittal shrugs. "Okay, good. Who wants to comment?"

There was the usual silence; no one ever wanted to be the first to speak up.

"I think it's pretty cool that Aeneas is the guy who founded Rome," said Jessica. "I always thought it was founded by two guys who were suckled by wolves as babies. I never knew it was Aeneas."

"That's according to Virgil, anyway," said Professor Dorian. "He wrote that Aeneas was a Trojan prince who defended his city against the Greeks. After the fall of Troy, he flees to Italy and becomes the first hero of Rome. Now that you've read *The Aeneid,* do you all agree he's a hero?" Dorian glanced around the room. "Anyone?"

"Obviously he's a hero," Jason said. "The Trojans thought so."

"What about his relationship with Queen Dido? The fact he abandoned her and she committed suicide? Does that influence your opinion of him?"

"Why should it?" Luke said. "Dido didn't have to kill herself. That was her choice and hers alone."

"And Aeneas had more important things to deal with," said Jason. "He had a kingdom to build. His men needed a leader. And anyway, Tyre wasn't even his homeland. He

60

didn't owe it any loyalty."

With mounting irritation, Taryn listened to her classmates justify the betrayal of Dido. Suddenly she couldn't stay silent any longer.

"He's not a hero!" she blurted. "He's a narcissistic asshole, just like Abelard. Just like Jason. I don't care if he went on to found the city of Rome. He abandoned Dido, which makes him a traitor."

The classroom went silent.

Then Jessica let out a mocking laugh. She never missed a chance to challenge Taryn in class, and as usual she went straight for the jugular. "Are we back to your old gripe, Taryn? It's the same thing you said about Jason and Abelard. You're obsessed with men betraying women."

"That's exactly what Aeneas did," Taryn pointed out. "He betrayed her."

"Why are you stuck on that theme? Did some guy do it to you?"

Cody put his hand on Taryn's arm, a touch that said: *Let it slide. She's trying to provoke you.* Of course he was right. She'd known girls like Jessica all her life, privileged girls who were handed everything they wanted. Girls who'd never seen the inside of a Goodwill store because they bought all their clothes brand new. Girls who used to bring their friends into the ice cream shop where she worked every summer, just so they could stand around, smirking, as she served them.

Oh yes, Taryn knew the Jessicas of the world, but they didn't know her.

Cody's hand tightened around her arm. She took a deep breath and silently settled back in her chair.

"Well, it's true, isn't it?" said Jessica, looking around the classroom. "That's Taryn's *thing*. Women getting betrayed."

"Let's move on," said Professor Dorian.

"Maybe it's personal for her or something," Jessica said. "Because it sure seems like she can't stop talking about men who —"

"I said, *let's move on*."

Jessica pouted. "I was only making a point."

"Leave Taryn out of it. She has a right to her opinion, and I'm glad she spoke up. Now let's get back to *The Aeneid*."

As he led the discussion in a different direction, Taryn focused on the man who'd come to her defense. She knew almost nothing about him. Not his background or his personal life or even what the *R* in Jack R. Dorian stood for. For the first time she noticed how tired he looked today, perhaps

62

a little depressed, as if these classroom squabbles had worn him down. He wore a wedding ring, so she knew he was married. Did he have a fight this morning with his wife, his kids? He struck her as one of the good guys — not a man like Aeneas or Abelard or Jason, but someone who'd stand by the woman he loved.

The way he'd stood by her today. She should thank him for it.

After the seminar ended and the other students filed out, Taryn lingered in the classroom, watching as he gathered his papers. "Professor Dorian?"

He looked up, surprised that she was still there. "What can I do for you, Taryn?"

"You already did it. Thanks for what you said in class. That thing with Jessica."

He sighed. "It was getting pretty hostile."

"Yeah. I don't know what I've done in this class to make her dislike me, but I seem to irritate her just by breathing. Anyway, thank you." She turned to leave.

"Oh. I almost forgot." He shuffled through a stack of papers and pulled out the essay she'd written last week, about Jason and Medea. "I passed these out at the beginning of class. Before you got here."

She stared at the A-plus scrawled in red at the top. "Wow. Really?"

"The grade is well deserved. I can see you put a lot of emotion into what you wrote."

"Because I really did feel it."

"A lot of people feel things, but not everyone can express those feelings as well as you do. After what you said in class today, I'm looking forward to your paper on *The Aeneid.*"

She looked up at him, and for the first time she registered the fact that he had green eyes, the same color as Liam's. He was not as tall as Liam, nor as broad shouldered, but his eyes were kinder. For a moment they just looked at each other, both of them hunting for something to say but not coming up with a single word.

Abruptly he broke off his gaze and snapped his briefcase shut. "I'll see you at the museum next week."

CHAPTER 6
TARYN

"Goddamn, he gave you an A-*plus*?" Cody said as they walked across the quad. "I worked my ass off on that paper, and I only got a B-plus."

"Maybe you didn't feel the theme deeply enough."

"Star-crossed lovers?" Cody stared straight ahead. "Oh, I feel it well enough," he muttered.

She was still beaming, still high. Professor Dorian's praise was like jet fuel pumped straight into her veins, and she was bursting to share the triumph. She pulled out her cell phone to call her mother, even though Brenda had probably just crawled into bed after her night shift at the nursing home. Only then did she notice that her mother had sent an email. The subject line made her stop dead in the center of the quad.

Time for you to come home?

She opened the email. It was several

paragraphs long. As Cody watched her, as other students streamed past her like schools of fish veering around a stone pillar, Taryn read and reread what her mother had written. No, her mom couldn't possibly mean this.

"Taryn?" said Cody.

She dialed Brenda's number, but the call went straight to voice mail, which of course it would. When her mother went to bed after her shift, she always muted her phone.

"What's wrong?" said Cody as she hung up.

Taryn looked at him. "My mom says if I apply to grad school, it has to be in Maine."

"Why?"

"The money. It's always about the money."

"Is that such a disaster? Going back to Maine?"

"You know it is! Liam and I had it all worked out. We're staying in Boston. It's what we planned."

"Maybe his plans have changed."

"Don't," she commanded.

Taken aback by her glare, Cody fell silent. He glanced up at the clock tower and said, timidly, "We're, um, going to be late for class."

"You go. I'll see you later."

"What about those essay questions? I thought we were going to work on them together."

"Yeah, sure. Tonight. Come over to my place."

He brightened. "I'll bring a pizza."

"Okay," she muttered, but she wasn't looking at him; she was still staring at her phone. She didn't even notice when he walked away.

Her mother sounded exhausted on the phone. It was four in the afternoon, and for a nurse's aide who worked the graveyard shift at Seaside Nursing Home, it was the equivalent of the crack of dawn, but Taryn couldn't wait any longer to speak to her.

"You don't seem to understand how important this is," Taryn said. "I can't go back to Maine."

"And what are you going to do after you graduate?"

"I don't know yet. I'm thinking about grad school. My grades are good enough, and I'm sure I could get into some school here."

"There are perfectly good schools here in Maine."

"But I can't leave Boston." *I can't leave Liam* was what she was thinking.

"Not everything we want in life is pos-

67

sible, Taryn. I've tried to keep up with your tuition payments, but you can't get blood from a stone. It's been hard enough for me, keeping up with this second mortgage. Now I've got nothing left to borrow against, and I'm already working double shifts. You have to be sensible."

"This is my *future* we're talking about."

"I *am* talking about your future. About all these loans you'll have to pay back someday, and for what? Just so you can brag you went to some fancy college in Boston? What about my retirement? I haven't saved a penny for myself." Brenda sighed. "I can't do this for you anymore, honey. I'm tired. Since your father left, it seems all I ever do is work."

"It won't be this way forever. I promised I'd take care of you."

"Then why don't you come home? Come home now and live with me. You can get whatever education you need up here. Maybe get a part-time job to help pay for it all."

"I can't go back to Maine. I need to be —"

"With Liam. That's it, isn't it? It's all about being with *him.* Being in the same city, the same school."

"A degree from a good school makes a

difference."

"Well, *his* family can afford it. I don't have that kind of money."

"We will someday."

Another sigh, this one deeper. "Why are you doing this to yourself, Taryn?"

"Doing what?"

"Betting your whole future on a boy? You're so much smarter than that. Didn't you learn anything when your father walked out? We can't rely on them. We can't rely on anyone but ourselves. The sooner you wake up and —"

"I don't want to talk about this."

"What's going on, honey? There's *something* going on. I can hear it in your voice."

"I just don't want to go back to Maine."

"Has something happened between you and Liam?"

"Why do you think that? You have no reason to think that."

"He's not the only boy in the world, Taryn. It's not healthy to spend all your time mooning over him, when there are so many other —"

"I have to go," Taryn cut in. "Someone's at the door."

She hung up, deeply rattled by the call. She desperately wanted to talk to Liam, but she'd already left three voice mails on his phone, and he hadn't called back yet. Outside it was starting to snow, but she couldn't stand being cooped up inside her tiny apartment for even another minute. She needed to take a walk and clear her head.

She didn't think about where she was going; her feet automatically took her there, following the same route she'd traveled so many times before.

It was dark by the time she reached Liam's apartment building. Standing on the sidewalk, she looked up at his windows. His neighbors' lights were on, but his windows were dark. She knew his last class of the day had ended hours ago, so where was he? She didn't dare enter his apartment now because he might come home any minute and catch her there, but she was so starved for a glimpse of him she couldn't leave. Not yet.

Right across the street was a juice bar. She walked in, ordered a glass of acai berry, and claimed a seat by the window. Through the veil of lightly falling snow, she kept watch on his building. It was now dinnertime, and she thought of all the evenings they'd spent together in his apartment, gorging on take-out food. Pad thai from Siam House. Burgers and fries from Five Guys. They'd eat at his coffee table while they watched TV, and

70

afterward they'd slip out of their clothes. Into his bed.

I miss you. Do you miss me?

The temptation to call him was so powerful that she couldn't resist it. Once again, her call went straight to his voice mail. He was busy studying, of course, because he was determined to get into law school, and he must be preparing for the LSAT. That was why he'd turned off his phone.

She ordered a second glass of acai berry juice and slowly nursed it along, making it last so they wouldn't ask her to leave the shop. Liam was probably studying in the library; maybe that was where she should go. She'd pick a table on the first floor near the restrooms, and she'd spread out all her books and work on that paper for Professor Dorian's class. Liam was bound to notice her when he walked past to the restroom. He'd be impressed by how focused she was, how dedicated to her classwork. So much more than just the poor hometown girl he'd known since middle school. No, she was someone bound for bigger things, someone who was his perfect match in every way.

Her cell phone rang. *Liam.* Her hands were shaking as she answered: "Hello?"

"I thought we were studying at your place tonight. You're not answering your buzzer."

She slumped back in the chair with disappointment. It was only Cody. "Oh God. I forgot about it."

"Well, I'm standing outside your building now, and I've got the pizza. Where are *you*?"

"I can't meet you tonight. Can we do it another time?"

"But we were gonna go over those essay questions for Dorian's class. I brought all my books and notes and everything."

"Look, I've got a lot of things on my mind. I'll call you tomorrow, okay?"

The silence that followed was leaden with disappointment. She pictured him hulking outside her building in his mountainous down jacket, his baseball cap powdered with fallen snow. How long had he been standing in that bitter cold, waiting for her?

"I'm sorry, Cody. I really am."

"Yeah." He sighed. "Okay."

"Talk tomorrow?"

"Sure, Taryn," he said and hung up.

She looked across the street at Liam's window; it was still dark. *A little longer,* she thought. *I'll sit here just a little longer.*

■ ■ ■ ■

AFTER

■ ■ ■ ■

After

CHAPTER 7
FRANKIE

The boyfriend's name is Liam Reilly, and he seems like just the sort of boy every mother hopes her daughter will bring home. He is blond and strapping, clean shaven, and neatly dressed in chinos and an oxford shirt. As Frankie and Mac step into his apartment, he asks politely if they would like coffee. Too few young people these days seem to respect cops, and even fewer would extend the courtesy of offering them coffee. As the three sit down in Liam's living room, Frankie notices a stack of law school brochures on the coffee table — yet another detail that impresses her. He is nothing like the unkempt musicians her twin daughters have recently dragged home, boys with no obvious ambitions beyond landing their next gigs. Boys who are afraid to look Frankie in the eye because they know she is a cop. Why couldn't her girls bring home a Liam instead? He is a doctor's kid, courteous and articulate, and he tells them he's already been accepted to two law schools. He has no arrest record, not even an outstanding parking ticket, and he seems genuinely shocked by the news of his ex-girlfriend's death.

"You had no inkling that Taryn would kill herself?" Frankie asks him.

Liam shakes his head. "I know she was upset when I broke up with her. And yeah, sometimes she could act a little psycho. But *kill* herself? That's not like Taryn at all."

"What do you mean by 'a little psycho'?" says Mac.

"She was stalking me." He sees Mac's raised eyebrow. "Seriously, she was. It started off with her calling me and texting me at all hours. Then she started sneaking into my apartment while I was out."

"You caught her in here?"

"No, but one of the girls next door saw her leave the building one morning. Taryn never returned my key, so she could've come in anytime she wanted. And then I noticed that things were missing."

"What things?"

"Stupid little things like my T-shirts. At first I thought I just misplaced them, but then I realized it had to be her, taking my stuff. That was creepy enough. Then it got even worse."

"You mentioned she kept calling and texting you," says Frankie.

"I finally had to block her. But then she just used another student's cell phone to call me."

"So she *did* have a cell phone."

Liam gives her a quizzical look, as if the question is absurd. "Yeah. Sure."

"Because we never found her phone."

"She definitely had one. She was always complaining that her mom could only afford to buy an Android."

"If we do find that phone, would you know how to unlock it?" Mac asks.

"Yeah. Unless she's changed her pass code."

"What is her pass code?"

"It's, um . . ." The boy looks away. "Our anniversary. The day we kissed for the first time. She was kind of sentimental about it, and she kept bugging me to celebrate it with her, even after . . ." His voice trails off.

"You said she kept texting you," says Frankie. "Can we see those texts?"

He pauses, no doubt wondering if there is anything on his phone he shouldn't reveal to a cop. Reluctantly he pulls out his iPhone, unlocks the screen, and hands it to Frankie.

She scrolls through the list of conversations until she finds the string of texts from Taryn Moore. They are two months old.

Where RU?

Why didn't U show up? I waited over two hours.

Why RU avoiding me?

Call me PLEASE. This is important!!!!!!

The girl's mounting desperation is apparent in these texts, but Liam did not respond to any of them. Silence is a coward's way out, and that's what Liam chose to be. By not responding, he left the girl screaming unheard into the void.

"I guess you've talked to her mom," Liam says. "I hope Brenda's okay."

"It was a difficult conversation." It was in fact heart wrenching, even though Frankie was not the one who actually broke the news. That unfortunate task went to a police officer in Hobart, Maine, who knocked on Mrs. Moore's door and informed her in person. When Frankie called a few hours later, Taryn's mother sounded exhausted from crying, her voice barely a whisper.

"Brenda was always nice to me," says

78

Liam. "I felt kind of sorry for her."

"Why?"

"Her husband ran off with another woman when Taryn was ten. I don't think she ever got over her dad leaving them."

"Maybe that's why she freaked out when you left her."

He winces at the parallel. "It's not like we were engaged or anything. It was just a high school thing. Except for growing up in the same town, we didn't have much in common. I'm planning to go to law school, but Taryn didn't have any plans, not really. Except maybe getting married."

Frankie looks down again at Liam's iPhone. "These are the most recent text messages she sent you?"

"Yeah."

"These were sent back in February. There's been nothing since then?"

"No. It all stopped after we had this big blowup at a restaurant. I was having dinner with my new girlfriend, Libby. Somehow Taryn found out we were there, and she barged right into the dining room. Started screaming at me, in front of everyone. I had to drag her outside and tell her, once and for all, that we were finished. I think that's when she finally realized it really *was* over between us. After that, her texts stopped. I

79

figured she'd moved on, maybe found a new boyfriend."

"Her mother didn't say anything about her daughter having a new boyfriend."

Liam shrugs. "Brenda wouldn't necessarily know. Taryn didn't tell her everything."

Frankie thinks about the secrets her own daughters have kept from her: The birth control pills that she found in Gabby's underwear drawer. The boy who'd been sneaking into Sibyl's bedroom, until the night Frankie pulled her service weapon on him. Yes, girls were very good at keeping secrets from their mothers.

"*Was* there another boyfriend?" Mac asks.

"I don't know of one," says Liam.

"Ever see her with anyone else?"

"Just that classmate of hers. Guy who hung around her all the time. I don't know his name."

"You think she was involved with him?"

"You mean, like her *boyfriend*?" He laughs. "No way."

"Why not?"

"If you saw him, you'd understand. The kid's as big as a blimp. She probably let him hang around with her out of pity. I can't think of any other reason."

"Friendship, maybe? A dazzling personality?"

"Yeah. Sure." Liam snorts, because he can't imagine being supplanted by a fat kid. He has the blind self-confidence of someone who knows damn well he's good looking, who has never doubted his self-worth. Frankie decides she does not like this boy after all.

"Why do you think she killed herself, Liam?"

He shakes his head. "Like I said, we lost touch. I wouldn't know."

"She was your girlfriend. You've been together since high school. You must have some idea why she did it."

He thinks about it for a moment, but only for a moment. As if the question isn't important enough to rack his brain over. "Really, I don't." He glances down at his Apple Watch. "I'm meeting someone in twenty minutes. Are we done here?"

"What an asshole," says Frankie as she and Mac eat lunch in the Boston PD canteen.

"Comes with being a golden boy," says Mac. "I knew a few kids like him when I was growing up. Arrogant jerks. Thought they were something special, when all they did was hit the genetic lottery. Wish I'd gotten a few of those genes."

"What's wrong with your genes?"

"You mean, aside from the fact I've got diabetes, male-pattern baldness, and rosacea?"

"I don't think rosacea's genetic, Mac."

"No? Well, somehow, I caught it from my mom." He hoists the ham-and-cheese sandwich to his mouth and takes a giant bite. Given his weight and his hypertension, ham and cheese are not what he should be eating, but that sandwich looks damn tempting to Frankie, compared to her Caesar salad. Frankie doesn't even like salads, but this morning she glimpsed her reflection in the ladies' restroom, and it confirmed what her ever-tightening waistband already tells her. Salads it will have to be until her trousers stop pinching. Until she doesn't grimace every time she glances in a mirror.

"So you got any plans for tonight?" he asks.

"I think it'll be TV and bed." She resignedly spears a romaine leaf with her fork and chews it without enthusiasm. "Why do you ask?"

"If you've got no plans tonight, Patty's got this cousin."

"Of course she does."

"He's sixty-two, has a good job, owns his own house. And he's got no criminal record."

82

"Ah, a real winner."

"Patty thinks you'd really like him."

"I'm not in the market, Mac."

"But don't you ever think about getting married again?"

"No."

"Seriously? Someone to come home to every night? Someone to grow old with?"

"Okay. Yeah." Frankie puts down her fork. "I do think about it. But there aren't any Romeos beating down my door at the moment."

"This cousin's real nice, and Patty's anxious for you two to meet. We can keep it casual, just a double date with beer and burgers. If you get antsy, you just have to give me the signal, and you can make your escape."

Frankie picks up her fork and listlessly moves lettuce around on her plate. "Does her cousin know I'm a cop?"

"Yeah. She told him."

"And he's still interested in meeting me? Because that usually stops 'em cold."

"Patty says he likes strong women."

"Who are also armed?"

"Just don't wave it around. Be your usual charming self. It'll be great."

"I don't know, Mac. After that last blind date . . ."

"You know why that went wrong? It's 'cause you let your daughters set it up. Who the hell sets up their mom with a bartender?"

"Well, he *was* pretty hot. And he made a mean martini."

"You should always *start* with the background check." He gives a bow. "And yes, you can thank me for that. At least with Patty's cousin, you know right off the bat he's okay."

Okay. When had *okay* become the best she could hope for in a man? When did she stop seeking the thrill of raging hormones and a pounding heart and settle for the merely acceptable?

"What's this cousin's name?"

"Tom."

"Tom what?"

"Blankenship. He's a widower with two grown kids. And like I said, I ran a background on him. Not even a parking ticket."

"Sounds like stellar dating material."

Tonight is billed as nothing more than beer and burgers at a pub on Brighton Avenue, so why is she still standing in front of her closet, debating what to wear? She has not been on a date in months, not since the hot-but-larcenous bartender. She doubts this

84

evening will turn out any better, but there is always that chance, that cruel glimmer of hope, that this man could be *the one,* and she doesn't want to blow it. So she stands perusing her closet for just the right outfit.

Not the blue dress, which she outgrew about two sizes ago. She yanks it off the hanger and tosses it onto a growing pile that's bound for the Goodwill donation bin. Her green dress has stains in the armpits, so into the donation pile that goes as well. Defeated by her pitiful wardrobe, she finally rakes out her tried-and-true black pantsuit. It's who she is anyway, a pantsuit kind of gal.

Finally dressed and ready to go, she walks into the living room to collect her coat from the closet.

Her daughter Gabby looks up from her magazine and makes a face. "Oh, Mom. Are you really going to wear *that,* tonight?"

"What's wrong with it?"

"This is supposed to be a date, not a court appearance. Why not put on a dress? Something sexy?"

"It's thirty-three degrees outside."

"Sexy requires sacrifice."

"Says who?"

"Says this article." Gabby flips the magazine around to show her mother a photo of a dewy-faced model in a red leather mini-dress.

Frankie scowls at the six-inch heels. "Yeah. No."

"C'mon, Mom, just make an effort. Sibyl and I think you'd look pretty tasty in spike heels. You can borrow mine."

"First of all, daughters should not use the word *tasty* and *Mom* in the same sentence, unless it refers to food. And second, I really don't care if I look tasty."

"Yes, you do."

"Okay, maybe I do." Frankie thrusts her arms into the sleeves of her coat. "But not for some guy I've never even met."

"Wait. Did *Mac* set up this blind date?"

"Yes."

Gabby groans and looks back at her magazine. "Then you might as well just go as you are."

"Wish me luck. I might be home late."

Gabby flips a page. "I doubt it."

". . . and then when our kids were still in high school, she went to culinary school and got her degree at age forty-four. Started a whole new career when she opened her own catering business. Man, did we eat well, the kids and me! She picked up a ton of clients up on Beacon Hill, doing their Christmas parties, New Year's, bar mitzvahs . . ."

Frankie glances at her watch, takes another gulp of beer, and wonders how to gracefully slip out of the pub and go home. How much more can the man say about his saintly wife, Theresa, who's been dead now for seventeen months? Not a year and a half but a precise seventeen months, his status as a widower tallied the same way parents tally a toddler's age. That's how fresh his loss still feels to him.

When Frankie first glimpsed her date across the pub, sitting with Mac and Patty, she had high hopes for the evening. Tom is trim and clean shaven, and he still possesses most of his hair. When they shook hands, his grip was firm, and he looked her in the eye as he smiled. They ordered drinks and chicken wings for the table. She told him she had twin daughters. He told her he had daughters too. Then he started talking about his late wife.

That was two pitchers of beer ago.

Patty announces brightly: "I'm off to the ladies' room." As she stands up, she gives her husband a poke in the arm.

"Hm? Oh yeah, I'll get us another round of beer," says Mac and obediently rises from his chair as well.

Frankie knows exactly why they are leaving her alone with Tom-who-has-no-criminal-record. Patty views every unmarried acquaintance as a personal challenge, and Frankie has been her most vexing project.

Left alone at the table, both Frankie and Tom sit in painful silence for a moment, both of them staring at the platter of now-ravaged chicken wings.

"I'm sorry," he sighs. "I guess I'm not lighting any fires for you."

This is true, but Frankie wants to be kind. "I can see this is all too soon for you, Tom. It takes time to heal. Until you do, you shouldn't force yourself to get back into circulation."

"You're so right. This is my first date since . . ." His voice trails off. "But Patty's been nagging me for months to get back in the game."

"Yeah, she's a force of nature."

He laughs. "Isn't she, though?"

"But you're not ready."

"Are you?"

"It's not so fresh for me."

He looks at her. "I'm sorry. Here I've been talking about Theresa all evening, and I should have asked about your husband. What happened to him?"

"Patty didn't tell you?"

"All she told me was that it was a few years ago."

She is grateful for Patty's discretion. It's painful enough that so many of Frankie's colleagues know the truth. "He had a heart attack. It was completely unexpected." *In more ways than one.* "It happened three years ago, so I've had time to adjust."

"But do we ever, really? Adjust?"

She considers the question. Thinks about the months after her husband, Joe, died, when she lay awake at night, tormented by questions that have no answers. By grief mingled with rage. No, she will never really adjust, because now she questions everything she once believed in, everything she took for granted.

"The truth is I'm still not over his death," she admits.

"In a way, it's kind of comforting, knowing that I'm not the only one who's having a hard time."

She smiles. "I think you must have been a really good husband."

"I could have been a better one."

"Remember that, if you ever get married again. But right now, I think you should just take care of yourself." She reaches for her purse. "It was nice meeting you, Tom," she says, and she means it, even though there

89

are no sparks between them, and there probably never will be. "It's late, and I should head home."

"I know this wasn't the world's best date, but can I call you sometime? When I *am* feeling ready?"

"Maybe. I'll let you know."

But as she walks back to her apartment, Frankie already knows they won't be seeing each other again. Sometimes there are no second chances at happiness. Sometimes, merely being content with your life is enough. The air is so cold it feels like she's inhaling needles, but it reminds her she is alive.

Unlike her husband. Unlike Taryn Moore. Unlike all the other lost souls whose bodies have passed beneath her gaze.

She takes another deep breath, grateful for its sting, and walks the rest of the way home.

■ ■ ■ ■

BEFORE

■ ■ ■ ■

CHAPTER 8
TARYN

She really should be a better friend to Cody. He was the one person who always answered his phone when she needed a favor, the one person who tolerated her bad moods. The two of them were the black sheep of the flock, and ever since they'd met last year, when he'd chosen the seat next to hers in Western Lit, they'd been hanging out together, if only because black sheep always recognized their fellow outcasts. So yes, she really *should* be nicer to him, but sometimes it irritated her, the way he was always hovering nearby, trying to be helpful. Trying to burrow his way deeper into her life. She wasn't blind; she knew why he saved her a seat in class, why he shared his class notes and slipped her candy bars when she was hungry. She would never like him the way he *wanted* her to like him, and how could she, when there was so much about him she found unattractive? It wasn't just his waddling walk or the crumbs that always stuck to the front of his sweaters. No, it was his sheer neediness that annoyed her, even though she did understand where it came from. Like her, he was the kid who never fit in, the kid who was desperate to prove himself.

She looked at him across the library table, where they both sat working. For the past hour he'd been hunched in his chair, working on the class paper that was due in two days, but he had tapped out scarcely two sentences on his laptop. As usual he was wearing his red baseball cap with the grease-stained bill, and it was pulled so low over his forehead that she couldn't see his eyes.

"Why don't you ever take that thing off?" she asked him.

"Huh?"

"Your hat. I never see you without it."

"It's the Red Sox."

"Well, you should at least wash it."

He pulled it off, leaving a hat-shaped indentation in his baby-fine blond hair, and smiled down at the brim. "My dad bought this for me when we went to a Red Sox game. They lost that day to the Yankees, but it was still pretty great, being in the stands. Eating hot dogs and ice cream. Having my dad there with me." Cody caressed the grease stain on the brim, like Aladdin rubbing his magic lamp, hoping for the genie to appear. "It was the last day we spent together. Before . . . you know."

"Where's he living now?"

"Somewhere in Arizona. I got a card from him at Christmas. He said maybe I could come visit him one of these days. Said he'll take me camping."

No, he won't, she thought. Because dads who left their families never kept any of the promises they made. They didn't want visits. They didn't want to be reminded of the kids they'd abandoned. They wanted to forget they even existed.

Cody sighed and mashed the Red Sox hat back onto his head. "You ever see your dad?"

"Never. Not in years. He doesn't care, and I don't either."

"Of course you care. He's your dad."

"Well, I don't." She stuffed her books and papers into her backpack and rose to leave. "Neither should you."

"Taryn, wait."

By the time he caught up with her, she was already out of the building and walking so fast across the quad that he was panting hard just to stay apace.

"I'm sorry I mentioned your dad," he says.

"I don't want to talk about him. Not ever."

"Maybe you need to talk about him. Look, I know he walked out on you, but so did my dad. It's something we just have to live with. It hurts, but it also makes us stronger."

"No, it doesn't. You know what it makes us? Damaged. It makes us rejects."

She halted in the center of the quad and turned to face him. He flinched, as if she were about to strike him. As if he were afraid of her, which he probably was, on some level. Afraid of losing her or infuriating his one good friend on this campus.

"When someone says they love you, it should mean forever," she said. "It should be something you can count on, something you can stake your life on. But my dad, he couldn't be bothered to stick around. He left the people he was supposed to love. I hope he burns in hell."

Cody stared at her, taken aback by her fury. "I'd never do that to you, Taryn," he said softly.

The breath suddenly whooshed out of her; so did the rage. "I know."

Cody touched her arm, tentatively, as if she might singe him. When she didn't pull away, he put his arm around her shoulder. His touch was meant to be comforting, but she didn't want him to get the idea there could ever be anything between them, not in the way he hoped.

She pulled away. "I'm done studying for the night. I'm going home."

"I'll walk you there."

"No, I'm fine. See you tomorrow."

"Taryn?" he called, so plaintively that she couldn't just walk away. She turned to see him standing alone under the lamppost. His hulking body cast a mountainous shadow. "Liam's not worth it," he said. "You can do better. A lot better."

"Why are you talking about him?"

"Because that's what this is really all about, isn't it? It's not about your dad leaving you. It's about Liam ignoring you. Shutting you out. You don't need him."

"You don't understand anything about him and me."

"I understand more than you think. I understand he doesn't deserve you. What I don't understand is why you won't let him go, when there are other guys who'd be better for you. Who *want* to be with you." She couldn't see his eyes in the shadow of his baseball cap, but she could hear the longing in his voice. "I know you've been with him forever, but that doesn't mean it's going to last."

"It's what we planned. It's why I'm on

this campus. Because we promised to stick together, no matter what."

"Then why isn't he here? Why doesn't he answer when you call?"

"Because he's studying. Or he's in class."

"He's not in class now."

She pulled out her cell phone and dialed Liam's number. The call went straight to voice mail. She stared at the screen, and a possibility dawned on her, one she'd refused to consider.

"Give me your phone," she said to Cody.

"Is something wrong with yours?"

"Just give it to me."

He handed his phone to her and watched as she called Liam. It rang three times, and then she heard: "Hello?"

"I've been calling you all day. You never called back."

There was a long silence. Too long. "I can't talk now, Taryn. I'm in the middle of something."

"In the middle of what? I need to see you."

"What's this number you're calling from?"

"It's my friend's phone. I haven't been able to reach you. I thought maybe you accidentally blocked me."

"Look, I have to go."

"Call me? Call me later, no matter what time it is."

"Yeah. Sure."

The connection cut off. She stared at the phone, stunned by how abruptly Liam had ended the conversation.

"So what did he say?"

Cody had been watching her the whole time, and she didn't like his knowing look. She slapped the phone into his hand. "None of your business."

CHAPTER 9
JACK

"I'm still guessing this back pain is nothing but a strained muscle," said Charlie as Jack drove him to his hospital appointment. "I don't know if these x-rays are necessary. And you sure didn't need to drive me there, boyo."

"No problem. It's my day off."

"On a Friday, huh? Nice schedule you got there."

"The perks of being a university professor." Jack glanced at his father-in-law, whose face had suddenly tightened with what he had to assume was pain. "You hurting?"

"A little." Charlie gave a wave. "Nothing Tylenol can't fix. Anyway, aches and pains come with the age. Wait till you're seventy; you'll see how hard it is just getting out of bed in the morning. Maggie says maybe all I need is physical therapy or a massage or two. I'm just hoping she doesn't insist I go to a yoga class or some fool thing."

"Yoga's good for you."

Charlie snorted. "Can you see me in one of those tighty-tight outfits, doing the downward beagle or whatever they call it?" He looked at Jack. "This summer if I'm feeling better, maybe we can all go on a biking trip out west." He reached into his jacket pocket and unfolded a glossy travel brochure. "Look at this. Backroads has a trek in Bryce Canyon. That's something I'd like us to do together, while I still can. After all, I'm now a card-carrying septuagenarian." He drew out the syllables as if pronouncing the word for the first time.

"Yeah, but a young sep-tu-a-gen-ar-ian."

"When I was with Cambridge PD, I didn't take nearly enough vacations. I spent too much precious time with the goddamn scum of the earth. Assholes you'd never miss if they got popped in the head with a bullet. Instead I should've taken more trips with Annie. Gone on that Alaska cruise she always wanted to take. Jesus, I regret that. Now I've gotta make up for lost time." Charlie looked at Jack. "So see if Maggie can get that time off in June. About ten days."

"I'll ask her."

"And the trip is on me. All expenses paid."

"Really? How come?"

101

"Because I'd rather enjoy my loot while I'm still alive and not have you spend your inheritance on memorial gutters."

"That's very generous of you. But we still need new gutters."

"You work on getting her to take some time off." He looked at Jack again. "Getting away together would be good for both of you."

"We could certainly use a vacation. A chance to unwind."

"And do other things."

"Other things?"

He winked. "I'm still hoping to see a grandchild one of these days."

"I'm hoping so, too, Charlie."

"So when's it going to happen? I hope while I'm still young enough to throw him baseballs."

The subject of children was so painful that for a moment, Jack didn't respond. He just kept driving, wishing he could avoid even thinking about the question.

"She's still shook up about that last miscarriage, isn't she?" Charlie said.

"She took it pretty hard. We both did."

"That happened a year ago, Jack."

"Doesn't make it hurt any less."

"I know, I know. But you're both still young. You've got plenty of time to have

102

kids. My Annie was almost forty-two when she finally had Maggie. Greatest gift God could've given me. You'll know what I mean when you're holding one of your own."

"I'm working on it," was all Jack could think of saying.

"Then think about Bryce Canyon, okay? The two of you in a romantic hotel room. It'd be a great place to start."

Jack did think about it. That afternoon, as he sat grading papers in the Garrison Hall Dunkin' café, the Bryce Canyon brochure kept calling to him. He set aside the stack of student essays and stared instead at the brochure's tempting vistas and suntanned faces. A week together in a beautiful place was exactly what they both needed. Maybe Charlie was right; maybe it was time to try again for that baby.

"Professor Dorian?"

Through the noisy buzz of conversation in the café, he almost missed the greeting. Only when she repeated it did he finally look up to see Taryn standing beside his table, backpack slung over her shoulder. She flicked a strand of hair off her face, a gesture that seemed more nervous than casual.

"I know it's your day off, but they told me in your office that I might find you here," she said. "Do you have a few minutes to talk?"

He slipped the brochure into his briefcase and gestured to the chair across from him. "Sure, have a seat."

She draped her parka over the chair and sat down. Although they regularly met in class and had on occasion chatted in passing, this was the first time he'd sat and studied her closely. Tawny eyes shone from an open, intelligent face. She wore no makeup, making her appear both innocent and vulnerable. A hairline scar above her full lips made him wonder how she'd been injured — perhaps a childhood spill off a bicycle? A tumble from a tree?

She took out her laptop and set it on the table. "I've just come up with a topic for my final paper, and I want to run it by you," she said, getting straight to business. "I'm thinking of writing about Dido and Aeneas, because it's their story I keep coming back to. Well, her story, anyway."

"Yes, it was apparent in class that you felt a connection with Queen Dido. What will be your focus?"

"They're clearly both passionate characters, but their passions are at odds with each other. He cares more deeply about his public duty, and he betrays her to fulfill his destiny. She's completely invested in her love for him, and she makes the ultimate sacrifice for that love."

"Public duty versus private desire. Duty versus love."

"Exactly. In fact that might be a good title — *Duty versus Love.*" She tapped out some notes. "I've read what other scholars have written about *The Aeneid,* and I hate how so many of them view Dido as a stereotypical female — irrational, emotional, even pitiful. They believe her femininity threatens Aeneas's masculine ideals of power, virtue, and order."

"And you don't see it that way."

"Not at all. And I suspect Virgil agreed with me. He portrays her as a complex woman, a proud and powerful queen, right up until the moment when Aeneas betrays her. And then she takes her fate into her own hands. Even directs the construction of her own funeral pyre."

"You think Virgil's sympathies lie with Dido?"

"Yes, she was seduced and abandoned. It's also obvious in the difference in their speeches. Dido's are filled with emotion. Aeneas is all about authority and destiny. He lacks the very passion that makes Dido so human, so real. Virgil shows us that *she's* the true hero."

"Interesting premise. If you can link this with your Medea paper, you could even turn this into a graduate thesis someday. If you decide to pursue a doctorate."

Her eyes lit up at the possibility. "Wow, I hadn't thought about it as a thesis, but yes! A paper about how women pay the price when their passions threaten men. We see that theme with Abelard and Heloise. We see it with Hemingway. When a woman's need for love becomes too great for her man." Her face clouded over. "We see it in real life too."

Before he could catch himself, he said, "Sounds like you're speaking from experience."

She nodded as her eyes suddenly filled up. She looked away to recenter herself.

He didn't know what real-life experience had fueled her focus on this theme, but he recalled Jessica's comment that Taryn seemed obsessed with men who betrayed women. "Sometimes writing can be a healing experience. You know, empowering yourself to deal with hurt and doubt."

She nodded and wiped her eyes, making her look all the more vulnerable — and making him want to comfort her. But he caught himself. "It sounds like a fine topic.

I'm impressed by how deeply you've thought about these themes," he said. "Are your parents academics?"

She gave an embarrassed shrug. "Hardly. My parents divorced when I was ten years old. And my mom works as a nurse's aide. We live in this little town called Hobart, up in Maine."

"Hobart? I've been there. It was years ago, when my wife and I went white-water rafting." Back in the days when he and Maggie had still taken vacations.

"Then you know it's in the middle of nowhere. Just a little mill town."

"But it appears to have produced a budding scholar."

She smiled. "I'd like to be. There are so many things I'd like to be."

"What other English courses are you taking?"

"Eighteenth-century lit, with Professor McGuire."

He tried to keep a poker face. Ray McGuire's office was next to Jack's. At the beginning of the term, he had complained to Jack that the current crop of female students was distinctly unattractive. "But keep your eyes out for this girl named Taryn Moore. She's the stuff wet dreams are made of."

Now he understood what Ray had meant.

Taryn got up and put on her jacket. "I'm going to dive right into this paper. Thank you."

"And if you're thinking of grad school, let me know. I'll be happy to write a letter of recommendation."

Together they walked out of the building. The breeze ruffled her hair, and with the sunlight streaking it in shades of red and gold, she looked like a Pre-Raphaelite siren.

"See you in class," she said and gave a little wave.

For a long moment Jack stood on the sidewalk, and as he watched her walk away, he felt like a sad cliché. Here he was, just another married college professor coveting a female student. How needy. How pathetic.

No, he wasn't just another professor. He was the youngest full professor in the English Department, and someone who loved his job and who last year had been honored with an Excellence in Teaching Award. Moreover, he was privileged to teach in Boston, the most collegiate city in America and most desirable venue for college teaching. For every opening in English departments throughout eastern Massachusetts, hordes of PhDs rained down applications. Also, Jack had tenure, so coveted because no other profession granted employees lifetime contracts — and the only way to lose it was to get caught doing something illegal or profoundly stupid.

Like romancing your student.

He pulled out his phone and texted Maggie. He'd managed to snag two tickets to tonight's Boston Symphony Orchestra performance, and he asked where she wanted to meet for dinner beforehand.

Five minutes later she texted back: No time for dinner. I'll see you at the BSO. Meet me outside the entrance at 7!

Even though they wouldn't dine together, at least he'd be spending an evening with his wife. A night at the symphony was just what they both needed.

On that cold February night, only a few people were standing outside the Massachusetts Avenue entrance to Symphony Hall. The program tonight was Schumann's cello concerto, one of Maggie's favorites, and she'd been looking forward to this concert for weeks. Almost as much as Jack had been looking forward to a date with his wife.

He stood curbside, waiting for a glimpse of her, but at 7:15 p.m., there was still no sign of Maggie.

At 7:20 he spotted Ray and Judy McGuire hustling up the sidewalk from the CU garage.

"Are you panhandling?" Ray said.

"I should be, given my salary."

Ray laughed and shook Jack's hand. "So where's that beautiful bride of yours?"

Jack glanced at his watch. "She should be here any minute now."

"Great. See you at intermission." They climbed the steps and disappeared inside the building.

Ten more minutes passed. Jack's face was numb, but he stayed at the curb, bouncing up and down to keep warm, fingering the tickets in his coat pocket. Now he was worried. Had she been in an accident? He dialed her phone but got only her voice mail.

He left a message: "Are you okay? Where are you?"

At 7:45, his cell phone rang at last. *Maggie. Thank God.*

"Jack, I'm so sorry! I have an emergency here, and I really can't leave right now."

"Isn't there anyone else who can cover for you?"

"No. Not for this patient." In the background, Jack could hear the ominous beeping of a medical alarm. "I've gotta go. I'll see you at home." She clicked off.

He stood there in disbelief, shivering in the cold and hollow with disappointment. He thought about calling it a night and just heading home, but that would be a waste of an expensive concert ticket. He walked into the building just as the lights blinked, announcing that the performance was about to start. As he followed the usher down the aisle, Jack was acutely aware that he was the only patron still not seated. The usher pointed him to a row with every seat occupied, except for the conspicuous gap of two. Jack sat down and laid his coat on the empty seat. The woman to his right glanced at him, no doubt wondering why his seatmate was an overcoat.

As the house lights dimmed, he noticed the couple to his left was holding hands. Others in front were whispering last-minute thoughts, one woman leaning into her mate and kissing him on the cheek.

God, how he wanted Maggie there. He wanted her to be holding his hand, whispering in his ear, kissing his cheek. Instead she was across town, huddled over a patient who needed her. *But I need you too. And I miss you.*

The hall burst out in applause as the conductor walked onto the stage. Jack could not focus on the music. He scarcely registered the performance and was only aware that the Schumann concerto was over when the audience again applauded.

He grabbed his coat and pushed his way out and up the aisle for the exit.

It was nearly eleven o'clock when he pulled into his driveway and parked beside Maggie's Lexus in the garage. The house was dark except for one dim light in the kitchen. She was no doubt already in bed, he thought, so he was surprised to find her sitting at the kitchen counter with a glass of wine. She looked exhausted, her face ashen, her eyes sunken deep in shadow.

"Are you okay?" he asked. "What happened?"

She swallowed more wine. "One of the residents was too ill, so I had to pinch-hit. The patient's fine, but I really couldn't get away. So how was the concert?"

"It would have been better with you there."

"Sorry." She took another sip of wine. "Feel like snuggling?"

Her code for lovemaking. "You mean now?"

"Yes, now."

He squeezed her hand, and together they walked up to the bedroom.

Afterward, when Jack lay beside his sleeping wife, he wondered if this was how it would be from now on. If sex was something they did instead of dealing with the real issues between them.

He stared up into the dark, listening to her breathe softly beside him. And an image floated into his mind. A woman with tawny eyes, her windblown hair streaked with sunlight.

CHAPTER 10
TARYN

Liam must have ratted her out. That was the only reason she could think of for why she'd been asked to visit room 125 in Dickinson Hall, where the placard on the door read: OFFICE FOR UNIVERSITY EQUITY AND COMPLIANCE, DR. ELIZABETH SACCO, TITLE IX COORDINATOR.

The email Dr. Sacco had sent her yesterday hadn't mentioned why Taryn needed to visit her, but of course it was about Liam. One of his neighbors, probably one of the blondes, must have told him she'd been slipping into his apartment while he was out. Or he'd gotten tired of all her phone calls and texts, so he'd filed a complaint about her. It hadn't had to come to this. All he'd had to do was sit down with her, talk to her. She'd remind him of all their years together, their good memories, the many ways their lives were joined. They'd wrap their arms around each other, and everything would go back to the way it used to be between them. This was just a misunderstanding; that was what she'd tell Dr. Sacco.

Taryn knocked on the door and heard: "Come in."

The woman sitting behind the desk greeted her with a neutral expression, and it bothered Taryn that she could read so little in that face. Dr. Sacco was in her forties, with neatly clipped blonde hair and a navy-blue blazer that would look at home in a bank or a corporate boardroom.

"Taryn Moore, right?" Dr. Sacco said, brisk and businesslike.

"Yes, ma'am."

"Have a seat." She gestured to the chair facing her desk, and Taryn sat down. Lying on the desk were half a dozen file folders, and Taryn quickly scanned the labels, searching for Liam's name, but Dr. Sacco swept up the files so quickly that Taryn couldn't get a look at them before they went into the out-box.

"Thank you for coming in today, Taryn."

"I'm not sure why I'm here. Your email didn't say."

"Because we need to keep this matter confidential. I'm the coordinator for Title Nine Equity and Compliance. Are you familiar with what my office does?"

115

"Sort of. I looked it up online before I came."

"Title Nine prohibits discrimination based on gender, and my office enforces those standards. Whenever there's a complaint alleging sex discrimination or harassment involving students or staff, it's my duty to investigate. If I find the complaint has merit, we take disciplinary action, which can mean anything from counseling to outright dismissal. If the matter is serious enough, we refer it to law enforcement."

Dismissal. Was she about to be expelled? She thought of all the student loans she'd taken out, all the double shifts she'd worked every summer to pay for tuition. And she thought of her mother dragging herself home at dawn after another exhausting night of changing bedpans at the nursing home, just so her daughter could attend Commonwealth. It had to be Commonwealth, because she needed to be with *him*. *Would you really do this to me, Liam?*

"We take every complaint seriously," said Dr. Sacco. "I need to hear what both sides have to say, and I document everything. So after you and I have talked, I'll ask you to sign a statement."

Taryn's hands were trembling. She kept them below the desk so Dr. Sacco couldn't

116

see them and know how scared she was about the possibility of expulsion. She'd sneaked into Liam's apartment only half a dozen times — well, maybe it was a dozen times — but she never took anything of value. She took only things he'd never miss, things that mattered only to her. Or was this about all the phone calls and texts? She thought back to the times she *might* have gone too far, all the things she probably should not have done, like reading his mail or stealing his pillowcase or following him around campus. Merely minor infractions, really.

". . . so far I've interviewed two other students, but I'll be checking with the rest of the class to see if they experienced the same issues with him."

Taryn blinked, suddenly registering her words. What was she talking about? She'd missed something. "The class? Which class?"

"Star-Crossed Lovers."

Taryn shook her head. "I'm sorry, I don't know what this is all about."

"Professor Jack Dorian. What has been your experience with him?"

All at once a breath whooshed out of her, and for a moment all she could do was sit without speaking, too relieved to say a word.

117

So this was not about Liam at all. This was about something else entirely.

Dr. Sacco frowned at Taryn's silence. "Do you have anything to say about him?"

"Why are you asking about Professor Dorian?"

"Because there's been a complaint filed against him, by one of his female students."

"Who?"

"I can't reveal her name, but she's in your nine-fifteen seminar. You probably witnessed the interaction she's talking about."

"What did she say happened?"

"She said Professor Dorian made comments that were sexist and demeaning. She said he targeted her in particular, but other women in the class were just as upset about what he said."

"I never witnessed anything like that."

"Maybe you missed class that day, so you didn't see it."

"I haven't missed any of his classes. He's my favorite teacher."

"So he didn't say anything that offended you?"

"No." Taryn paused. "What would happen to him if he *had* done something like that?"

"It depends how offensive the comments were. A simple warning might suffice. But if it were serious, I might recommend disciplinary action."

"Could he actually lose his job?"

Dr. Sacco hesitated. Picked up a pen and rocked it between her fingers. "For truly serious infractions, yes. It's happened. In this day and age, the university tries very hard to be sensitive to our students' needs. In the past, bad behavior might have been overlooked, but not now. We take every complaint seriously."

"Who made this complaint?"

"As I said, I can't give you any names."

"Was it Jessica?"

Dr. Sacco's lips pressed together in a tight line. That was all the confirmation Taryn needed.

"So it *is* her." Taryn snorted. "Well, I'm not surprised."

"Why do you say that?"

"She's been a total jerk in class, and he called her on it, in front of everyone. Plus he gave her a C-minus on her last paper. You don't *do* that to girls like Jessica. There are consequences."

"She told me that Professor Dorian made sexually denigrating remarks that made her feel personally attacked. Did you witness such behavior?"

"No. Never."

"She claims he said, and let me quote

119

from her complaint, 'that he could under-stand a teacher having an affair with a student.' " She looked up at Taryn. "Did he say that?"

Taryn hesitated. "Well, maybe he said something like that. But it was in the context of the theme we were discussing. It was in reference to the characters in our as-signed reading." She shook her head in disgust. "You know what? This is a bullshit complaint. *I'm* the reason Jessica's going after him."

Dr. Sacco frowned, bewildered. "You?"

"Jessica and I got into an argument in class. It became pretty nasty, and Professor Dorian stepped in to defend me. That pissed her off, so she turned on him."

"I see."

But *did* she see? She thought of the tight clique of girls that always surrounded Jes-sica, girls who trailed in her wake like simpering ladies-in-waiting. Would any of them dare to contradict her, or would they all corroborate Jessica's version of the truth? She might be the only student to defend Dorian, and suddenly it seemed vital that she did. He'd stood up for her, and now she'd stand up for him.

"Professor Dorian would never harass a student. I don't know what she thinks she's doing, but Jessica certainly didn't tell you the truth. And I'll sign a statement."

"In his defense?"

"Absolutely. I've never met a teacher who's so passionate about his material. When he talks about Romeo and Juliet or Aeneas and Dido, you *feel* their pain. He's one of the best teachers you have in this university. If you fire him because of what some spoiled bitch says, then you're everything that's wrong with the Me Too movement."

Dr. Sacco was clearly taken aback by her ferocity, and for a moment she couldn't muster a response. Staring at Taryn, she tapped her pen on the desk like a jittery metronome. "Well," she said, "you've certainly given me an alternative viewpoint. I'll take that into account."

"Do you need me to sign a statement?"

"What you've just told me is sufficient. But if I receive any more complaints about Professor Dorian, I'll need to talk to you again."

Taryn was about to walk out of her office when she stopped and turned back. "Are you going to tell him what I said about this?"

"No. This conversation was confidential."

So he'd never know that she was the one

who'd defended him. This would be her own little secret.

For now.

CHAPTER 11
JACK

Over the weekend, Charlie sent Maggie and Jack yet another brochure for the Bryce Canyon biking trip he'd been urging them to join. It featured alluring photos of visitors riding in tandem through the canyons and raising their glasses of wine at group dinners. There was a wide spectrum of ages, from millennials to people who looked Charlie's age, and he'd scrawled across the page: *We can be in these pictures too!* At seventy, Charlie was in great shape, biking and working out regularly at the gym. "Why the hell not do this?" he said over the phone. "I'm ready to sign on when you are. Let's carpe the diem while we still have the diem to carp."

That Tuesday, Charlie's diem began to cloud over. Because of his back pain, he couldn't do any heavy lifting, so Jack stopped by his place to fill the log hoop for his wood-burning stove.

"The doctor called me this morning," Charlie said, trying to sound casual as Jack tossed another log onto the stack. "He wants to do more tests on me."

Jack clapped sawdust from his hands. "What kind of tests?"

"An MRI scan, to start with."

"How come?"

"He said the x-rays showed some anomalies in my spine. But he won't tell me what it means."

Jack felt a nugget of ice pass through his heart. "Does Maggie know?"

"I'm not sure I want to bother her about it. She's got enough things to deal with."

"It could be just scarring from your fall off the bike a few years ago. You did crack your spine then."

"Whatever. I'm scheduled for Thursday."

Rarely had Jack pondered Charlie's inevitable mortality. In the fifteen years he'd known him, Charlie had been the picture of health, and his eventual death seemed abstract, some event in the vague future. As Jack drove back to campus, he didn't want to consider the possibility that something was seriously wrong with Charlie. Nor did he want to think about how it would devastate Maggie.

His phone chimed with a new email.

As he waited at a stoplight, he glanced down at a message from someone named Elizabeth Sacco. He didn't recognize the name, but he saw she had a university email address. He opened the message and read it with mounting alarm:

Dear Prof. Dorian:
In my role at the university, I am responsible for looking into all reports of gender discrimination, including sexual harassment and assault. My office was recently made aware of a report that alleges you violated the University's Title IX Policy.

Incident Summary: A student alleges that you made inappropriate comments in English 3440 "Star-Crossed Lovers" during a discussion about male teachers in various literary texts having affairs with their students.

This university takes these allegations seriously, and I would like to schedule a meeting to discuss the allegations.

Please know that you are welcome to have an adviser or advocate accompany you. Additionally I would greatly appreciate your not discussing this matter with anyone so as to preserve the integrity of the inquiry.

I look forward to hearing from you soon.

The instant he was back in his office, he checked the university website, and there she was: Dr. Elizabeth Sacco, Title IX Initiatives Office. He only vaguely recalled that the university even had such an office, dedicated to sexual harassment claims.

These charges were ridiculous. Never before had he been accused of impropriety. For several minutes he sat trying to compose himself before he responded. If he sounded defensive, it could antagonize Dr. Sacco. If he sounded dismissive, she might be offended that he didn't take the charge seriously.

He forced out a neutral response and told her he was free to meet the next day, at her convenience.

For the rest of the day, he was weighed down by an indefinable guilt, wondering if he had indeed committed some awful offense. His mind kept spinning awful possibilities, creating an apprehension that the complaint would snowball, take on a life of its own. What if Sacco chose to side with the student, who he assumed was female? What if they made him the sacrificial lamb at the altar of political correctness? How ironic, since he'd always been a proud defender of women's rights. Now he might be lumped in with the likes of Harvey Weinstein. Or maybe he was overreacting. Maybe this was just a misunderstanding and Elizabeth Sacco was simply doing her job, following up on unfounded rumors.

But the next morning, while he stood outside the door labeled **OFFICE FOR UNIVERSITY EQUITY AND COMPLIANCE,** he felt as if he were about to step into Kafka's *The Trial,* where Josef K. woke up one day to discover he'd been arrested for an unknown crime and faced his own execution.

He opened the door, and the receptionist flashed him a cool smile. "Professor Dorian?"

"Yes."

"Dr. Sacco's expecting you. Come this way."

. . . to the chopping block.

He'd been expecting an ogre, but the woman who greeted him seemed pleasant enough, in her early forties and dressed in a somber gray pantsuit. With her short hair and owlish glasses, she reminded him of a clergywoman.

He settled in the chair across from her, suppressing the urge to blurt: *Why the hell am I here?* This was the office that dealt with claims of sexual discrimination, harassment, and abuse. Last year, it had investigated the rape of a female student by a drunken hockey player. The complaint against him seemed absurd by comparison, and he wondered if this was simply a student's revenge for a bad grade he'd given.

They exchanged a few tense pleasantries about the recent snowstorm and the miseries of New England weather. She told him she was from South Florida and, until a few years ago, had seen snow only in movies. Then a few beats of silence told him the pleasantries were over.

"I understand how unsettling this may be for you," she said.

" 'Unsettling' doesn't come close. I thought at first your email was some kind of hoax, because I've never been accused of anything like this. This is not me."

"I'm simply trying to determine the facts, and I hope to resolve this in a way that satisfies everyone. As I wrote in my email, a student in your Star-Crossed Lovers class complained about comments you made."

"What comments?"

"You made this student uncomfortable when you spoke approvingly about teachers having affairs with students. Is that an accurate assessment of what you said in class?"

"Absolutely not! My comment was only in reference to characters in novels. I think I used as examples *The Human Stain* and *Gone Girl.* Are you familiar with those?"

"I saw the movie *Gone Girl.*"

"Then you remember that Ben Affleck's character took up with one of his students."

"Yes, I remember."

"And are you familiar with the letters of Abelard and Heloise?"

"They were lovers from the Middle Ages, as I recall."

"He was a teacher, and she was his young student. I simply pointed out that Heloise and Abelard may have inspired other writers to explore teacher-student affairs in contemporary fiction. And how these situations are driven by the characters' circumstances."

She nodded. "I was an English major. I understand the point you were trying to make."

That was encouraging. "The male characters in these novels are all flawed and vulnerable. They have unhappy marriages, or they're lonely, and they're hungry for

129

intimacy. That leads to the affairs. I was not advocating any such behavior, and it's ludicrous to think that I was. I mean, what instructor would do that?"

"Yes, I understand. But you can appreciate, given current events, that we're especially sensitive to any hint of sexual misconduct."

"Of course. I'm all in favor of disciplining men who harass and abuse. But I can't believe anyone in class felt threatened by a discussion of fictional teachers having fictional affairs with fictional students."

She looked at her notes. "The student who filed the complaint also reported that you said you understood why it could happen. Why a professor would have an affair with a student." She looked up at him.

He felt his face flush in anger. "That's not what I said. In fact —"

"Professor Dorian." She held up her hand. "I also interviewed other students, and one in particular described the incident exactly as you just did. She was very insistent that you were discussing only characters in a book, and nothing else."

She. Was it Taryn Moore who'd defended him? It had to be.

"So I'm going to assume this complaint was merely a misunderstanding."

130

He released a sigh of relief. "Then . . . that's it?"

"Yes. However, for future reference, you might consider including trigger warnings on your syllabi. Other professors are doing that, alerting students that some of the course material might be offensive because of violence, sexual abuse, racism, et cetera."

"I know others are doing that, but I have a problem with trigger warnings."

"Why?"

"Because feeling uncomfortable is what a college education is all about — being exposed to disturbing aspects of human experience. We're talking about twenty-something adults who are exposed to a lot worse in the daily news. I'm not going to infantilize them."

"I'm certainly not going to tell you how to teach your courses. But just consider it."

He got up to leave.

"Just one more thing," she said. "The university strictly prohibits retaliation against anyone involved in a Title Nine investigation."

"I wouldn't do that even if I knew who complained." But he did know, or he had a pretty good idea. He could picture Jessica now, exchanging sly winks and conspiratorial whispers with her roommate, Caitlin, whenever they disagreed with anything he said. And he remembered the C-minus he'd scrawled on Jessica's paper, a grade she'd angrily challenged.

But he would not retaliate. He'd simply show up for class and carry on as if nothing had happened. He shook Elizabeth Sacco's hand, thanked her for dropping the charge, and walked out, feeling fifty pounds lighter.

And thinking: *Thank you, Taryn.*

CHAPTER 12
JACK

"What did the student complain about?" Maggie asked as they drove to the clinic to meet Charlie. They were both feeling anxious about his appointment, and to fill the silence, he'd mentioned his meeting with the Title IX coordinator.

"We were discussing the letters of Heloise and Abelard. You know, the two lovers from the twelfth century," he said, as if that explained things. But it didn't.

"Heloise and Abelard? Isn't there an exhibit about them at the MFA? I saw a banner for it on one of the buses."

"Right. The exhibit opens this week."

"So what do Heloise and Abelard have to do with your Title Nine issue?"

Suddenly he wished he had never brought up the subject. Since the complaint had been dismissed, he felt exonerated, a victim of a vengeful student. On some level, he'd thought that sharing the situation with Maggie would neutralize any suspicions she might have. But on another level he felt as if he were recklessly confessing to a crime he'd never committed. "I explained to the class that the Heloise-and-Abelard affair served as a model for contemporary stories like *Gone Girl* and others."

"Wasn't Abelard her teacher?"

"Yeah."

"And he was a lot older than she was?"

"Yeah. As a result of the affair, he was castrated and served out his days in a monastery. And Heloise was shut away in an abbey."

"Why did the student report you to the Title Nine office?"

"It was a dumb misunderstanding. And the charges were dropped."

"Jack, what was the complaint? What did you say to make the student uncomfortable?"

"I said — I told them there might be reasons why a teacher would have an affair with a student." Out of the corner of his eye he could see her staring at him.

"And have you?"

"Have I what?"

"Had an affair with a student?"

"Jesus, Maggie!" he snapped. "Why would you even ask that?" Was he protesting too much? As if, in some dark recess of his consciousness, he had actually considered the possibility?

"It's just that . . ." She sighed. "My job's been crazy lately. It's gotten hard to carve out enough time for us."

"I miss it, you know. The way we used to be."

"You think I don't miss it too?" She looked at him. "I'm trying, Jack. I really am. But there's so much I have to juggle. So many people who need me."

"And what happens if we ever have kids? How are they going to fit into your schedule?"

She stiffened and turned away. At once he regretted mentioning the possibility of a child, knowing how devastated she'd been by her last miscarriage. The ghost of that lost baby still haunted them both. "I'm sorry," he said.

She stared straight out the window. "That makes two of us."

Charlie was the last patient on Dr. Gresham's schedule for the day, and they found him sitting all alone in the waiting room, holding a tattered copy of *National Geographic* in his lap. It had been only a few days since Jack had last seen Charlie, and he was shocked by how much older he looked today, as if the sand in his hourglass was spilling away ever more rapidly. Charlie smiled as they walked in and tossed the *Nat Geo* onto the coffee table, where it landed on the pile of other ancient magazines.

"You made it," he said.

"Of course we made it, Dad." Maggie bent down to give her father a hug. "You didn't need to drive here on your own. We could have picked you up."

"Trying to take away my car keys already? You'll have to pry them from my cold dead hands." He gave Jack a nod. "Thanks for joining me on this happy occasion."

"Sure thing, Charlie."

"Getting older is all fun and games." He winced and shifted in his chair. "The fact Dr. Gresham needs to *discuss* the MRI results in person tells me it's about to get a whole lot more fun."

"It doesn't necessarily mean anything," Maggie said, but Jack doubted Charlie was fooled by her reassurance. The false optimism in her voice was obvious.

"Mr. Lucas?" It wasn't the nurse calling Charlie's name, but Dr. Gresham himself. He stood holding a medical chart, his expression determinedly neutral. A bad omen, right there in his face.

With a groan, Charlie rose from the chair, and they followed Dr. Gresham down a short hallway to his office. No one said a word; they were all girding themselves for what was coming. Maggie and Jack eased Charlie into a chair; then they sat down flanking him, the three of them facing Dr. Gresham across the desk. Gresham placed his hands on the chart and took a deep breath.

Another omen.

"I'm glad you could be here with your father, Maggie," Gresham said. "You can help explain things to him later, if what I say isn't completely clear."

"I'm not an idiot," cut in Charlie. "I spent forty years as a cop. Just tell me the truth."

The doctor gave an apologetic nod. "Of course. I wanted to tell you this in person because I'm afraid the news isn't good. The MRI shows a number of osteolytic lesions in your thoracic spine. It explains the pain you've been having, and —"

"Osteo what?"

"Areas of bone destruction. There's some danger of collapse and compression of T5 if it's not treated with radiation, and fairly soon. As for the primary —"

"So it's cancer."

Dr. Gresham nodded. "Yes, sir. That's

what it appears to be."

Charlie looked at Maggie, who'd been shocked into silence. Maggie, who understood every word and yet couldn't produce any of her own.

"There are also multiple nodules in both the left upper lobe and right middle lobe of the lungs. Several of them are peripheral enough for a transthoracic needle biopsy. My best guess is adenocarcinoma. At this stage, with bone metastases —"

"How long?" Charlie cut in.

Maggie reached for his hand, tried to hold it, but Charlie pushed her away, asserting he was still in control. He was not about to play the meek patient just because he couldn't understand what these doctors were saying about him.

"It's, um, hard to say," Dr. Gresham answered.

"Months? Years?"

"It's not possible to predict these things. But some stage-four patients can live for a year or more."

"Treatment?" Charlie asked. His voice was brusque and unemotional, while Maggie looked like she was about to crumble.

"At this stage," Gresham said, "the treatment is palliative. Radiation for the bone lesions. Narcotics as needed for the pain. We'll do everything we can to keep you comfort-able and maximize your quality of life."

"Dad," Maggie whispered. Again she reached for his hand, and this time he let her take it. "Jack and I will be right beside you every step of the way."

"Fine," Charlie snorted, "but I'll deal with it in my own way. If I have to go down, I'll go down swinging. Screw cancer!"

He shoved himself out of the chair. Anger made him push past the pain, and suddenly he was the tough old Charlie that Jack knew, the Charlie who wasn't afraid to face down thugs in a dark alley. As he strode out of the office, Maggie hustled after him. Jack heard the outer door slam shut.

"Thanks, Doc," he said, rising to his feet. "I'm sorry about how he took the news."

"No one takes this kind of news very well." Dr. Gresham shook his head. "I'm sorry it couldn't have been better. The next few months are going to be tough on you all. Let Maggie know she can call me anytime. She'll need all the support she can get."

When Jack walked out of the building, he found Charlie and Maggie standing beside his car. He was flushed and clearly angry as he waved her away.

"I can drive home on my own."

139

"Dad, please. It's no problem. You need to let us help."

He shook his head. "I don't need a baby-sitter! I'm going home to pour myself a double scotch." With a grunt, he climbed into his car and slammed the door shut.

"Dad." Maggie rapped at the car window as Charlie pulled out of the parking space. "Dad!"

Jack reached for her arm. "Let him go."

"He can't just take off like this. He needs —"

"Right now he needs his dignity. Let's allow him that much."

Maggie pressed her hand to her mouth, trying not to cry. He took her in his arms, and they held each other as the sound of Charlie's car faded away.

CHAPTER 13
JACK

It was a little before ten a.m. when Jack arrived at the Museum of Fine Arts. Over the main entrance hung a giant banner announcing the new exhibit: **ETERNAL LOVERS: ABELARD AND HELOISE,** with an image of the iconic pair in a passionate embrace. His Star-Crossed students were already waiting on the front steps, and as he approached, Jessica and Caitlin fixed him with sullen looks. He spotted Taryn standing off to the side, and he wanted to thank her for defending him against the Title IX accusation, but he'd have to do it later, in private. Certainly not while Cody Atwood hovered nearby, as he was today. Instead, he gave Taryn a smile and a nod, and it was enough to make her face light up.

"Professor Dorian?" said a young woman standing near the entrance.

"Yes. You must be Jenny Iverson," he said. She nodded. "Assistant to the curator. I'll be taking your class on a tour of the new exhibit. So welcome, everyone!"

As he followed the group up the marble steps to the second floor, he reminded himself not to reveal any grudge he might have against Jessica, even though he was certain she'd been the source of that Title IX complaint. *Keep your cool, Jack. Just smile at the little jerks.* They passed through the Rabb Gallery, past Maggie's favorite painting in the entire museum: Renoir's *Dance at Bougival.* He paused to admire the image of the two dancers, the woman in a red bonnet, the man in a straw hat, both so joyously in love. Twelve years ago, he'd proposed to Maggie before this very painting. *Let that always be us,* he'd said to her then.

How different their lives looked today.

They arrived at the Farago Gallery, where the walls were covered with a dizzying display of oil paintings and triptychs and engravings, all featuring Heloise and Abelard. In the center of the room were glass display cases with fourteenth-century illuminated manuscripts of the lovers' letters. On the far wall hung movie posters and recent translations of their story — evidence that their tragic tale had become timeless.

"This exhibit was timed to open around

Valentine's Day, for reasons which should be obvious," said Ms. Iverson. "Instead of dinner and a movie, maybe a perfect date night will be a trip to this museum!"

"Most boring date ever," Jack heard Jessica mutter behind him. He chose to ignore it.

"I understand you've already read the letters of Abelard and Heloise, so you know their love story. How an affair between a teacher and his brilliant, beautiful student pitted Christian devotion against sexual passion."

He noticed Cody looking sideways at him.

"As much as we want to believe this was a true story, the authenticity of the letters has never actually been established, and some scholars argue they're merely fiction."

"What do you think?" Taryn asked her.

"There's such passion in these letters; I prefer to believe they're real."

"Or they could just be erotic fantasies written by some horny monk," Jessica said.

Iverson responded with a tight smile. "Perhaps."

"Does it really matter who wrote them?" Taryn said. "They so beautifully immortalize a doomed love affair. I'm guessing they were the inspiration for other tales about star-crossed lovers. Maybe even *Romeo and Juliet.*"

"Excellent observation," said Ms. Iverson.

As they moved on, Jack heard Jessica whisper to Caitlin, "Brownnosing little bitch."

They passed by a Pre-Raphaelite painting of the doomed couple, golden-haired Heloise adorned in lustrous silk, Abelard with a head of dark ringlets. In the painting beside it was a completely different version of Abelard, depicted as a medieval scholar in a cowled hood. He looked more like a wizard than a teacher as he kissed an innocent Heloise.

"He looks like Voldemort putting the moves on Hermione," Jason said to a few chuckles.

"Maybe she did it for the A-plus," Jessica said.

Jack saw Cody flash Taryn a frown. What the hell was the scuttlebutt in class? Did they really think there was something going on between him and Taryn?

He wanted the tour to be over, but unfortunately, they were moving on to sexier depictions of the pair. They stopped before a nineteenth-century oil painting showing Abelard holding Heloise's hands against her bared breast. Behind them, her menacing uncle Fulbert lurked in a shadowy doorway. But it was the rosy glow of Heloise's breast that held Jack's gaze, a breast unmarred by age or the relentless pull of gravity. He was acutely aware of Taryn standing beside him, her gaze on the painting as well. She was close enough for him to catch the scent of her hair, to feel her sweater brush against his arm.

Abruptly he turned and moved on.

They came to the final group of illustrations, depicting Abelard's punishment.

"As you already know, since you've read the letters," said Ms. Iverson, "Heloise's uncle Fulbert had Abelard castrated as punishment for the affair with Heloise. So some of these images are quite disturbing."

They certainly were. One black-and-white eighteenth-century engraving showed Abelard laid out on a canopied nuptial bed with two men holding down his legs while Fulbert performed the castration. Heloise stood restrained as she watched the scene, screaming in horror. In another etching, Abelard was held down, his head covered by a hood, while a black-robed priest wielded a knife between Abelard's legs.

The final painting, *The Farewell of Abelard and Heloise,* by Angelica Kauffman, showed nuns leading a weeping Heloise from Abelard, the lovers' arms stretched out to each other as they were forever separated.

"She goes to a convent. He gets his balls cut off," Cody said. "I think it's pretty clear who got the worst of it."

"Not Abelard," Taryn said. "He got what he wanted, even if he did spend the rest of his life sexless and in a monastery."

"Thanks for meeting with me," Taryn said an hour later as she and Jack sat at a table in the MFA's restaurant. "I probably should have scheduled an appointment during office hours."

"We both have to eat lunch. We might as well have our meeting here."

"Yeah, but . . ." She looked around the dining room as a waiter glided past with four glasses of wine on his tray. "The coffee shop would have been fine too."

"The food's much better here." He shook out his napkin with a nonchalance he wasn't quite feeling. Professors often had lunch with their students, yet he felt a twinge of guilt, sitting here with Taryn. This restaurant was where he and Maggie had celebrated their engagement, right after he'd proposed to her in front of Renoir's dancers.

The waiter came to deliver their drink orders, iced tea for Taryn and a pinot noir for him. He took a sip to center himself.

"To be honest," he said, "I thought this restaurant would offer more privacy. Because I wanted to thank you for coming to my defense about that Title Nine complaint against me."

"How do you know I'm the one who defended you?"

"Elizabeth Sacco told me one of the female students in the class stood up for me. I realized it *had* to be you."

"It was supposed to be confidential," she said as a smile twitched on her lips. "The complaint was ridiculous anyway. I can't believe anyone was triggered by what you said."

"Neither can I," Jack said.

"About affairs between teachers and students?"

"I was talking about a book. I wasn't advocating any such behavior."

"But would you?"

"Would I what?"

"Ever have an affair with a student?"

He felt his heart take a gulp of blood. "I'm a married man. And it's strictly forbidden by university rules. Besides, I'm twice the age of my students."

"You talk like you're ancient or something."

"Compared to you, I am."

She smiled. "But not so old I wouldn't date you."

The coquettishness of her response disturbed him, but he let it pass. He took another sip of wine. "Rules aside, it's just not something I would ever do. Because it's wrong."

She nodded. "And that's what makes you different. You care about right and wrong. About loyalty. A lot of people in this world wouldn't give a damn about that." She pulled up her museum-shop bag. "Want to see what I bought?"

"Sure." He was relieved to change the subject.

She pulled out a box from which she extracted a white ceramic statue of a woman, a dagger gripped in her hand. Carved at the base of the statue was the name *Medea.*

"You didn't buy anything about Abelard and Heloise?"

"No, because *this* is more my kind of woman."

"Medea?"

She read aloud the description on the box. " 'In Greek mythology, Medea punished her unfaithful husband by murdering their two children. Wounded by infidelity, blinded by jealousy and anger, Medea contemplates her pending crime.' " She looked at him. "She's a far more interesting character than Heloise, don't you think?"

"Why?"

"Because Medea's not passive. She's active. She uses her rage to take command of the situation."

"By murdering her children?"

"Yes, it's horrible, what she does. But she doesn't spend the rest of her life whining *woe is me.*"

"And you find that admirable?"

"I find it worthy of respect." She placed the statue back in the box and stuffed it into her backpack. "Even if men might find the idea terrifying."

"Terrifying?"

"Female rage." She looked straight at him, and the fierceness of her gaze unsettled him. "That's what I'd like to write about. Medieval literature emphasizes female passivity. It saddles women with all those *thou shalt not*s. We're not allowed to be immodest or wanton or rebellious. But Greek mythology celebrates our power. Think of Medea and Hera and Aphrodite. They don't passively accept male infidelity. No, they *react* to it, sometimes violently. And they . . ."

Her voice suddenly dropped away. She

was no longer looking at Jack but over his shoulder. He turned to see what had caught her attention, but all he noticed was a young couple walking past the hostess stand and out of the restaurant. He looked at Taryn and was alarmed by how pale her face was. "Are you all right?"

She shot to her feet and yanked her jacket from the chair. "I have to go."

"What about your lunch? It's still coming."

She didn't answer. She dashed out of the restaurant, just as the waiter returned to their table.

"Your lobster rolls," he said and set down two plates.

Jack looked at the chair where Taryn had been sitting. "I think you should box up her order."

"Isn't she coming back?"

He glanced at the exit. Taryn had vanished. "I don't think so."

CHAPTER 14
TARYN

They were half a block ahead of her, unaware that she was following them, although she was staring so fiercely surely they could feel the heat of her gaze on their backs. Who was that girl with Liam? How long had this been going on between them? It was obvious that something *was* going on, just by the way he draped his arm over her shoulders, by the way their heads tipped together. In her high-heeled boots, she was almost as tall as he was, and the cinched belt of her down jacket emphasized a model-thin waist and slim hips. Tight blue jeans showed off impossibly long legs.

Her stomach churned, and suddenly she felt so sick she reeled against a streetlamp and retched into the gutter, vomiting up sour-tasting water. For a moment, all she could do was hang on to that icy pole as people passed by her. No one asked if she was okay. No one stopped to offer a kind word. Though surrounded by pedestrians and traffic, she was all alone, invisible.

When at last she lifted her head, Liam and the dark-haired slut were nowhere to be seen.

It was only a ten-minute walk to Liam's off-campus apartment. When she arrived and rang his buzzer, no one answered. She let herself into 2D to wait for him.

The instant she stepped into his apartment, she sensed there was something different in the air — the way it smelled, the way the molecules themselves seemed statically charged as they swirled around her. What had once belonged to her was now foreign terrain, claimed by a usurper, and she'd been blind to what was now so obvious. She remembered the alien cartons of yogurt she'd seen in his refrigerator, the Stanford Law School brochure in his stack of mail, and the fact his bed had been so neatly made. It was *her* doing. The Bitch. She'd managed to slither her way into her territory, and Taryn had missed all the signs.

She sat on the sofa facing the bookcase, where the photo of Liam and herself used to be. Instead of their picture was a small crystal globe, something she didn't recognize. It caught the wintry light from the window, and she couldn't stop staring at it.

Yet another item that did not belong there.

Her hands were numb from the cold. From the shock. She tucked them inside her jacket and hugged herself. There was no one else here to hug her because Liam was now hugging someone else.

All afternoon and into the evening, she waited for him. She heard his neighbors on the second floor come home: The Abernathys returning from their boring jobs back to their boring lives. The blondes, giggling and chattering as they jangled keys. And from across the hall came the clang of virtual swordsmen in combat as the geeky grad students battled it out in some video game. But here in Liam's apartment, there was only silence.

She didn't remember falling asleep. She only knew that when she woke up on the sofa, it was dark, the building was silent, and her cell phone battery was down to 6 percent. It was exactly 4:45 a.m., and he'd never come home.

He was with her, of course. Staying with her. Sleeping with her.

She left Liam's building and walked through the bitterly cold darkness to her apartment. She passed a twenty-four-hour coffee shop and smelled fresh-baked croissants, but she had no appetite, even though she hadn't eaten a thing since yesterday. It seemed like a lifetime ago. A time when she'd thought Liam was still hers.

Before the Bitch had stolen him away.

By the time she reached her apartment, she was so chilled she didn't even bother to undress but just pulled off her boots and crawled into bed, shivering. Thinking about Liam and *her*. This was the first time in all their years together that he'd strayed. This new girl was new to him, alluring only because she was fresh meat, and he didn't yet know her flaws. Everyone had secrets, and surely she did too. A shoplifting arrest? An abortion? A boyfriend she'd cheated on? If she had any secrets at all, Taryn would ferret them out.

And she knew just the person who would help her.

"I don't want to do it," Cody said.

They were sitting in the student union food court, and as usual he'd loaded up his lunch tray with all the things he shouldn't be eating: three slices of pizza, an order of french fries, and an extra-large Pepsi. There was no green vegetable in sight, unless you counted the flecks of bell pepper trapped in the congealing mozzarella. Taryn sat across from him, nursing only a cup of coffee

because she was too keyed up to eat anything, and she was so frustrated by Cody's
intransigence that she wanted to shove his
tray off the table, just to force him to look
at her.

"I'm not asking you for a lot," she told
him.

"You're asking me to spy on some girl I
don't even know."

"That's why you have to be the one to do
it."

"Why don't you?"

"Because Liam might spot me. But he
doesn't know you. You can follow them
anywhere, and you'll never be noticed."

"Now you want me to *follow* them too?"

"It's the only way to know what they're
up to. You're the one who's seen all those
Jason Bourne movies. This is exactly what
spies do. They blend into the crowd and
become as invisible as ghosts. You'll be my
personal secret agent." She leaned forward,
her voice dropping to an intimate whisper.
He was looking right at her now. His mouth
might be full of pizza, but all his attention
was on her. She saw the glint of excitement
in his eyes at the thought of Cody Atwood,
secret agent. He was no Jason Bourne, but
he was all she had.

"What do you want me to do?"

"Find out who she is. Her name, her hometown, whether she lives on campus or off. Find out her secrets."

"How am I supposed to do that?"

"You're the spy. You should know what to do."

He was silent for a moment, rubbing a greasy hand on his chin as he mulled over how his hero Jason Bourne would handle the assignment. "I guess you'll want photos," he said. "I can dust off my Canon."

"Great."

"And I'll need my telephoto lens."

"You have one?"

"My grandpa gave me his old lens a few years ago. Haven't used it in a while, but I'll dig it out. So how do I find this girl? You haven't even told me her name. Where do I look for her?"

"Begin with Liam."

He sighed and sank back in his chair. In that instant she knew she was losing him and she'd have to do something quick to reel him back.

She put her hand on his arm. "You're the only one I can count on, Cody."

"It's not really about the girl, is it? It's still about Liam."

"I need to know what she's up to. What she's planning."

"Why?"

"Because I don't trust her. And I need to look out for my friends."

"By spying on him? On her?"

"I'd do it for you too. If I thought you were tangled up with the wrong person, I'd step in to protect you."

"You would?"

"It's what friends do. We watch out for each other." And she truly meant it. She might not be in love with Cody or attracted to him, but she would never let anyone hurt him. It was a matter of loyalty.

"What if they catch me spying on them? I could get in trouble."

"You're too smart. I'm sure you'll be good at this."

He perked up, her chubby-cheeked Jason Bourne with a grease-smeared chin. "You really think so?"

"I know so."

He sat up straighter. Took a deep breath. "So where do I find Liam?"

Her name was Elizabeth Whaley, and she lived in an apartment building two blocks from campus.

Cody turned out to be a better spy than Taryn had expected, and in only two days, he'd tracked down the girl's apartment. It was a building that Taryn had walked past many times before, never imagining that this was where her enemy lived. The building was new, with underground parking, which meant the girl had money. That would impress Liam, and it would impress his parents even more. The girl was thin, fashionable, and rich.

There had to be *something* wrong with her.

Taryn waited across the street from the building until she saw a young man carrying a sack of groceries climb the steps to the front door. As he let himself in, she was right behind him, and they both stepped inside. No one ever felt threatened by a pretty girl, certainly not a girl who was smiling at them. He smiled back at her as they both got into the elevator, which quickly filled with the scent of green onions and cilantro from his sack of groceries. On the third floor he stepped off, but she stayed on until the fourth floor.

It was *her* floor. The enemy's.

Taryn paused outside 405, listening. She heard no voices, no music, no sounds of anyone at home. But she was not planning to knock on that door anyway; instead, she knocked at 407, where the sound of a TV told her the occupant was at home.

A bedraggled woman wearing blue jeans answered the door. Her blonde hair was uncombed, and her eyes were hollow with fatigue. Somewhere in the apartment, a baby started crying. The woman glanced toward the sound, then looked back at her visitor.

"I'm sorry to bother you," said Taryn. "Do you happen to know your neighbor very well? The one next door?"

"You mean Libby?"

Libby. Short for Elizabeth. "Yes," said Taryn.

"I run into her once in a while. Say hello in the elevator. Why?"

"Have you had any, um, concerns about her?"

"You mean like noise?"

"Or other things."

The baby cried louder. "Excuse me," the woman said and ran into a bedroom. She returned holding the baby, who fussed and squirmed in her arms. As she jiggled it, she asked: "Is there some sort of problem with Libby?"

"This is kind of, um, delicate."

"If there's something I should know, I'd really like to hear it. Since I'm living right next door to her, with a baby and all."

"I know Libby from the building where

159

she used to live. And we had, um, issues with her. Have you noticed anything?"

This had gotten her attention. Even as the baby wriggled and whimpered, the woman mulled over the question, no doubt reviewing every interaction she'd ever had with her neighbor. "Well, she's kind of a cool cat. And I don't think she's a big fan of babies. At least, not my baby."

Okay. Keep going.

"And there was that party she threw last month. You could smell the pot all the way down the hall. Some of the kids were drunk, and I know they weren't all of age. It went on till way past midnight, kept me and my husband awake. And the baby too."

"That's pretty inconsiderate."

"No kidding." The woman was just getting started, trawling her memory for every irritation, every slight, as she jiggled the baby to keep it quiet. "Then there's that boy she keeps bringing over. I mean, if they're having sleepovers, why doesn't he just make it official and move in? But I guess he can afford having his own apartment. I sure didn't have that kind of money when I was in college."

That boy. Was she talking about Liam?

"Oh, and there were the FedEx packages that went missing, down by the mail slots.

160

We never did find out who took them. Did that happen in your building? Did things go missing there too?"

Taryn didn't answer. She was thinking about Liam sleeping in another girl's bed. A girl who had no right to him. No, there could still be a mistake. She didn't know for certain it was Liam.

"Please don't tell her I was here," said Taryn.

"Should I be worried? Should I tell the building supervisor?"

"Not yet. Not until I have proof."

"Okay. Thank you for warning me." The woman cast a nervous glance toward 405. "I'll keep an eye on her."

So will I.

On her way back to the elevator, Taryn paused once again outside 405. She thought about how easy it would be to wait here until Elizabeth Whaley returned home. How easy it would be to follow her into her apartment and pull a knife from the kitchen drawer. She wondered how hard you had to push to make a blade sink into flesh, and how deep it had to go to pierce the heart. She considered all these things.

Then she left the building and walked home.

■ ■ ■ ■

It was seven fifteen on Friday night when her phone dinged with a text message from Cody.

When she opened it, at first she didn't understand the significance of what she was looking at. It was a blurry photo taken through a window, and half the frame was filled with a man's shoulder in the foreground. Then she focused on the couple seated in the background. The woman's back was turned, but Taryn could see she had long dark hair and was holding a glass of red wine. The man seated across from her also held a glass of wine, raised slightly as though in a toast, and the camera had caught him in midlaugh. It was a face she knew all too well, and it was smiling at another woman.

Feverishly she tapped out a reply to Cody: Where is this?

He answered: Emilio's on Concord St.

She knew exactly where Emilio's was. She remembered standing outside the restaurant with Liam when they were freshmen, salivating over the menu posted in the front window. She remembered him telling her, "One of these days, when we have some-

162

thing big to celebrate, I'll bring you here."

He never had. Instead he was there with *her,* laughing and sipping wine.

She texted Cody: R they there right now?

Should be. I left only ten minutes ago.

A roar whooshed inside her head, and she pressed her hands to her temples to block out the sound, but it was still there. The sound of her heart pounding. Breaking.

It was a fifteen-minute walk to Emilio's, and the whole time she thought about where they must be in their meal. By now the bread and appetizers would have been cleared away, and they'd be on the main course. She imagined the woman twirling pasta on her fork, Liam slicing into his forty-two-dollar veal entrée. That was what he'd go for, the priciest item on the menu, if only to impress his date. She picked up her pace, her boots pounding the sidewalk in determined march tempo. She could not let them slip away from the restaurant before she confronted them. This must happen tonight, now. Her hands were clenched in fists, ready for battle. This *was* battle, and she thought of Achilles and Aeneas, Sparta and Troy. That war had been fought over a woman. This war would be fought between women. By the time she stepped into Emilio's, she was flushed and sweating in her down jacket. Inside, over the background music of soft jazz, she heard the clink of chinaware and the happy buzz of conversation. In the bar, a cappuccino machine roared, frothing milk.

"Can I help you?" the hostess asked.

Taryn pushed right past her into the dining room and spotted Liam at a table near the window. The chair across from him was empty, but there was a woman's sweater and a purse draped over the back. She'd gone to the restroom, and Liam was too busy scrolling through his smartphone to notice Taryn until she was standing at his table. His chin snapped up, and he stared at her in disbelief.

"Taryn? What are you —"

"Why are you here with her?"

"I don't know what you're talking about."

"I saw you two at the museum. And now you've brought her here."

"You've been spying on us?"

"Just tell me why you're with her."

"This is none of your business."

"It fucking well *is* my business."

"Okay, you have to leave. Now." He glanced around, scanning the dining room for help. The hostess was already walking toward them, high heels clacking across the

164

wood floor.

"Is this woman disturbing you?" she asked Liam.

"Yes, she is. Maybe you could show her out."

"Not till you tell me *why the fuck you're here with her*!" Taryn screamed.

Everyone was staring, but she didn't care. She didn't care that her hair was a wild tangle and her face was wind chapped and her voice was shaking. All she cared about was that Liam's shame was now out in the open for the world to see.

"That's *enough.*" Liam rose to his feet and said to the other diners: "I'm sorry about this, folks. This woman is crazy."

"I'm calling the police," said the hostess, already pulling out a cell phone.

"Liam, what's going on?" a new voice said.

Taryn turned to see the Bitch, who had returned from the restroom and was frowning at her. She was doe eyed and so very pretty.

"Why are you seeing my boyfriend?" Taryn demanded.

"I'm going to walk her outside," Liam said to the girl. "I'll be right back."

"But Liam —"

"Just wait here, okay, Libby?"

Liam hauled Taryn across the dining room

165

and out the door to the sidewalk. An icy wind was blowing, and he was only in shirtsleeves, but he was so fueled by rage he seemed impervious to the cold.

"Taryn, you are going to *leave me alone.* Do you understand?"

"So you've been cheating on me."

"Cheating? On *you?*" His laugh was like a slap in the face. "Do you think you and I are still together? It's *over.* It's been over for months, and there's nothing between us, okay? I told you that. I've been telling you since Christmas, but you're like a psycho with all your phone calls and emails and texts. Do you get it now? I'm *done* with you. So leave me the fuck *alone.*"

"Liam," she said softly. Then again, "Liam."

"Go home." He turned back to the restaurant.

"You love me. You told me so. Don't you remember?"

"Things change."

"*This* doesn't change! Not love!"

"We were kids. We didn't know any better."

"I knew. I've always known. The only reason I came to Boston was to be with you. You *asked* me to."

"But now it's time for both of us to move

on. We're not the same people we were in high school, Taryn. I'm heading to law school, maybe in California. I need to be able to *breathe*."

"Is *she* going to let you breathe?"

"At least she won't smother me. She has plans of her own."

"Meaning you."

"No, meaning she's going to do something with her life. She's applying to grad school, thinking about a career."

"You two are going away to grad school together?"

"Come on, Taryn. Don't make this harder than it already is. It was never going to work out between us."

"Because I don't have *her* ambition? Or is it because I'm just the girl from Mill Street and you're the doctor's kid?"

"It has nothing to do with where you came from. It's about where you're going, and about where I want to go. It's about having plans."

"But I had *you.*"

He sighed. "I can't be responsible for making you happy."

"All these years, you let me *believe* in us. You kept me around just so you could keep using me. Fucking me." Her voice was rising, loud enough that people inside Emilio's could hear her. Through the window she could see them staring. Let them. She hoped the Bitch was watching too. "I was just your whore, wasn't I?"

"Taryn."

"Just a whore you used and threw away. You bastard. You *bastard.*" She lunged toward him.

He grabbed both her wrists. "You're acting nuts! Stop it. *Stop it.*"

She fought him, sobbing as she pushed and punched, but he was too strong. She wrenched away, and he released her so suddenly that she stumbled backward and fell on her butt. Sitting on the icy sidewalk, she could feel the appalled gazes of people staring at her through the restaurant window. They'd seen the whole thing. They knew she was the one who'd attacked first. There was no blaming this on Liam.

"Go home, Taryn," Liam said in disgust. "Go home before you embarrass yourself even more than you already have." He walked back into Emilio's, leaving her alone and shivering on the sidewalk.

She could still feel all those eyes watching her as she slowly rose back to her feet. She couldn't bear to look at the window, couldn't bear to see them enjoying her humiliation. She just walked away, sore and limping from her fall on the pavement. She was so numb from cold and shock that she moved on automatic pilot. All she could hear were the same words echoing again and again in her head.

I'm not good enough for him. Not good enough. Not good enough. Not good enough.

Suddenly she glimpsed her reflection in a storefront window, and she halted, staring at her haunted eyes, her windblown hair. Was this what crazy looked like? Was this the moment she walked into traffic or threw herself off a building?

She took a deep breath. Scraped the tangled hair off her face and stood up straight. Liam thought she wasn't good enough.

It was time to prove him wrong.

■ ■ ■ ■

AFTER

■ ■ ■ ■

CHAPTER 15
FRANKIE

Sometimes this job is just too easy, thinks Frankie. The murder weapon, almost certainly covered with the killer's fingerprints, is already sealed in an evidence bag. The estranged husband now sits handcuffed in a patrol car outside. And his wife . . .

Frankie looks down at the body on the bed. The woman is dressed in a blue cotton nightgown, the hem scalloped with white lace. She lies curled up on her right side, her face nestled on a pillow that is now embedded with bits of scalp and brain matter, blasted there by the force of the gunshot. Judging by the wife's peaceful pose, she must have slept through the sound of the key turning in her front-door lock, which she had not yet changed. She slept through the footsteps treading up the hall to her bedroom. And she was sleeping when the figure approached her bed, a figure that, after eight turbulent years of marriage, would have been chillingly familiar.

"He won't stop blabbing," says Mac. "If only they were all like him."

Frankie looks up as her partner walks into the bedroom. His face is still florid from the wind, his rosacea inflamed worse than ever on this cold morning.

"Then you and I would be out of a job," she says and looks at the body again. Theresa Lutovic, age thirty-two. Maybe she was pretty once; it is now hard to tell.

"Restraining order was filed just last week. New locks were supposed to be installed tomorrow."

"She did everything right," says Frankie.

"Except for marrying the guy."

"Do the neighbors have anything to add?" she asks.

"Neighbors on the right didn't wake up until they heard the sirens. Neighbor on the left heard a bang, doesn't know what time it was, and went right back to sleep. If the asshole hadn't called it in himself, it might've been a while before anyone found her." Mac shakes his head in disgust. "No remorse, not one shred of it. In fact, he sounded like he's fucking proud he did it."

Proud of asserting his God-given right of possession, Frankie thinks, looking down at what had once been that possession. Did

174

this woman feel any inkling when she first met her husband that a blood-soaked bed was in her future? When they were dating, was there a hint — a glare, a sharp word — revealing the monster beneath his mask? Or did she ignore all the clues, lured in like so many women are by the promise of hearts and flowers and happily ever after?

"At least there aren't any children involved," Frankie says.

Mac grunts. "Thank God for small blessings."

Eddie Lutovic sits at the interview table with his head held high, his back as ramrod straight as a soldier's. As Frankie settles into the chair across from him, he does not meet her gaze but looks right past her, as if some phantom authority stands behind her. As if this matronly woman with bifocals and a navy-blue pantsuit cannot possibly be that authority. Frankie lets him stew in silence for a moment as she takes her time studying him. He could be considered a good-looking man, muscular and trim at thirty-six, his brown hair clipped short, his eyes an unnerving crystalline blue. Yes, she can see that some women might be attracted, even reassured, by his confident bearing. They'd think: *Here is a man who can take care of me, protect me.*

"Mr. Lutovic," she says. "In case you've forgotten my name, I'm Detective Loomis. I need to ask you a few more —"

"Yeah, you told me your name this morning," he cuts in, still refusing to look at her.

She lets his obvious disdain slide right past her. Calmly she says, "At five ten this morning, you called nine-one-one from your estranged wife's residence."

"That's my house. Not hers."

"Regardless of whose house it is, you called the emergency operator. Did you not?"

"I did."

"You informed the operator that you'd just shot your wife."

He gives a dismissive wave. "Why am I talking to you? I should be talking to Detective MacClellan."

"Detective MacClellan is not the one sitting here. I am."

"Everything I need to say, I've already said to him."

"And now you're going to say it to me."

"Why?"

"Because we're not leaving this room until you do. So let's just get on with it, shall we? Why did you shoot Theresa?"

At last he looks at her. "You wouldn't

understand."

"Try me."

"You think I *wanted* to kill her?"

"I think you must be angry that she was leaving you."

His glare could freeze water. "A man can only be pushed so far. That's *my* house she was living in. You can't kick a man out of his own *fucking house*!"

"Tell me about the gun you used. The Glock."

"What about it?"

"It's not registered. And since Theresa had a restraining order against you, you were in illegal possession of that weapon."

"The Second Amendment says I have a right to own a gun."

"The State of Massachusetts doesn't agree."

"Fuck the State of Massachusetts."

"And the State of Massachusetts will happily return the sentiment," she says and smiles. As they regard each other across the table, the gravity of his situation at last seems to sink in. Suddenly the breath goes out of him, and his shoulders sag.

"It didn't have to be this way," he says.

"But it is. Why?"

"You don't know how hard she made it for me. It was like she *wanted* to piss me off. Like she did things on purpose, to get me to react."

"What things?"

"The way she looked at other guys. The way she talked back if I called her on it."

"She asked for it, did she?"

He hears the disgust in her voice and raises his head to glare at her. "I knew you wouldn't understand."

Oh, but Frankie does understand. She's heard this excuse, or variations of it, too many times before. *Not my fault. The victim made me do it.* She could show him the list of calls his wife made to 911. She could show him the record of her last ER visit and the photo of her bruised face, and his answer would be the same: *Not my fault.*

It never is.

She sinks back, suddenly weary of her role in these three-act tragedies. Frankie is the character who invariably walks onstage too late, in the third act, after the damage is done. After the corpse is zipped into the body bag. If only she could have entered this drama earlier, when there was still time to warn the future Mrs. Lutovic: *Turn back now, before you fall in love with this man. Before you say* I do. *Before the beatings and the restraining orders and the ER visits.*

178

Before the zipper of a body bag closes over you.

But women in love are seldom dissuaded by the voice of experience. She thinks of her own impulsive daughters and all the nights she lies awake, waiting to hear the reassuring sound of their key in the door. How many hours of sleep has she lost as she watched the hours tick by, afraid to think of all the terrible possibilities?

She knows all too well what can go wrong. She saw it today, in the bedroom of a dead woman.

An officer escorts Lutovic out of the room, but Frankie remains in her chair, jotting down notes from the interview. It has all been recorded on video, but she is old fashioned enough to prefer the touch and permanence of paper. Words written in ink don't vanish into the ether or get accidentally deleted, and the act of writing them down helps sear the interview into her memory. Her phone dings with a text message, but she keeps writing, in a rush to record her impressions before they fade. But what will never fade is her disgust toward Eddie Lutovic. She is so focused on her notes that she scarcely notices when Mac walks into the room. Only when she hears him sneeze does she look up.

"ME's office just called. They want to know if we're coming," he says.

"To what?"

"The autopsy on Taryn Moore."

She looks down at her angry scribbles. Thinks of Eddie's leering face and his wife's blood splattered on the pillow. She shuts her notebook.

"It's not like we have to go," says Mac. "It's just a suicide."

"Are you absolutely sure about that?"

Mac gives a resigned sigh. "I'll drive."

CHAPTER 16
FRANKIE

In Frankie's experience, autopsies seldom reveal surprises of any significance. Occasionally the ME might turn up an extra bullet wound or an occult tumor or, in the case of one deranged senior citizen who'd shot up his neighborhood, a whopping case of brain rot known as Pick's disease. But most of the time, Frankie has already deduced the cause and manner of death even before the pathologist makes his first cut. Postmortems are often merely formalities, and Frankie is not required to attend them.

This one, she wishes she had skipped.

When she sees Taryn Moore's body laid out on the table, it is far too easy for her to imagine it belonging to one of her own daughters. Daughters she nursed and bathed, whose diapers she changed; daughters she watched blossom from plump toddlers into slim-hipped teenagers into beautiful young women. Now here is another mother's daughter, once equally beautiful, and the thought of that mother's loss is so painful she wants to walk out of the room. Instead she stoically ties on a paper mask and joins Mac at the autopsy table.

"Didn't know if you two were coming, so I got started without you," says Dr. Fleer, the pathologist. If she didn't know he was a fanatically health-conscious vegan and marathon runner, she would think he was seriously ill because he is cadaverically thin, his blue eyes staring from a disturbingly skull-like head. "I'm just about to open the thorax."

Frankie forces herself to focus on the torso as Fleer cuts through the exposed ribs with pruning shears. Standing beside her, Mac gives an explosive sneeze behind his paper mask, but it is the crack-crack of snapping bone that makes her wince.

"Sounds like you should go home, Detective MacClellan," Fleer says. "Before you infect us with whatever virus you're incubating."

"Why are you worried about a little virus?" Mac snorts. "I thought you vegans were invincible."

"It wouldn't hurt *you* to try going vegan for once. A few months into it, you won't

182

even miss those animal fats."

"When they make broccoli taste like steak, I may give it a try."

"You don't have a fever, do you? Myalgias?"

"It's just a head cold. This damp weather is hell on my sinuses. Anyway, I'm wearing a mask, aren't I?"

"Paper masks are not airtight, and you were already sneezing when you walked in. By now, your viral spray has been broadcast all over this room."

"Excuse me for breathing."

Fleer cuts through the last rib and lifts off the shield of breastbone, revealing the heart and lungs. He peers into the chest cavity. "Interesting."

"What's interesting?" asks Frankie.

"The aorta appears intact."

"Is that a surprise?"

"A five-story fall onto concrete usually results in far more intrathoracic trauma than I'm seeing in here. When a body hits the ground at that velocity, the heart jerks against its ligaments, and that can tear the great vessels, but I don't see any large-vessel rupture here. Probably because she was only twenty-two. People that young have much more elastic connective tissue. They can bounce back."

183

Frankie looks at the glistening heart of Taryn Moore and thinks about the trauma from which young people sometimes *don't* bounce back. A father who abandons you. A boyfriend breaking up with you.

"So it's the head injury that killed her?" says Mac.

"Almost certainly." Fleer turns and calls across the room to his assistant, who is setting up the instrument tray for the next autopsy. "Lisa, can you pull up Taryn Moore's skull x-rays so they can take a look?"

"What are we supposed to see there?" says Mac.

"I'll show you. To fracture a skull takes only five foot-pounds of force. You can get that much force just by falling three feet onto your head, and this was a five-story fall." Fleer crosses to the computer monitor, where Lisa has pulled up the skull films. "Based on these AP and lateral views, it appears she hit the ground, bounced, and hit the ground a second time. The initial impact caused this compression fracture of the squamous part of the temporal bone. The second impact fractured the frontal bone and resulted in the facial trauma. Using Puppe's rule, we know the sequence."

"Puppe's rule?" says Mac. "Does that have

184

something to do with dogs?"

Fleer sighs. "It's called *Puppe's rule* after Dr. Georg Puppe, the physician who first described the principle. It simply states that a fracture line will be stopped by any previous fracture line. And here, on this x-ray, you see where the bone has caved in? Based on the location, near the temporal fossa, I'd say there was very likely a rupture of the middle meningeal artery. When we open up the cranium, we're almost certainly going to find a subarachnoid bleed. But let me continue with the thorax." Fleer returns to the autopsy table and picks up a scalpel. He excises the heart and lungs, sets them in a basin, and moves on to the abdominal cavity. Swiftly and efficiently he removes stomach and bowel, liver and spleen. Frankie turns away, nauseated, when he slits open the stomach and empties the contents into a basin, releasing the sour stench of gastric juices.

"The last meal she ingested was . . . red wine, I'd guess," he says. "I don't see any food."

"She had macaroni and cheese in her microwave," says Frankie.

"Well, she never ate it. There's no solid food in here." Fleer sets aside the sectioned stomach and turns his attention to the hollowed-out abdominal cavity. The viscera he's removed so far are undiseased, the organs of a healthy young woman who should have outlived everyone around this table. Yet here they are, Fleer and Mac and Frankie, still alive and breathing, while Taryn Moore is not.

"As soon as I finish the pelvis, we'll open the cranium, and you'll see just how much damage a five-story fall can . . ." He pauses, his hands deep in the pelvic cavity. Abruptly he turns to Lisa. "Make sure you include a serum HCG in her blood work. And I'll want to preserve this uterus in formalin gel."

"HCG?" Lisa approaches the table. "Do you think she's —"

"Let's have Dr. Siu look at the uterine sections." He reaches for a syringe. "And we'll need to collect DNA from these tissues."

"DNA? What's going on?" Mac says.

Frankie doesn't need to ask; she already understands the reason for the DNA collection. She looks down at Taryn Moore's exposed pelvic cavity and asks: "How far along was she?"

"I don't want to hazard a guess. All I can tell you is her uterus is abnormally large, and it feels soft, almost boggy, to me. We'll preserve it in formalin and have a pediatric pathologist examine the sections."

"She was pregnant?" Mac looks at Frankie. "But her boyfriend said they broke up months ago. You think it's his baby?"

"If it isn't his, we've just opened up a whole new can of worms."

Fleer uncaps the syringe. "DNA is the answer to all life's mysteries."

"So now we know the reason she killed herself," says Mac. "She finds out she's pregnant. Tells the ex-boyfriend, who refuses to marry her. He says it's not his problem; it's hers. She gets so depressed she takes a flying leap off the balcony. Yeah, it all makes sense."

"It certainly seems like a logical scenario," says Fleer.

Mac looks at Frankie. "So are we finally satisfied this was suicide?"

"I don't know," she says.

"It's that goddamn cell phone, isn't it? It's still bothering you."

"What cell phone?" Fleer asks.

"The girl's cell phone is missing," says Frankie.

"You think it was stolen?"

"We don't know. We're still waiting for her wireless carrier to produce the call log."

"Okay," says Mac. "Just for the sake of argument, let's say this wasn't a suicide. Let's say someone pushed her off the balcony. How the hell are we ever going to prove that? We have no witnesses. We have no evidence of a break-in. All we know is she ended up dead on the sidewalk with a fractured skull."

A skull with two different fractures. Frankie crosses back to the computer, where Taryn Moore's x-rays still glow on the monitor. "I have a question about these separate fracture lines, Dr. Fleer."

"What about them?"

"You said she hit the ground, bounced, and hit it again. How do you know that?"

"I told you, it's based on Puppe's law. The compression fracture of the temporal bone came first. The second impact caused the fracture of the frontal bone."

"What if she *didn't* bounce? What if she only hit the ground once? Is it possible the first fracture happened *before* she even fell off the balcony?"

Fleer's eyes narrow. "You are suggesting two separate traumatic events."

"The x-ray doesn't exclude the possibility, does it?"

He is silent for a moment as he considers her question. "No, it doesn't. But if what you propose is what actually happened, that would mean . . ."

"This wasn't a suicide," says Frankie.

188

CHAPTER 17
FRANKIE

They sit at Mac's workstation, where a photo of his wife, Patty, tanned and wearing a smile and a bathing suit, is prominently displayed. At fifty-two, Patty is still trim and bikini-worthy, and that photo never fails to annoy Frankie because she herself has never felt bikini-worthy. Also because it smacks of bragging: *I've got a hot wife; what've you got?* Which seems more than a little insensitive since half their colleagues in the unit are divorced or on the verge of it. Still, she can't fault a man for being proud of his wife.

Frankie avoids looking at smoking-hot Patty, even though the photo is hanging right above the desktop computer, and she focuses instead on the video that's playing on Mac's monitor. It's footage from the surveillance camera mounted on the building across from Taryn Moore's apartment, and while her balcony is too high to be in the camera's field of view, this recording should have captured footage of her plummet to the ground, as well as the moment the Lyft driver discovered her body. Frankie dreads viewing the first event, that final split second between life and death, and her shoulders are tense as Mac fast-forwards the video and the time code rapidly advances from midnight to 12:30 to 1:00 a.m. A storm blew in from the west that night, and falling rain obscures the camera's view. Suddenly there is the body, magically materializing on the sidewalk. It is little more than a formless dark lump beyond beads of falling rain.

"Back up," says Frankie.

Mac rewinds to 1:10. The body is not there. They both lean forward, watching intently as the video now plays at normal speed.

"There she is," says Mac. He rewinds, frame by frame, and freezes the image.

Frankie stares at what is captured on the screen at 1:11:25. Taryn's falling body is merely a dark smear suspended in midair. They can make out no details of her face; they only know that they are looking at the last split second before she slammed onto the concrete.

"I don't see her cell phone anywhere," says Frankie.

"Maybe it fell somewhere out of frame."

"Let's see if anyone walks by. Picks it up."

Once again, the time code advances. At 1:20, a car drives past without stopping. At 1:28, another car. It is raining hard, and the drivers are no doubt focused on the road ahead as they peer through the water sheeting down their windshields. Car after car passes without stopping as Taryn Moore's body lies there unnoticed, slowly cooling. Considering the foul weather and the late hour, it is not surprising that no pedestrians walk past.

At 3:51, a black sedan glides into the frame. This vehicle does not drive past as the others did. Instead it slows down and stops, blocking the camera's view of the body. For a few seconds the sedan idles at the curb, as if the driver cannot decide whether to brave the rain and investigate or to simply drive on as everyone else has done before him. At last the car door swings open, and a man steps out. He circles around to the sidewalk, where he crouches out of view. Seconds later, he scrambles back into his vehicle.

"The nine-one-one call came in at three fifty-two," says Mac. "So this is our Lyft driver, right on schedule."

"He's being a very good citizen. I can't

imagine he'd steal her phone. So what happened to it?"

"You and that phone. Look, there's nothing here that changes our conclusion. We now know the exact time of death was one eleven. At three fifty-one, the Lyft driver finds her body and calls it in. Suicide's still at the top of the list."

"Let's see what the front-door camera shows."

The entrance to Taryn Moore's apartment building is around the corner from where her body landed, and the only available surveillance footage is from a camera mounted three feet above the front-door intercom. The camera is old and the video quality grainy, but it would have recorded everyone who entered the building.

Mac starts the playback at 9:00 p.m. At 9:35, they spot Taryn's neighbor Helen Ng, her hair plastered down by rain. It was Friday night in a college neighborhood, and as the clock advanced toward midnight, tenants continued to straggle home.

"There's gotta be at least eighty, ninety people living in that building," says Mac. "We gonna try matching names to every one of these faces?"

"Let's just keep watching. Maybe we'll get lucky and pretty boy Liam will show up."

"Still won't prove he killed her."

"It'll prove he's lying about the last time he saw her. And that's a start."

"Only a start."

At 11:00 p.m., a couple appears, shaking off the rain. The young woman nibbles on the man's ear, and as they step inside, he's already pawing at her breasts.

"That was not *my* college experience," says Mac.

At 11:45, two young men stumble to the door, obviously drunk.

At 12:11, a weary-looking Domino's Pizza deliveryman trudges in from the rain, holding an insulated delivery bag. Five minutes later he exits the building, carrying his empty bag.

Then, at 12:55, an umbrella appears. Unlike that garish paisley umbrella that Mac brought to the death scene, this one is black and anonymous, indistinguishable from a million other umbrellas, and the nylon dome hides whomever is holding it. Umbrella Person walks into the building without ever revealing his — or her — face to the camera.

Frankie leans closer. "Now this might be significant."

"It's just someone with an umbrella."

"Look at the time, Mac. It's just sixteen

minutes before Taryn Moore's body hits the sidewalk."

"It might be another tenant coming home."

"Let's see what happens next."

For the next thirty minutes, not much does happen. As the time stamp advances, no one else appears in the entranceway. The only movement captured on video is the occasional splatter of gust-driven rain blowing in. Everyone in the building, it seems, is home for the night.

No. Not everyone.

At 1:25 a.m., someone exits the building. It's Umbrella Person. Once again, Frankie cannot see the face, cannot even determine the gender. Shielded by that dome of black nylon, he or she moves unseen past the camera and slips away into the night.

"Go back," says Frankie. "Ten seconds."

Mac rewinds the video, and Umbrella Person is sucked backward into the building. Frankie scarcely dares to draw a breath as the video once again advances, but in slo-mo this time, frame by frame. The umbrella stutters into view. Just as it's about to move out of the frame, Mac freezes the image.

"Hey," he says. "Look at that." He points to the black bulge that peeks out behind the umbrella, a bulge whose glossy surface reflects a splash of light from the entrance-way lamp. "I think that's a trash bag," he says.

For a moment Frankie and Mac are silent, focused on the screen, where the video is now paused at 1:26 a.m. At that moment in time, Taryn Moore lay sprawled on the sidewalk around the corner, her skull shattered, her blood mingling with the rain.

"Maybe there's no connection," says Mac. "Even if there is, it's gonna be hard for us to prove."

"Then we'd better get to work."

CHAPTER 18
FRANKIE

The apartment's ancient elevator seems even slower tonight, wheezing as it carries its four passengers and their boxes of forensic equipment up to the fifth floor.

"At least this time we've got an elevator that works," says one of the crime scene techs.

"Last week, Bree and I had to haul this gear up a rickety ladder to get to a death scene. It was up on the roof."

"Well, tonight, ladies," says Mac, "I'm here to assist you." His gallant offer seems to impress neither Amber nor Bree, who respond with polite millennial smiles. Except for Mac, it is an all-woman team working the crime scene tonight, a sign of feminist progress that Frankie never imagined when she joined Boston PD over thirty years ago. It delights her to see so many young women like these two now patrolling city streets or arguing cases in the courtroom or gamely lugging heavy camera gear to crime scenes. Time and again, Frankie has told her twins that girls can do anything they put their minds to, as long as they work hard and stay focused and don't let boys distract them.

Someday, maybe they'll listen.

When they reach the fifth floor, Amber and Bree hoist up the two heaviest boxes of gear and carry them out of the elevator, leaving Mac to carry the lightest box.

He sighs. "I feel more obsolete every day."

"We're taking over the world," says Frankie. "Get used to it."

They all pause in the hallway to pull on latex gloves and shoe covers before stepping into Taryn Moore's apartment. Since Frankie's previous visit, nothing has been removed, and the *Medea* textbook is still lying on the kitchen counter where she last saw it, the woman's wrathful face glaring from the front cover.

Bree sets down her Igloo container of chemicals and surveys the room. "We'll start in here. But before I mix the luminol, let's give the place a once-over with the Crime-Scope." She points to the box Mac has just set down. "The goggles are in there. You might want to put on a pair."

While Amber and Bree set up the camera

and tripod, Frankie pulls on goggles to protect her eyes against any damaging wavelengths of light from the CrimeScope, which will be used for the initial survey of the room. While the CrimeScope will not detect occult blood, it will reveal fibers and stains that might warrant closer inspection.

Amber closes the drapes against the city glow and says, "Can you kill the lights, Detective MacClellan?"

Mac flips the wall switch.

In the abrupt darkness, Frankie can barely make out the silhouettes of the two young women who stand near the window. The CrimeScope's blue light comes on, and Amber sweeps the beam across the floor, revealing an eerie new landscape where hairs and fibers now glow.

"Looks like your victim wasn't much of a housekeeper," Amber observes.

"She was a college student," says Mac.

"This place hasn't been vacuumed in a while. I see a lot of dust and hair strands. Did she have long hair?"

"Shoulder length."

"Then these hairs probably belong to her."

The blue light skims toward the coffee table, illuminating a landscape of detritus shed by the apartment's now-deceased occupant. Long after Taryn's belongings are removed, after her body is laid to rest in a grave, traces of her presence will still linger in these rooms.

The CrimeScope beam zigzags across an area rug and up the back of the sofa, where it comes to an abrupt stop. "Hello," says Amber. "This looks interesting."

"What is it?" asks Frankie.

"Something's fluorescing on the fabric."

Frankie moves closer and stares at a glowing patch that seems to float untethered in the darkness. "It's not blood?"

"No, but it could be a body fluid. We'll test it for acid phosphatase and swab for DNA."

"You're thinking semen? Her vaginal and rectal swabs showed no evidence of recent sexual activity."

"This stain could be weeks, even months old."

"Hmmm. Semen on the back of the sofa?" says Mac.

"We're talking college kids, Detective," says Amber. "We can give you a long list of all the weird places we've found semen stains. And if you think about it, if a couple does it while they're standing up, the stain would hit the sofa right about at this height."

Frankie doesn't want to think about it.

She doesn't want to think about girls her daughters' age having sex in *any* position. "Can we move on to the luminol?" she asks. "I'm more interested in finding blood."

"Detective MacClellan, can you turn on the lights?"

Mac flips the wall switch. Where the patch once glowed, Frankie sees only dull green upholstery fabric. Whatever fluoresced under the CrimeScope is now no longer visible, yet she knows it's still there, waiting to reveal its secrets.

Bree opens the Igloo container and pulls out the bottles of chemicals that she'll combine to make luminol. Since luminol rapidly degrades, it must be mixed on the spot. "You might want to put on your respirators now," Bree says as she pours the components into a jar and gives it a shake. "And once we kill the lights, Detectives, stay right where you are so I won't bump into you in the dark. Okay, everyone ready?"

Frankie pulls on a respirator, and Mac flips the wall switch, once again plunging the room into darkness. Frankie hears the soft hiss of the spray bottle as Bree mists the room. Chemiluminescence has always seemed like dark magic to Frankie, but she knows it is merely the chemical reaction of luminol with the iron in hemoglobin. Long

200

after blood is spilled, even if it is wiped away and painted over, its molecular traces will remain, silently waiting to tell a story.

As the misted luminol settles onto the floor, the true story of Taryn Moore's death is revealed.

"Holy shit," says Mac.

Parallel lines light up at their feet like phantom railroad tracks, marking where blood has seeped into the cracks between the scuffed floorboards, beyond the reach of any mop or sponge. What was invisible under bright light now glows with the ghostly echoes of violence.

There it is. There's the proof.

"You recording this, Amber?" says Bree.

"Got it all on camera. Keep spraying."

The bottle hisses again. More parallel floorboard lines appear, like railroad tracks stretching across a black plain.

"I see a drag mark here," Bree says. "Looks like the victim was pulled in the direction of the balcony."

"I see it," says Frankie. "Trace it backward. Where do the drag marks begin?"

Another hiss of the spray bottle. Suddenly a wedge of fluorescence glows on a corner of the coffee table. The surrounding floor lights up with scattered bright pinpoints, like a starburst that slowly fades into a black periphery.

"Here," Bree says softly. "This is the spot where it happened."

Mac turns on the room lights, and Frankie stares down at where, only seconds before, splatters glowed like stars. All she sees now is the floor and an utterly ordinary coffee table, from which all visible evidence of violence has been washed away. Luminol has revealed the apartment's secrets, and now when Frankie gazes around the room, she can picture how it all played out. She sees Taryn Moore opening the door to her visitor. Perhaps the girl does not yet sense danger when she allows her killer to enter. Perhaps she even offers the visitor a glass of wine or a bite of the macaroni and cheese she is heating up in the microwave. Perhaps she never sees the attack coming.

But then it happens: a shove or a blow, sending the girl falling against the sharp corner of the coffee table. The impact fractures her skull and splatters blood on the floor. Now the killer drags the stunned girl toward the balcony. There he opens the door, letting in a rush of cold air, a scattering of rain. Is Taryn still alive as he lifts her over the railing, as he drops her from the balcony? Is she alive as her body plummets through the darkness?

The killer now sets to work erasing the evidence of what happened. He wipes the blood from the floor and the coffee table. He stuffs the stained rags or paper towels into a black trash bag. He leaves the balcony door wide open and the lights on, carries the bag out of the building, and vanishes into the night. He gambles that no one will look beyond what appears to be a suicide, that no one will take the time to search for any microscopic traces of blood that he could not erase.

But the killer made a mistake: he also took the girl's cell phone and probably destroyed it so it cannot be tracked. It is a small detail, one that might be easily ignored by investigators. After all, it's so much simpler for police to close this case and move on. That's what the killer is counting on: a cop who is too overworked or careless to consider all the possibilities or to follow up on each and every clue.

He doesn't know me.

■ ■ ■ ■

BEFORE

■ ■ ■ ■

BEFORE

CHAPTER 19
JACK

For a week, Taryn did not show up for class, nor did she respond to any of Jack's emails. Had she fallen ill? Returned home to Maine? Even Cody Atwood could not — or would not — tell him what had happened to her, and Jack was concerned enough to look up her Facebook page, hoping to find an update on her status, but she'd added no new posts in over a week.

By Monday, he was ready to call the school registrar and suggest a welfare check. So he was relieved when he heard a knock on his door that morning and looked up to see Taryn standing in the office doorway.

"Are you free to talk?" she asked.

"Of course! I'm glad to see you."

She walked in and closed the door behind her. He debated whether he should ask her to open the door again. After that complaint, he thought it wiser to never again confer with a student — female or male — with the door closed. But he hadn't seen Taryn since she'd bolted out of the restaurant at the MFA, and judging by her haggard face, she was in need of counseling. He let the door stay shut.

"I've been worried about you," he said as she sat down across from him. "Nobody seemed to know why you missed class last week. Not even Cody."

She sighed. "It's been a bad week."

"Have you been sick?"

"No. I just needed some time to think. And I've made a decision." She sat up straight, squared her shoulders. "I want to go to grad school. Is it too late to apply to the doctoral program here?"

"I'm afraid it may be. But it's not completely out of the question. The committee can make exceptions in special cases."

"Do you think I might be a special case?"

"You're doing solid A work in my class. And Professor McGuire told me your paper on Mary Wollstonecraft was extraordinary. He's chair of the graduate committee, so that bodes well." He paused, trying to read her face. To understand what had led her to make this abrupt decision. "Why are you suddenly interested in grad school, Taryn?"

Her lower lip quivered. She cleared her throat, steadied her voice. "I broke up with

208

my boyfriend."

"Oh. I'm sorry."

Her eyes pooled. She cleared her throat again, fighting tears. He ached to give her a hug but handed her a box of tissues instead.

"I don't mean to unload on you, but I didn't want you to think I've blown off your class. It's the best one I've ever had. And you're the best teacher I've ever had." She saw him frown and added: "Sorry if I'm embarrassing you. Anyway . . ." She took a breath. "This has made me rethink every-thing about my future. About what sort of life I want. It made me realize that I've been as passive and powerless as Heloise. I'm not the loser Liam thinks I am, and I'm going to prove it."

"Liam? That's your boyfriend?"

"Yeah." She wiped her hand across her eyes. "He thinks I'm not good enough for him."

"Well, that's just bullshit. There's a whole world of possibilities out there for you, and you don't need a graduate degree to prove your worth. You can do anything, be anyone you want to be. Why the hell would he think you're not good enough?"

"Maybe because he's a doctor's kid, and I'm just . . . just me." She wiped her eyes again. "We dated all through high school. I

209

assumed that someday we'd get married. That's what he used to tell me, anyway. But it's not going to happen now. Not to someone like me." She took a breath and sat up straighter. "I'm going to change that."

"Forgive me for asking, but are you applying to grad school for yourself? Or to prove something to him?"

"I don't know. Maybe it's both. Either way, it's something I need to do. I want to be like you."

"Like me?" he asked, surprised.

"Your life seems so perfect. Like you've got it all figured out."

He smiled. "Wait till you're my age. You'll realize no one ever has it all figured out."

"But look at what you do. It seems like you really love your job."

"Yes, I do. Being with young people, talking about the books I love. Doing research that fascinates me. If this is the career you want, I certainly think you're talented enough to make it happen."

"Thank you," she murmured.

"And as for this ex-boyfriend of yours, if anyone's a loser, he is for letting you go. Any other man would count himself lucky to have a woman as amazing as . . ." He stopped, suddenly registering the fervor in his own voice. She had heard it, too, and she was leaning in, her eyes transfixed on his face. He looked down at the desk. "Now. Let's talk about what you need to do to get into grad school."

"And I'll need scholarship money as well."

"Okay. But first things first. Let's see if we can get you into the program. There's an application checklist I can mail you. I'll write a recommendation letter, and I'm sure Professor McGuire will too. But even with a high GPA, you're going to be up against tough competition. There are only a few slots in the program."

"But you still think I have a chance?"

"I've read your papers, Taryn. I think you'd be a real asset to the program, and we'd be lucky to keep you here."

"I can't thank you enough."

Tears glistened on her eyelashes, and he had the reckless urge to reach across the desk and stroke away her tears. Instead, he looked at his watch, suddenly anxious to end the meeting.

"You're not like other professors. You're much more human and understanding."

Jack shrugged that off, feeling as if he were approaching a minefield. "In any event, if you want to drop by next week, we can talk about the paper you're writing. A strong thesis idea will certainly help your application."

"I'm already working on it."

He walked her to the doorway, where she lingered so close to him that he could smell the scent of her shampoo. He took a step away.

"Come by anytime, Taryn."

She squeezed his arm and walked out of the room. Even as her footsteps faded away down the hall, he could still feel that touch on his arm.

CHAPTER 20
TARYN

You can do anything, be anyone you want to be.

She heard his voice in her head, his words a mantra that she chanted to herself as she sat in the library, laptop open, books spread out on the table in front of her. *You can do anything. Be anyone.* What she wanted was to be respected. She wanted Liam to regret he'd ever left her. She wanted his mother to kick herself for thinking Taryn wasn't good enough to marry her precious son. She wanted the world to know who she was.

Most of all, she wanted to make Professor Dorian proud of her.

No one had ever expressed such faith in her, not any of her other teachers, not even her own mother, although in her defense, Brenda was so beaten down by life she couldn't foresee any better times. Taryn imagined herself driving up to Brenda's house someday in a brand-new BMW. She would hand Brenda a copy of her own book, hot off the press. She imagined her mother weeping with joy when she told her it was time to pack up her belongings and move out of that two-bedroom shack into the new house Taryn had bought for her.

But first she needed to get into grad school. And that meant she needed to finish writing this paper.

From the library stacks, she'd collected *The Iliad* and *The Odyssey* and half a dozen history books about the Trojan War. *The Aeneid* had whetted her appetite for stories about warriors and heroes and the choices they made. *Love or Glory?* That was the title she'd chosen for her paper, a theme that was already shouting at her from all these Greek myths and legends. While women wailed and grieved over their treacherous lovers — Queen Dido abandoned by Aeneas, Medea abandoned by Jason, Ariadne abandoned by Theseus — those lovers simply moved on in pursuit of glory, heedless of the hearts they'd broken. For men the choice was their destiny; for women, the result was always sorrow.

But not for her. She'd be the one to move on, to claim her own glory. *You can do anything, be anyone . . .*

"You're *still* here?" said Cody. He'd left

over an hour ago to have dinner, and now he was back. "It's almost nine o'clock. You'd better get some dinner before the cafeteria closes."

"I'm not hungry."

He plopped down in the chair across from her and frowned at all the books lying open on the table. "Wow, you're really serious about grad school."

"And nothing's going to stop me." She flipped a page and stared at the illustration of Agamemnon wielding a knife, about to slit the throat of his sweet young daughter Iphigenia. He was another coldly ambitious man who chose glory over love, who sacrificed his own child so the gods would send fair winds to hasten his ships to Troy. But he would pay for that monstrous act when he returned from the war. His wife, Clytemnestra, grief stricken over the death of their daughter, would have her revenge. Taryn imagined Clytemnestra's black rage as she cornered her husband in his bath. The knife in her hand. The triumph she felt as she thrust the blade into his chest . . .

"I don't get it, Taryn. Why's getting into grad school suddenly so important?"

"Because everything's changed. I've got plans now. I'm going to get my PhD. I'm going to teach and write books and —"

215

"Does this have something to do with Liam?"

"Fuck Liam." She glared at Cody. "He's nothing. He's not worth my time. I've got better things to do with my life now."

Cody blinked, taken aback by her fierce retort. "What happened? What's changed?"

She sat silent for a moment, tapping her pen on the table. Thinking about Jack Dorian and how he'd comforted her, praised her. And she remembered something else he'd said: that any man would count himself lucky to have a woman like her.

"*He* made the difference," she said softly. "Professor Dorian."

"How?"

"He believes in me. No one else ever has."

"I do, Taryn. I've always believed in you," he said, but Cody was just a friend, the kind of boy who'd be blindly loyal to the end. No, the one opinion she really cared about was Jack Dorian's.

She wondered if he was thinking about her, just as she was thinking about him.

"I need to work on this project," she told Cody. "I'll see you tomorrow."

She waited until he left the library before she turned her attention back to her laptop and typed in the name *Professor Jack Dorian.* Suddenly she was hungry to see his

216

face, hungry to know more about him. She clicked on his faculty profile page. In his photo, which had clearly not been updated in years, he was wearing a tweedy jacket and a tie, and his smile was approachable but bland. She thought of how his green eyes lit up when he laughed, and how silver now streaked the dark hair at his temples. She liked the Jack Dorian she knew now. He might be older than in this photo, and his laugh lines were a little deeper, but what mattered wasn't his age, only his heart and his soul.

And he'd opened his to her.

She read the faculty profile, committing the details to memory. BA Bowdoin College. PhD Yale. Three years as assistant professor at University of Massachusetts, four years as associate professor at Boston University. Full professor for the last eight years at Commonwealth. Author of two books about literature and society and more than two dozen published articles about topics ranging from universal themes in ancient myths to modern trends in feminist literature. She wanted to read them all, to immerse herself in everything he'd written, so that the next time they met, she could impress him. She scrolled down his long list of publications and came to a sudden halt, her gaze fixed on his personal information.

Spouse: Margaret Dorian.

Of course she knew he was married; she'd seen the gold band on his finger, but somehow she had blocked out that particular detail. She tried to set it aside, but the images were already in her head: Jack driving home. Walking through his front door. His wife waiting to embrace him, kiss him. Or were those images wrong? She thought of the day in class when he'd looked weary and defeated, as if something had gone wrong at home. Maybe his wife wasn't there to greet him with a kiss. Maybe she was a woman who berated him, belittled him.

Maybe he was desperate for someone who'd make him happy.

She searched online for *Margaret Dorian, Boston*. It was an unusual enough name, so it was easy to find the right woman. The top three links were all for Margaret Dorian, MD. On Rate My Physician she'd earned a top score, and one patient had written a comment about *Dr. Dorian's compassion and kindly bedside manner*. The online Whitepages had the contact details for her medical practice in Mount Auburn Hospital, Cambridge.

She hopped onto the Mount Auburn website and clicked on the link for Margaret Dorian, MD.

In her photo she was wearing a white doctor's coat and a smile. She had brown eyes and shoulder-length red hair, and although she was still attractive, Taryn could see signs of middle age creeping into her face, around her eyes, her mouth. While no longer young, she was accomplished, and her patients liked her. Taryn thought of the long hours a doctor must work, the nights, the weekends. Did her husband feel neglected? Did he spend too many nights alone, longing for company?

She went back online to look for their address. It wasn't hard to find; on the internet, there were no secrets. Google Maps took her right to their Arlington neighborhood, and on street view she could see their house, a two-story white colonial with a front lawn and neatly trimmed shrubs. On the day this street-view photo had been taken, the garage door was open, and a silver sedan was parked inside. On satellite view, she spotted no signs of children on the property — no bikes, no toys, no play set in the backyard. They were childless, which made it all the less messy should they ever split up. Should he meet someone else with whom he'd rather spend the rest of his life.

She returned to the photo of Dr. Margaret
Dorian. Still pretty, yes.
But maybe Jack was longing for more.

CHAPTER 21
JACK

"I'd say Taryn Moore's a shoo-in," Ray McGuire said. He'd just come out of the grad committee meeting, and he stood in Jack's doorway, grinning at him. "Her application's so strong we waived the deadline requirement."

"That's great! She'll be thrilled to hear it."

"Official acceptance letters don't go out for another few weeks, but the vote was unanimous. She's got a three-nine-something GPA. And her letters of recommendation all read like she's the next Gloria Steinem."

Jack couldn't help but feel a bolt of pride. "She's really psyched about the program."

"I hope she didn't apply to Harvard."

"Nope. Just here. This was her first choice."

"Excellent. The writing sample she submitted was a paper she wrote for you on

The Aeneid. I'm not up on classical scholarship, but it actually looks publishable. An elegant analysis that Virgil's really telling us, through subtext, that instead of committing suicide, Queen Dido should have thrust that sword into Aeneas." He laughed. "Kind of a scary take on it, actually." He turned to leave, then paused. "By the way, if she joins our program, she'll raise our female hotness average from its current minus five. But I guess that's not very PC of me to say, eh?"

"You are a superficial sexist pig."

Ray smiled. "Yeah, and proud of it."

A day later, Taryn practically danced into Jack's office.

"Thank you, thank you, thank you!" she burst out and leaned across his desk, her hair spilling over her shoulders, her face aglow.

"I take it you've heard some good news?" he said, smiling.

"Yes! Professor McGuire stopped me in the hall just now, and he said it's almost certainly going to happen!" With a joyful sigh, she dropped into the chair facing his desk. That was how comfortable she'd become with him. They'd spent so much time together discussing her application and her thesis that she now needed no invitation to make herself at home in his office. "And it's all because of *you*."

"Taryn, I wasn't the one who wrote those papers. Or earned those grades."

"But you showed me the possibilities. You made me believe in myself."

Flustered by her praise, he couldn't think of anything to say. They regarded each other for a moment as he took in the beautiful disarray of her hair, the pink flush of her cheeks. She was more tempting than any Heloise could ever be, and he felt as bewitched as Abelard.

He looked down at his desk, hunting for a distraction, and saw the conference brochure he'd received a few weeks earlier. A welcome change of topic.

"This might interest you," he said, handing the brochure to her.

"A conference on comparative lit?"

"It's at the UMass campus in Amherst. Some of these presentations might interest you. Maybe even give you ideas for a future dissertation. Some of the best scholars in your field will be there."

She studied the session titles he had highlighted. " 'The Invention of Men'?"

"About how classical literature is ultimately the history of men."

She read the description. " 'Beginning

with Homer, male writers and historians have focused only on men, leaving women as mere shadows in history.' " She looked at him. "It's a talk by Maxine Vogel!"

"So you're familiar with the name?"

"She's one of the best-known feminist critics in the world."

"She recently published a paper very similar to your interpretation of Heloise."

"Oh my God, I'd love to go. Is it too late to register?"

"I don't think you'd have a problem getting in."

"I wonder if there's bus service to Amherst. Since I don't have a car."

"I'm going too. I can drive you and any other students who want to attend. I'll mention it in class, see if we can drum up some interest."

She frowned at the conference fees. "Oh. I'd need to pay for a hotel."

"I'll check with Ray McGuire to see if he can come up with student travel funds. Especially since there's a good chance you'll be joining our grad program."

She smiled at the brochure. "My first-ever literary conference. I just know I'm going to love it."

Taryn stood on the edge of the campus

quadrangle, where she'd promised to be waiting for him. Even from half a block away, he could spot her slim figure, dressed in dark-pink tights and a black jacket, her hair fluttering in the wind.

No other students. Just Taryn.

This was a mistake. He knew it, of course, but he couldn't back out now, not after he'd promised to drive her to the conference. Not after all the arrangements had been made.

He pulled up at the curb. She tossed her overnight bag into the back seat and slid in beside him.

"Isn't anyone else coming?" he asked.

"Just me."

"I thought you were going to talk a few classmates into joining us. I assumed Cody, at least, was coming."

"I tried, but no one else was interested." She flicked back her hair and smiled. "Oh well. Looks like it's just you and me, Professor."

A mile down the avenue at Copley Square, he turned onto the Mass Pike west, his stomach churning. Taryn and he, alone in a car, headed out of town like two lovers. As they entered the tunnel under the Prudential Center, he asked himself, *What are we doing? What am I doing?* As soon as they

225

arrived at the hotel, he needed to call Maggie. If only to remind himself he was married. That he was doing this for only the right reasons.

Although she'd registered late, a few rooms had still been available at the conference hotel, which was a short walk from the campus where the sessions would take place. As they headed into the lobby and approached the reception desk, he felt his heart rate quicken. Did they look like lovers? Had anyone noticed they'd arrived in the same car? He glanced around the lobby, which looked like the lobbies of countless other corporate hotels, and was relieved to see no one he knew.

"Your key, sir," the desk clerk said, handing Jack the envelope with a key card to room 445. "I can put you both on the same floor," he offered.

Before Jack could respond, Taryn said: "That'd be nice."

The clerk gave her the key to room 437. Four doors away from Jack's room, but still far too close for comfort.

I'm her teacher. She's my student, he reminded himself as they stepped off the elevator on the fourth floor. *We're here for the conference, nothing else.*

"See you in a bit?" she said as they approached his door.

"Um, yeah."

"Lobby in twenty minutes?"

"Okay."

He let himself into the room, and as the door swung shut behind him, his breath whooshed out. *Okay. Okay, this will be fine,* he thought.

Time to call Maggie.

He sat on the bed and dialed her cell phone, needing to hear her voice. To be reminded of what they had together, all the history, all the love. But the call went to voice mail, and all he heard was, "This is Dr. Dorian. I'm unavailable to answer your call."

He disconnected and sat slumped on the bed. He had skipped lunch, and his stomach felt hollowed out, not from hunger but from nervousness. He was standing on the edge of an abyss, trying to keep his balance and not tumble into the darkness.

Half an hour later, he and Taryn walked into the building where other attendees milled about, greeting colleagues and checking billboard posters and schedules. Maxine Vogel's lecture, "The Invention of Men," was about to start, and the auditorium was filling fast. They claimed two seats on the aisle, and Taryn opened her laptop to take notes.

"I'll see if I can introduce you to her after the speech," he said.

"What should I say?"

"Ask about her latest research and take it from there. Every scholar loves to talk shop, and flattery never hurts."

"Okay. Okay. God, this is so exciting." She looked around at the attendees waving hellos and shaking hands, a world of scholars that she longed to join someday. The auditorium lights dimmed, and her attention snapped forward to the screen, where the first slide was now displayed. It was a woodcut print of a woman in a flowing gown, bent over her loom.

Maxine Vogel walked to the podium, where she stood bathed in the spotlight. "I'm sure you all recognize the woman in this slide. Penelope," said Dr. Vogel, sweeping an arm toward the screen. "For twenty long years, she remained ever faithful, ever patient, spurning all suitors as she waited for her husband, Odysseus, to return from the Trojan War. Scholars and poets point to her as the example of perfect womanhood." Vogel turned to her audience and snorted. "What utter bullshit."

And with that, she had the audience spellbound.

Jack glanced at Taryn and saw her lean forward, so rapt with attention that she'd forgotten to take notes. She was too focused on Vogel's defense of unconventional heroines, the women whose unruly passions and inconvenient desires pitted them against the mores of society. No wonder Vogel was a star in her field; he felt a twinge of envy at how completely she captivated her audience. And he envied Taryn, too, for all the possibilities in her future. Possibilities that he could feel slipping away with each passing year.

When Vogel's lecture ended and the lights came up again, Taryn was already on her feet and moving up the aisle toward Vogel. There was no need for Jack to introduce them; Taryn was a self-guided missile, aimed straight for her target. From across the auditorium, he saw her shake hands with Vogel, saw the older woman smile and nod as they walked together toward the room where the conference cocktail party awaited.

Mission accomplished, he thought. Taryn was doing fine on her own, and now was the time to make his escape.

He returned to his room alone, showered, and climbed into bed. He was annoyed that

229

Maggie hadn't called back, but then he saw the email she'd sent an hour ago:

Spending the night with Dad. He's having a rough time with back pain. Hope conference is going well — call you in the morning.

Of course, she'd be at her father's. They had no idea how much longer Charlie had left to live, and she wanted to spend every free moment she had with him.

He decided not to call her again tonight. He turned off the lamp and had just settled back on the pillow when his phone rang. Maggie?

But it was Taryn's voice he heard. "Are you in your room?" she asked. "I need to tell you something!"

"Can it wait until breakfast? It's eleven thirty."

"But this is so exciting I can't wait! I'll be right up!"

With a sigh, he turned on the lamp and got dressed. He'd just buckled his belt when he heard her knock on the door. He opened it to find Taryn standing in the hallway, holding up a bottle of wine.

"Why the wine?" he asked.

"You're not going to believe this. Maxine

230

suggested we coauthor a paper together! Just her and me!"

Maxine. Not Dr. Vogel. "Seriously? How did that happen?"

"I told her I thought Queen Dido has been completely mischaracterized by male scholars. I said it's because Dido challenged their ideals of masculinity. And she *loved* the premise." Taryn gave a laugh of triumph. "Can you imagine it? My name would be right under hers on the paper!"

"That's pretty astonishing," he said, genuinely impressed. "And I hope you realize how generous she is to be doing it. Most scholars with her stature would never even consider —"

"Let's celebrate! I had the bartender uncork this for us." She hunted down two glass tumblers in the room, filled them with wine, and handed one to Jack.

How could he refuse? She was practically dancing with joy, and he couldn't help smiling at her triumph. They clinked glasses and sipped. "Congratulations, Taryn," he said. "You're well on your way!"

She took another gulp of wine. "And it's all because of you."

"I wasn't the one who charmed Maxine Vogel."

"We talked for hours at the cocktail party,

brainstorming our paper. We could've kept going, but the bar was closing. Luckily I took a ton of notes."

"Good thinking," he said, his head buzzing from the wine. He'd scarcely eaten dinner, and now he was paying for it as the alcohol roared straight into his bloodstream.

She drained her glass, poured another, and topped off his. "We'll have to collaborate by email. You know, I send her pages, and she sends me comments and suggestions. Then we coedit the final version, and she'll submit it. She knows the editors of all the major journals. And to think none of this would have happened without you, Jack." Her eyes were huge, dark pools. "I wouldn't be here if you hadn't encouraged me."

He suddenly registered the fact that she'd called him Jack, not Professor Dorian. When had that started? When had they slipped into such easy familiarity? He knew he shouldn't have more to drink, but he gulped down the wine anyway and set down the empty glass.

She moved toward him so swiftly he didn't have time to react. He felt her breath against his hair as she whispered: "Thank you."

He stood paralyzed as she kissed him. This was not a thank-you peck. This was a full-lip kiss that lasted longer than any thank-you. Her tongue slipped into his mouth, and he felt his stomach drop away, felt his body respond.

This can't be happening.

"I want you," she whispered, and she slipped her hand into his trousers. Found him already, involuntarily, erect.

He groaned and tried to pull away.

"Jack, please," she begged. "Just for to-night. Just you and me."

This is so wrong.

But it was happening, and he was unable to fight it. Unable to resist the hunger that had been building all these weeks. Already their mouths were joined, their bodies moving against each other. He didn't remember how their clothes came off. Her naked body was a sculpted work of beauty — tight and athletic, long and firm. He didn't remember who led whom to the bed, but suddenly there they were, and he was on top of her, thrusting between her thighs as she gave tiny yelps of pleasure.

And then it was over, and they lay side by side, saying not a word.

She turned to kiss him, and he felt the wetness on her face, the heat of her cheeks. She took his hand and kissed his palm as well. "That was wonderful," she whispered.

"That was everything I dreamed it would be."

He didn't answer. He simply lay beside her in silence, thinking that he had just lost something precious. And he would never get it back.

CHAPTER 22
TARYN

He lay beside her, silent and still, but by the pattern of his breathing, she knew that he was awake. She wanted him to wrap her in his arms. She wanted him to say all the things lovers should say after they had feasted so joyously on each other's bodies, but he did not say a word, and she could guess why.

He was thinking about his wife. About how everything had changed because they'd just made love.

She reached for his hand. He didn't pull away, but neither did he squeeze hers. His hand lay rigid in her grasp, and she could feel the tension coursing through him. That was how she knew he had never before strayed from his wife, and it made what had just happened between them all the more significant. She was his first.

"You're feeling guilty. Aren't you?" she asked.

"Yes."

"Why?"

He turned to look at her. "How can I not feel guilty? I shouldn't have let this happen. I can't believe I —"

"Jack." Gently she stroked his face. "You're feeling guilty only because you're a good man."

"A good man?" He shook his head. "A good man would have resisted temptation."

"Is that all I am to you? Temptation?"

"No. No, Taryn." He touched her face, cupped her cheek in his hand. "That's not what I'm saying at all. You're beautiful and brilliant and everything any man would want. And you should be with someone who's better for you than I am."

"You're the one I want."

"I'm twenty years older than you."

"And twenty years wiser than any boy my age. All these years, the only one I cared about was Liam. I thought he was the best there was, the best I would ever find. Now I realize how shallow he is, how shallow most boys are. You made the difference. You showed me what I've been missing."

He sighed. "This was a mistake."

"For me? Or for you?" She couldn't hide the edge in her voice, the unmistakable note of anger, and when he frowned, she knew she was on the verge of losing him. At once she smiled and reached out for his hand. She pressed it against her face. "Even if it was a mistake, it's one I'll never regret. Not for as long as I live. Because I'm in love with you."

"Taryn . . ."

"Don't say anything. You don't have to tell me you love me. You don't have to pretend I'm what you want."

"My God, you're every man's dream."

"I only want to be *your* dream."

They stared at each other, drinking in each other's gazes. She knew he was tormented by guilt. A good man would be, and that was why she was willing to be patient and give him time to see how much she meant to him, how much better she was for him than his wife. She'd let him go home to her. Let him lie in bed beside that wife and think of *her,* long for *her* instead.

"I don't want any man but you. I know you think I'm too young for you, but I'm old enough to know who I want to spend the rest of my life with."

"There's not just you and me to think of. There's also . . ."

"Your wife."

At those two words, his hand went as still as a corpse's. "Yes," he whispered.

She pulled away from him and sat up on the side of the bed. "I understand. I really do. But I need you to know that for me, this isn't just a onetime thing. This is much, much more. I could make you so happy."

He didn't respond. The silence stretched on, and she wondered if he was afraid to admit the truth even to himself. Afraid to reveal how much he wanted her, needed her.

"Look, just think about who you want in your bed and in your life," she said. "I can wait, Jack. I can wait as long as it takes for you to make up your mind."

She took her time buttoning her blouse, zipping up her pants. As she got dressed, he watched her in silence. Even as she walked out the door, he said nothing. It was better that way. Let him regret not saying all the words he should have said.

That night, in her own hotel room, Taryn slept more soundly than she had in weeks.

The next morning, when she came down to breakfast, she found him sitting alone in a booth, a plate of scarcely touched ham and eggs in front of him. He looked terrible, his eyes bloodshot, his skin gray. While he looked haggard, she felt at her freshest and most radiant. She slid onto the bench facing him, and he gazed at her with such hunger it was all she could do not to smile.

"Good morning," she said quietly.

He nodded. "Good morning."

"Everything I said last night is still true."

He looked down at his coffee cup. "Let's not talk about it."

"Okay." She could be casual. She could be breezy. Let him see how mature she was about this.

The waitress approached with a coffeepot, and Taryn smiled at her. "Two fried eggs over easy and hash browns, please."

"Coming right up."

As Taryn waited for her order, Jack picked half-heartedly at the food on his plate, which by now had to be cold. She thought of the long drive home in a car with this silent man, and she was determined not to let him associate her with despair. No, she must be the light in his life, the woman he turned to not just for sex but also for love and laughter and joy. "I can't wait to get back to work on my project," she said. "This conference has been such an inspiration."

"Has it?"

"It's opened a new world for me, and I've got a dozen different ideas spinning in my head for other papers after this one."

He couldn't help smiling at her enthusiasm. "That's how I felt when I started grad school."

"Like you won't live long enough to get all your ideas down on paper."

"Yes."

"Do you still feel that way?"

He shrugged, a gesture of weariness and defeat. "Life gets complicated. Responsibilities. Obligations."

She leaned toward him and placed her hand on his. "You shouldn't let them suck out the joy in what you do. I won't let that happen to me."

"I hope it doesn't. I hope you stay as passionate as you are now. In fact, I wish I could steal some of that passion from you."

"You don't have to steal it, Jack. You just have to find your own again. And I can help you —"

"Jack Dorian! How nice to see you again. It seems like forever since our last conference together."

Taryn looked up to see a woman with silver-streaked black hair. She recognized her as one of the presenters at the conference. Her name tag said *Dr. Greenwald, Univ. of CT.* The woman glanced down at the table, where Taryn's hand was still touching Jack's, and her smile faded to a look of consternation.

Taryn pulled her hand away.

Jack went pale but still managed to greet

Dr. Greenwald with a stiff, "Hello, Hannah. I don't think I've seen you since, uh, Philly."

"Right. It was the Philly conference." She looked at Taryn, studying her as closely as if she were the subject of her next paper.

"This is Taryn Moore," Jack said. "I'm advising her on her senior project."

"So . . . she's your student."

"Yes, I am," Taryn cut in brightly. "Professor Dorian's been giving me great advice, as he does all his students."

"What's your project?" Dr. Greenwald asked.

"It's a paper that explores the theme of romantic betrayal in classical epics. He's introduced me to other scholars and pointed me to all sorts of relevant resources."

"I see."

But what *did* she see? Taryn wondered. That Jack's face had stiffened to a stony mask? That he was staying in the same hotel with a student half his age?

"I'll be interested in reading that paper," said Dr. Greenwald. She gave a brisk nod to Jack. "Hope to see you at another conference. And say hello to Maggie for me."

As Dr. Greenwald walked away, Taryn studied Jack's face. Just the mention of his wife had made his lips snap taut. He knew how this looked, and so did she.

Abruptly he slid out of the booth and tossed some cash on the table. "That should be enough to cover us both. I have to go pack, and you should too. I just got an alert there's a snowstorm headed our way, and we need to get going before the roads get nasty."

"Aren't you going to finish your breakfast?"

"I'm not hungry. I'll see you in the lobby in an hour."

She looked down at the fifty dollars he'd left on the table. It was far more money than he needed to leave, and it was a measure of just how desperate he was to escape. The waitress brought her eggs and hash browns. Unlike Jack, she had not lost her appetite. She devoured it all.

They said hardly a word to each other during the drive back to Boston. When they finally pulled up in front of Taryn's building, he did not get out of the car, did not offer to carry her overnight bag or walk her upstairs to her apartment. He just sat behind the wheel, shoulders slumped.

"Do you want to come in for a cup of coffee?" she offered.

"I need to get back to campus. Catch up on some work."

"Well, now you know where to find me. I'm on the fifth floor, apartment 510." She stepped out of the car. "Come by anytime, day or night." As she walked into the building, she knew he was watching her, but she didn't look back. Not once.

CHAPTER 23
JACK

He'd never known guilt could be so annihilating.

After he dropped off Taryn, instead of heading to campus, he drove home. He needed time alone to center himself and maybe knock back a stiff drink or two. Maggie should still be at Charlie's house, so at least he wouldn't have to face her yet. He'd have a few hours to resume his role of happily married man and upstanding English professor.

But as he pulled into the driveway, he saw Maggie's Lexus parked in the garage, and his heart clenched. Why was she home so early? Had someone emailed her that he was at the conference with another woman? Had someone seen Taryn slip into his room just before midnight?

As he got out of the car, his phone chirped with a text message. It was from Taryn.

Last night we shared something that I will never forget. I love you.

Panicked, he deleted the message and powered off the phone, as if to erase the last twenty-four hours. For several minutes he sat in the garage trying to compose himself, but his heart wouldn't stop thudding, and he half imagined it exploding out of his chest when he entered the house. But he could not sit in the garage forever. He inhaled the final breath of a condemned man, stepped out of the car, and walked into the kitchen.

Maggie was sitting at the counter, sipping a cup of tea.

"Hey, you. I'm glad you missed the snow-storm," she said, smiling. "How was the conference?"

He shrugged. "Like every other conference."

"How many students went with you?"

"What?"

"You said you were going to bring a few students with you."

"Oh. Um, three." When had he gotten so glib at lying?

"Lucky students. I never had a professor invite me to any conferences. Such great exposure for them."

Great exposure. "Yeah."

He was the *Allegory of Deceit*. A man who cheated on his wife. Who could tell lies on cue. A teacher who'd just slept with his student.

"We're supposed to get ten to twelve inches of snow tonight," she said. "So what do you say we send out for a pizza, light a fire, and snuggle up?"

Snuggle up — her old synonym for love-making. A little over twenty-four hours ago, he had snuggled up with Taryn. "Sounds great."

While she changed clothes, he ordered a pizza from Andrea's, made a fire, and opened a bottle of Malbec. He filled two Waterford crystals, and as he set them down on the coffee table, he was tormented by the memory of Taryn filling their wine-glasses. The memory of what had happened after that.

He dimmed the lights to mask his shame. When she came down, Maggie was dressed in her pajamas and bathrobe, her face glow-ing. "The snow's starting already. Maybe next year we should go someplace warm for a change. Aruba or Saint John."

His nerves were buzzing. He could only respond with a rote, "Sounds good." Saint

John was where they'd spent their honeymoon.

She frowned at him. "Are you okay?"

"Yeah, why do you ask?"

"I don't know; you seem so distant. Did something happen?"

"No. I'm just a little wiped out. All that traffic, with this storm blowing in and all."

"And being with all those students, you're probably constantly onstage," she added. "Well, you did a good deed, and I'm sure they all got something out of it."

"Maybe."

Taryn's voice echoed in his head: *Jack, please. Just for tonight.*

They went upstairs. Made love with the lights off so she couldn't read his face. When they were done, they lay next to each other in the darkness.

"Was that okay for you?" Maggie whispered.

"Of course."

"Sometimes I forget to say it, but I love you."

"I love you too," he said, thinking that he had to end things with Taryn. He couldn't live a double life, and he was not going to betray his wife again.

While Maggie slept, he tossed and turned, unable to think of any way to right all the wrongs he'd committed. Desperate for sleep, he finally reached for the bottle of Ativan and gulped down two pills. As he lay waiting for the drug to take effect, he thought: *This is not going to end well.*

CHAPTER 24
TARYN

For the better part of spring break week, she stayed away from Jack. She spent her evenings working on her "Love or Glory?" paper, hauling home books from the library. She exchanged half a dozen emails with Dr. Maxine Vogel to discuss the paper they were cowriting about Queen Dido. She stayed busy and focused because it was all part of her plan: Get into the doctoral program. Impress the department. Most of all, impress Jack.

She had no doubt he was thinking about her. How could he not be after what had happened between them? She imagined him lying awake beside his wife while longing for her instead. Had he told his wife about her yet? Eventually he would have to, and how relieved he'd feel when it was all out in the open. To start a new life, one must burn the old one.

And Sunday afternoon, when she received

his text message, she knew he was finally ready to choose her.

At five fifteen that evening, her apartment bell buzzed.

She let him into the building, and by the time he climbed the stairs and rang her doorbell, she had already stripped off her blouse, her jeans. Half-naked, she opened the door, and he stepped into her apartment.

There was no need for words, for any preamble at all. She wrenched open his shirt, unzipped his trousers, and reached for him. He grabbed her hands as though to stop her, but she could feel he was already hard and ready for her. It took only a few strokes to make him surrender. With a groan, he shoved her toward the sofa, spun her around, and took her from behind. She cried out in pleasure as he thrust into her again and again, his need so urgent that he had no time to be gentle. This was a desperate fucking, and it was exactly what she wanted, what she craved. While he thought he was taking her, she held all the power, and when she climaxed, it was a cry of triumph. He was hers. He was hers.

They collapsed, panting, onto the sofa, where their naked bodies lay entwined. She pressed her cheek against his chest, listening to the gradual slowing of his heart. Here was where he belonged, and he knew it. Not with a wife who no longer thrilled him but with *her*. It was why he was here, why he could not stay away. She'd never doubted he would show up at her door.

She was half-asleep when he rose from the sofa. Only when he sat down to tie his shoes did she stir fully awake and see that he was already dressed and preparing to leave.

"Why are you going?" she asked.

"I have to. I'm supposed to meet my father-in-law for dinner."

"Just your father-in-law? Or your wife too?"

The guilty look on his face was all the answer she needed. He reached down to stroke her cheek, and then he turned away.

"I love you, Jack."

Her words paralyzed him. For a moment he stood torn between leaving and staying. Instead of the words she hoped to hear, the words a lover should speak, there was only silence.

"Taryn," he finally said. "You know I care about you. But what happened between us — it never *should* have happened."

"Why are you saying this? Right after we made love?"

"Because it's not fair to you. You're so much younger than I am, and you have your whole life ahead of you. I'd be like a rusty old anchor, slowing you down."

"That's not really what you mean."

"Yes, it is."

"No, you're thinking about *yourself*. About how our affair affects *you*."

With a look of defeat, he sank onto the sofa. "People are starting to notice. Starting to talk."

"So what? Let them."

"I could lose my job. Which might threaten your application to grad school."

That was something she hadn't even considered: that if Jack Dorian went down, he could drag her down as well. He had been her most powerful advocate. Without his support, without his letters of recommendation, what chance did she have?

"Then we have to be careful," she said. "We might — we might need to stay apart for a while longer."

He looked up at her, and she didn't like the expression of relief she saw in his eyes. "I agree."

"But only for a few weeks. Only until it's safe, right?"

He rose back to his feet without answering and went to the door.

"Jack? You know I'll wait for you. As long as it takes."

He didn't look back at her. "I'll call you."

■ ■ ■ ■

AFTER

■ ■ ■ ■

CHAPTER 25
FRANKIE

Flanked by boxes filled with her dead daughter's belongings, Brenda Moore looks as worn down and used up as the sofa she's now sitting on. She is only forty-one, and once perhaps she was as attractive as Taryn, but life has not been kind to this woman. Her skin has the sickly pallor of a night shift worker, and judging by the length of her gray roots, it has been months since she last visited a hairdresser. Her tattered jeans and flannel shirt — practical attire for cleaning out a dead daughter's apartment — hang shapeless on her bony frame, and her hands are raw and chapped, no doubt a consequence of frequent handwashings at her nursing home job. Everything about her radiates defeat, and no wonder. What more devastating blow can life deliver than the death of your child?

"This place needs to be cleared out and cleaned up by next week," she says and gives a weary sigh. "The fifteenth. Or I'll owe another month's rent on it."

"Given the circumstances, I'm sure the landlord will make an exception," says Frankie.

"Maybe. But it's not something I'm counting on." She looks down at the box of her daughter's clothes and reaches in to stroke a sweater, as if comforted by its feathery softness. "I haven't even started cleaning yet. Or would you rather I not? I mean, I've watched those CSI shows, so I know the police like things kept as is, until they've finished all those tests."

"No, we've finished with this apartment. You're fine to do what you need to do."

"Thank you," the woman murmurs. There is no reason to thank them, but she seems like a woman who is grateful for any courtesies. "I wish I had more information for you. But my girl and I, we weren't as close as we used to be. It kinda broke my heart, you know? You raise your kid and you love her and you want to stay part of her life. But then they grow up, and they push you away . . ." She clutches her daughter's sweater, desperately wringing it in her fist.

Frankie cannot imagine the pain this woman is feeling, the heartbreak of collecting your dead child's clothes, folding them, pressing them to your face. Clothes that will be hard to surrender because they still carry her daughter's scent.

"When was the last time you spoke to Taryn?" Mac asks.

"It was a few weeks ago, I think. She hadn't called me in a while, so I had to call her."

"How often did you usually speak?"

"Not often enough. Not since we had that argument, back in January."

"About what?"

"I wanted her to come home to Maine after graduation. I told her how tight the money's been and how I couldn't afford to keep sending her more. Oh, she got upset. So upset we didn't talk to each other for weeks."

"Didn't she see your side of it?"

"No. She couldn't. All she could think about was being with *him.*"

"That would be her boyfriend, Liam Reilly?"

Brenda sighs. "I knew it was never going to work out, the two of them. I've been telling her that for years, but she never believed me."

"Why didn't you think it would work?" asks Frankie.

Brenda looks at her. "You said you've met him."

"Yes. We interviewed him right after Taryn died."

"And did you think he'd ever marry a girl like my daughter?"

Frankie doesn't know how to answer this, and she's taken aback that any mother would have such a harsh opinion of her own child. "Taryn was a lovely girl," she says.

"Yeah, she was pretty. Prettiest girl in town. And she was smart, so smart. But that's not good enough for *them.* His mother made that plain enough to me."

"His mother told you that?"

"She didn't have to. In our town, there's certain families that just don't marry each other. Your kids may go to the same school, and you shop at the same grocery store, but there are lines you don't cross. That's what I told Taryn, because I didn't want her to waste her best years hoping and waiting. Gamble your heart on the wrong boy, and you'll pay for the rest of your life." She looks down again at the sweater and says softly: "I sure did."

"Tell us about him," says Mac.

"Liam? Why?"

"We understand they were together a long time."

260

"Since they were kids. The only reason she applied to Commonwealth was because *he* was coming here. Everything she did was for him."

"Did he ever hurt your daughter?"

"What? No." Brenda is clearly startled by the question. "At least, she never said anything."

"Would she tell you about it? If he had hurt her?"

She looks back and forth at Mac and Frankie, trying to understand why they're asking these questions. "I don't know that she would tell me," she finally answers. "These last few weeks, she didn't speak to me at all. If only I'd stood by her. If only I'd supported her, no matter what. I could have scraped together more money. I could have —"

"This is not your fault, Brenda," Frankie says gently. "Believe me, her death had nothing to do with you."

"Does it have to do with Liam?"

"That's what we're trying to find out. Did you know they'd broken up?"

Brenda shakes her head and sighs. "I'm not surprised."

"So she didn't tell you about their breakup."

Brenda looks down again at the sweater

261

she's been obsessively stroking. "It seems she didn't tell me a lot of things."

"Liam said they broke up months ago," says Frankie. "He said Taryn was upset and she had a hard time accepting it."

"And was *he* upset?" Brenda snaps. "Did it bother him at *all* that my girl was dead?"

"He did seem shaken up by the news."

"But he'll move on. Men always do."

"Mrs. Moore," says Mac, "was there anyone besides Liam in your daughter's life? Another boyfriend, maybe?"

"No. He was the only one."

"Are you sure of that?"

Brenda frowns. "Why are you asking about other boyfriends? Is there something you know that I don't?"

Mac and Frankie look at each other, neither one wanting to break the news.

"I'm sorry to tell you this," says Frankie. "But your daughter was pregnant."

Brenda cannot speak. She presses her hand to her mouth to stifle the sob, but the sound spills out anyway, a high, keening wail that breaks Frankie's heart because she is a mother, too, and this is a mother's shriek. Brenda rocks forward and hugs herself, her body shaking with quiet sobs. It is terrible to watch, and Mac looks away, but Frankie does not. She forces herself to bear witness to the woman's agony, waiting silently, patiently, until Brenda's sobs finally fade away.

"Then you didn't know," Frankie says.

"Why didn't she tell me? I'm her mother! I *should* have known! Whatever she wanted, I could have helped her. We could have raised that baby together." Suddenly she lifts her head and looks at Frankie. "What did *he* say about it?"

"We haven't asked Liam yet. We wanted to talk to you first."

"I can just imagine how *he* would take the news. And his parents? Their precious son marrying a girl just because he got her pregnant? Certainly not if it's *my* daughter." Brenda sits up straight, anger stiffening her spine. "So that's why she killed herself. Because that boy wouldn't marry her."

Frankie doesn't immediately respond, and the silence makes Brenda frown.

"Detective Loomis?"

"There's a great deal we don't know," Frankie finally says.

Brenda looks at Mac, then back at Frankie. The woman is not clueless; she understands there is something crucial they haven't told her. "Earlier, you asked me about Liam. About whether he's ever hurt Taryn. Why?"

"We're looking into every possibility."

"Did he hurt her? *Did he?*"

"We don't know."

"But you'll find out, won't you? Promise me you'll find out."

Frankie looks her in the eye and says, mother to mother, "I will. I promise."

CHAPTER 26
FRANKIE

Golden boy Liam is not looking so golden this morning. Only a week ago, Frankie considered this aspiring lawyer a nice catch for anyone's daughter. Now he is squirming in his chair and avoiding her gaze, proving he is every bit as flawed as any of the boys her own girls bring home. Maybe even worse.

"I swear I told you the truth. I *did* break up with Taryn back in December," he says. "But she wouldn't accept it. I showed you my phone. You saw how she kept calling me, texting me. Sometimes she'd just pop up without warning, wherever I happened to be. I'd turn around and there she'd be. She kept stalking me, until that blowup in the restaurant I told you about."

"You told us you broke up with her last December," says Frankie. "But when was the last time you had sex with her?"

That question, asked by a woman his

mother's age, makes him flush. He looks at Mac, as if hoping another man will rescue him from this predicament, but Mac merely stares back, stone faced. "I don't remember," Liam mumbles. "Like I said, we broke up over Christmas."

"And the last time you had sex?"

"Um, around then. I think."

"You don't sound sure."

"Why does it matter?"

"Trust me, it matters. And we want the truth, Liam. You're a smart boy, and you're headed to law school. So you know what happens when you lie to a police officer."

At last he seems to register the gravity of the situation. When he finally answers, his voice is barely audible. "Maybe it was, um, January."

"When in January?"

"Right after we got back from Christmas break."

"At which time you already had your new girlfriend, didn't you? Libby's her name?"

He glances at the bookcase, where there is a framed photo of a stunning brunette, her lips pursed seductively for the camera. Quickly he averts his gaze, as if ashamed to even look at it. "I didn't mean to sleep with her," he says.

"What, did Taryn force you?"

"I felt sorry for her."

"So it was a pity fuck," says Mac.

"I guess it was, in a way. She showed up here one night, out of the blue. We'd already broken up, and I wasn't *planning* to sleep with her."

"Because you and Libby were already involved."

His head droops, and he looks down at his own shoes. Pricey athletic shoes, a brand a doctor's kid would own. "You don't know what Taryn was like. She was relentless. No matter how many times I told her we were through, she didn't believe me. She wouldn't stop texting me, harassing me. Following me around. It went on for weeks."

"Did she know you were seeing someone else?" Frankie asks.

"Not at first. I didn't tell her about Libby because I knew she'd go ballistic. She probably thought she could still get me back, and that's why she showed up here that day." At last his gaze rises to meet Frankie's. "She walked in and just took off her blouse. Stripped off all her clothes. Unbuckled my belt. I didn't want to do it, but she was so *needy.*"

His message is obvious: *I'm the victim here.* No doubt that is what he truly believes, that Taryn overpowered *him.* That he was too weak willed to resist her advances. Weakness comes in many forms, and Frankie can now see that weakness in this young man's face.

"When did you find out Taryn was pregnant?" Mac asks.

Liam's chin snaps up. "What?"

"When did she tell you?"

"She was *pregnant*?"

"You're saying you didn't know about it?"

"No! I had no idea!" The boy looks back and forth at Frankie and Mac. "Are you serious?"

"Tell us again when you last had sex with Taryn," says Frankie. "And remember, it's never good to lie to a cop. When we get back that pathology report, we're going to know the truth."

"I'm not lying!"

"You lied to us before, about when you last had sex with her."

"Because it *looked* bad. I was with Libby, and —"

"And a pregnant ex-girlfriend would present quite the problem for you, wouldn't it?" says Mac. "I imagine your hot new girlfriend wouldn't be happy about it. In fact, Libby would probably be so pissed off, she'd drop-kick you out of her life."

"I didn't know," Liam murmurs. "I swear

268

I didn't."

"And what a bummer, having to be a father at your age. You're only twenty-two, right? How can you go to law school when you've got a kid to support? It would blow up all your wonderful career plans."

Liam is silent, stunned by the nightmarish scenario Mac is painting.

"Did you offer to pay for an abortion? That's how other young men would probably handle it, young men who want to have a real future. Is that why you went to her apartment Friday night? To talk her into getting rid of the baby?"

"I didn't."

"I'm guessing she said no. I'm guessing she wanted to keep it."

"I didn't know about any baby!"

"She was about to ruin your life, Liam, not to mention your new romance. Goodbye, Libby. Goodbye, Stanford Law School," Mac continues relentlessly. "Taryn stood between you and your future. She was never going to go away. She was gonna keep her claws buried in you 'cause you were her golden ticket in life. I get it, son. I know exactly why you did it. Any guy would understand."

Liam jumps to his feet. "I didn't do anything wrong, and you're trying to make it sound like I did! I'm going to call my dad."

"Why don't you just sit back down and tell us the truth?"

"I know my rights. And I don't have to say another word." Liam stalks into the bedroom and slams the door.

"Did you really think he was going to confess?" says Frankie.

Mac shrugs. "A cop can always hope."

Through the closed bedroom door, they can hear Liam talking to his father. "It's nothing but bullshit, Dad. No, I didn't say anything incriminating. That's why I'm calling you. I need to know if I should call a lawyer."

Mac looks at Frankie. "That's it. Now he's not gonna tell us anything."

Of course he won't, she thinks. With a rich dad and the best lawyers you can buy, pretty boy just might skate away. But not if she can help it.

When Liam emerges from the bedroom, his face is flushed and his lips are tightly pressed together. "I'm going to ask you to leave," he says.

"Make it easy on yourself, son," says Mac. "Just tell us what happened."

"Am I under arrest?"

Mac sighs. "No."

"Then I don't have to tell you anything. Now, I'm waiting for a call from a lawyer. Please leave."

They have no choice. They both stand up and head to the door. But there Mac pauses and turns.

"If that's your baby, Liam, you know we'll be back."

"It's not mine! It — it can't be."

"Then whose is it?"

"I don't know!" He lets out a breath that's almost a sob. "Maybe — maybe that fat kid knows who it is. He was always around her."

"Tell us his name."

"I don't know his name. Maybe he's on her Facebook page or something."

"We've already looked at her Facebook page," says Frankie. "She had dozens of friends on there. Help us narrow it down."

Liam scrapes his hand through his hair. "Maybe . . . wait." He pulls out his phone and scrolls through his calls. "After I blocked her, Taryn used someone else's cell phone to call me. The number should still be on the log. Here." He hands the phone to Frankie. "That's the number she called me from. It could be that kid's phone."

Frankie pulls out her own phone and dials the number on Liam's screen.

It rings three times, and then a male voice

271

answers: "Hello?"

"I'm Detective Frances Loomis, Boston PD. May I ask who I'm speaking to?"

"Um, w-what?"

"I need to know your name, sir."

There is a long silence followed by a broken sigh. "Cody. My name is Cody Atwood."

CHAPTER 27
FRANKIE

Although he's managed to pull himself together for this interview, it's clear that Cody Atwood has been crying. His eyes are swollen, and his cheeks are bright pink, like a baby who's just had his face slapped, and in the wastebasket nearby is a mound of wadded-up tissues. He slouches on his sofa, a misshapen lump among the puffy throw cushions, and he says nothing as Mac scrolls through the messages on the boy's iPhone. The handover of the phone was a willing surrender, with no warrant necessary, which makes Frankie think the boy is either innocent or completely clueless. Or perhaps he's just too distraught to think straight. Certainly he's not stupid; he's intelligent enough to make it to his senior year at Commonwealth, and Frankie takes note of the English lit and calculus textbooks on his desk.

His apartment is larger and considerably

nicer than Taryn Moore's. It has a new stainless steel refrigerator, freshly painted walls, and on the bookshelf is a Canon camera with a missile-size telephoto lens. Money must not be an issue for Cody Atwood's family. Despite his obvious trappings of privilege, the boy himself radiates neediness. Cody hugs himself, as though trying to make himself shrink from view, but when you're as large as this boy, there's no way to hide your size.

"You and Taryn sure did exchange a lot of text messages," Mac says.

Cody nods. Wipes a hand across his nose.

"You two were pretty close, huh?"

A barely audible, "Yeah."

"Like, boyfriend-and-girlfriend close?"

Cody's head droops. "No."

"What was your relationship?"

"We hung out."

"What does that mean?"

"We studied together. Went to some of the same classes. And sometimes, I'd do things for her."

"Things?"

"Like take notes for her when she couldn't make it to class. Lend her money when she came up short. She was on a pretty tight budget, and I wanted to help."

"Awfully nice of you. Not many boys

would lend a girl money when she's not an actual girlfriend. Did you expect something in return?"

Cody's head tips up, and Frankie can finally see his eyes, which are no longer half-hidden by the baseball cap. "No! I'd never —"

"Did you want anything in return?"

"I just wanted her to — to —"

"Like you?"

Cody's cheeks flush an even brighter pink. "You make me sound like I'm some kind of loser."

In truth, that's exactly what Mac *is* doing, and Frankie feels sorry for the boy. She feels sorry he must navigate a world dominated by all the privileged Liam Reillys who have never known rejection.

Before Mac can ask his own question, she quietly interjects herself into the conversation. "You really cared about Taryn. Didn't you, Cody?" she says gently.

Her kindness disarms him. He wipes his eyes and turns away. "Yeah," he whispers.

"She was lucky to have such a good friend."

"I tried to be. I hated seeing her get hurt. And I'm sorry I let her talk me into spying on them."

"Spying on whom?"

"Liam and his new girlfriend. I followed them with my camera, and when I saw them together at the restaurant, I told Taryn. That's when she fell apart." He wipes his drippy nose. "She could've come to *me*. I would've done anything."

"Yes, I think you would have."

"But it's like she couldn't even *see* me. There I was, ready to help. I would never have taken advantage of her, the way *he* did. I think that's what broke her heart. That's why she did it." Cody shakes his head in disgust. "I don't know why he hasn't been fired."

Frankie is confused. She looks at Mac, then back at Cody. "Are we still talking about Liam?"

"No. Professor Dorian."

"A teacher?"

"Yeah. We both took his English lit course. I could see there was something going on between them. The way she looked at him. The way he looked at *her*. I complained to the school, but nothing happened to him. He's still teaching, while Taryn — Taryn . . ." Cody slowly exhales, and his head droops. "No one ever fucking listens to me."

Mac is already tapping on his smartphone, searching for information. "This professor, what's his first name?"

276

"Um . . . Jack."

"And he's in the English Department?"

"Yeah."

"Cody," says Frankie. "You said you complained about him to the school."

"I talked to some lady in the Title Nine office. She said — she promised — she'd follow up on it."

"What exactly did you tell her?"

"I said something was going on between them. I thought he was taking advantage of Taryn. Everyone in the class could see she was getting special attention. It made me sick to think about it. Her involved with a guy that old."

"How old?"

Mac looks up from his smartphone. "Forty-one, according to his bio. *Real* old."

"Do you think they were actually having an affair?" Frankie asks Cody.

"I'm sure of it. That's what I told the lady at Title Nine."

"Do you have any proof?"

Cody hesitates. "No," he admits. "But I could hear it in her voice, whenever she talked about him. How her life was going to change because of him. How she thought they could have a future together. The guy is *twice* her age."

Which must make me seem ancient, thinks

Frankie. But at forty-one, Jack Dorian is still in the prime of life. Mac shows her his smartphone screen, where he's pulled up Jack Dorian's photo. She sees an intelligent face, a full head of hair. Yes, he is definitely attractive enough to catch a woman's eye.

"He should be fired for what he did to her," says Cody.

But what *did* Jack Dorian do? Was it merely a flirtation between teacher and student? Did their relationship veer into something dangerous? Or was Cody Atwood so obsessed with Taryn that he couldn't abide any man showing an interest in her — even if that interest was perfectly innocent?

"Do you think Professor Dorian is the kind of guy who might hurt a woman?" Mac asks.

At this question, Cody goes very still. "Why are you asking that question?"

"Maybe you could just answer it?"

"The school says she killed herself. That's what they said on the news too." He looks at Frankie. "Are you saying that's not true?"

Frankie doesn't answer, because the truth is still unclear to her. The deeper they dig into Taryn's death, the larger the cast of characters they uncover. And now they've added one more name: Jack Dorian.

"She was my friend," says Cody. "I want to know what really happened!"

Frankie nods. "So do we."

■ ■ ■ ■

BEFORE

■ ■ ■ ■

CHAPTER 28
JACK

For three weeks, Taryn had stayed away from him, but Jack continued to twist in self-loathing. He had gone to her apartment to end their affair and, in one mindless moment, had yielded again to his goddamn id. Yes, she had wanted it. Yes, she had opened the door already stripped down to her underwear. Yes, she had moaned in delight and said she loved him. Still, he couldn't help feeling that he was the one who had taken advantage of her, assaulted her.

Since that day, he had seen her only in class and never alone. No more private meetings in his office or strolling together out of the classroom. When she did attend class, she sat in stiff silence, scribbling notes and fixing him with hard looks that set off a frisson of guilt, as if he had betrayed her. But he did not love her, and he'd never suggested they had a future together. He would never leave Maggie for her. And he was determined to tell her this point-blank the next time they were alone. He had led them both astray, and he was the one who would take full responsibility.

He just needed to find the opportunity — and the courage — to say it.

His dread of that conversation overshadowed any sense of celebration when he and Maggie went out to dinner for his birthday. They always celebrated their birthdays at the same restaurant, Benedetto's in Harvard Square, and their tradition included a champagne toast with Veuve Clicquot and a shared appetizer of calamari. After tonight, he vowed, he would take the first steps back to normalcy. To being a good husband again. Charlie's failing health had been a burden on them both, and they needed this chance to get away, just the two of them. To remember the Jack and Maggie they once had been.

He ordered his usual glass of champagne and was surprised when Maggie asked for only sparkling Pellegrino.

"What? No Veuve Clicquot?" he asked.

"Not tonight. Not for the next seven months." Smiling, she handed him an envelope. "Happy birthday, honey."

Puzzled, he opened the envelope, expecting to find a birthday card inside, but the card he pulled out was decorated with balloons and floating babies. Not a birthday card at all but something else. Something that only slowly dawned on him.

She beamed. "Are you ready to be called Daddy?"

He stared at her, not certain he'd actually heard what she'd said. "Oh God. Really? *Really?*"

Maggie blinked away tears. "Yes. Really. I didn't want to tell you until I was absolutely sure everything was fine. I saw my OB this morning, and she said it all looks perfect. The ultrasound, the blood tests. It's going to be an October baby. Just in time for Halloween."

Maggie's face suddenly shimmered out of focus as his vision blurred over. *A baby.* He wiped away his own tears. *Our baby.*

"Think of it, Jack. This Christmas there'll be three of us. Our first Christmas together as a family!"

His chair legs scraped across the floor as he jumped to his feet. He scrambled around the table and threw his arms around her. "I love you. God, I love you."

"I love you too," she sobbed. For a moment they forgot they were in a restaurant. Forgot everything except that they were in each other's arms and this miracle was about to change their lives forever.

"And this time," Maggie said, "it will be fine. I can just feel it. Everything will turn out absolutely fine."

But everything was absolutely not fine.

On Monday morning, he found an envelope in his office mailbox addressed only to *Jack*. It contained a card with an illustration of Abelard and Heloise in a passionate embrace, and handwritten inside was a line from Heloise's fourth letter to Abelard: *Heaven commands me to renounce that fatal passion which unites me to you; but oh! my heart will never be able to consent to it.*

It was not signed, nor did it have to be.

In fury, he took the card into the men's restroom, tore it into pieces, and threw them into the toilet. Standing in the bathroom stall, watching the bits of paper flush away, he tried to steady his shaking hands. He'd hoped the problem would resolve on its own, that Taryn would lose interest in him or find another object of her affection. Now he realized the problem was not going away by itself. He had to end this now, before it blew up his life.

When he walked into the seminar that morning, there she was in her usual seat, this time wearing an alarm-red sweater. Her eyes sparkled as she met his gaze, a look that said: *You'd better pay attention to me.* He did not acknowledge her but simply scanned the group, feigning normalcy, wishing he were any other place than in this classroom.

The week's assignment was *Romeo and Juliet,* and he plunged straight into his prepared comments about the Montagues and Capulets, how their enmity led to the tragic deaths of their children and how love could transcend even the most stubborn of hostilities. As he ended his comments, his gaze passed over Taryn, and he had a sudden flash of her face gasping in orgasm.

Quickly he looked away and asked, with a note of desperation in his voice, "Was this tragedy preordained by fate? What's the role of free will in the story?"

To his relief, Jason picked up the thread. "The prologue says the lovers are star crossed, which implies their fate is already decided."

"Okay."

"And in act one, Romeo talks about fearing some consequence hanging in the stars from the night's revels. So Shakespeare seems to say that fate rules their lives. That it was all predestined."

He glanced at the wall clock, wishing it

would move faster, but he also dreaded what would follow. Today, he'd tell her. Today this would end. And he had no idea how Taryn would react.

Beth raised her hand. "Romeo says he was 'Fortune's fool.' He knows he has crappy luck. So a lot of what happens in the play does seem fated."

Taryn spoke up. "So you both think Romeo did *nothing* out of his own free will? I can't imagine Shakespeare actually believed that."

"What do *you* think he believed?" Beth asked.

"Shakespeare might have believed that *some* things are meant to happen. That two people are *fated* to fall in love." She aimed a look at Jack that made his stomach drop.

Taryn, don't.

"But if you believe entirely in fate," said Taryn, "then you believe we have no control over our futures. That some higher power decides everything for us, good and bad. That means there are no coincidences in life, no accidents, no laws of nature, and no free will."

Jessica gave a bored sigh. "We're talking about a play. Not real life."

"But it's a reflection of real life. Even if lovers are *destined* to meet, even if they're *destined* to fall in love, what they do next is of their own free will. People are ultimately responsible for their own actions." She looked straight at Jack. "And for the consequences they suffer because of those actions."

"Why did you want to meet out here?" Taryn asked as they walked together down a path winding through the frozen marshes of the Fenway. It was late afternoon, an icy wind was blowing, and no one else was nearby to overhear their conversation. It was the perfect place for him to finally tell her the painful truth.

"I wanted to talk to you in private," he said.

"We could have talked in your office. At least it would've been a lot warmer."

"My office isn't private enough." Because even a closed door would not muffle any shouts or sobs. He had no idea if she'd take this calmly or if he'd have to endure a hysterical outburst. No, this needed to be said far away from anyone who knew him.

"What's going on, Jack?"

He pointed to a bench. "Let's sit down."

"Ooh. This sounds serious," she said, but the playful note in her voice told him she had no idea how serious the conversation

289

was about to become. She sat and smiled expectantly. What did she think he was about to say? That he'd fall to his knee and propose marriage? That he'd pledge his undying love? How the hell had he let a simple fling grow into this uncontrollable monster?

He sat down on the bench beside her and sighed, and his breath puffed out in a cloud of steam. As she watched him, he struggled to recall the speech he'd planned to deliver, but under her expectant gaze, all the pretty words vanished. So he simply said what needed to be said, ruthless though it was.

"I have to end this, Taryn. We can't see each other anymore."

She shook her head, as if not certain she'd heard him. "You don't mean this, Jack. I know you don't."

"I absolutely do mean it."

"This isn't you. This is your wife, isn't it? You told her about us. And now she's forcing you to —"

"This is my decision and mine alone."

"I don't believe that. I don't believe you'd *choose* to throw away what we have. Did she threaten to tell the school? Are you afraid of losing your job — is that it?"

"This has nothing to do with my wife. I haven't told her a thing. This is just not go-

290

ing to work between us."

"Yes it will." She reached out and clutched his sleeve. "I'm ready to be whatever you want me to be. We could be so happy! I could *make* you happy."

"Taryn, you are beautiful and brilliant, and someday you'll find the man who deserves you. Someone you *will* make happy. But that man isn't me. It can't be me."

"Why?" Her voice rose to a hysterical pitch. *"Why?"*

"Because my wife is pregnant."

CHAPTER 29
TARYN

He continued to speak, but she was unable to hear anything he said beyond that one sentence.

My wife is pregnant.

She thought about what that meant. She pictured them together in bed, making love. How long ago had the wife conceived? Had it happened after the start of the semester, after he'd met Taryn? These past few weeks, she had imagined him unhappily married to a woman who no longer excited him, a woman he no longer desired. She had imagined him fantasizing about *her,* wanting *her,* yet all this time he'd been living with his wife, fucking his wife. Even though he was married to the woman, to Taryn this felt like a betrayal.

". . . what you and I had was beautiful, but it was also very wrong. It never should have happened. I take full responsibility, and I'm sorry."

Suddenly she focused on him. "You're *sorry*?"

"For letting it get out of control. For hurting you. I'm a married man, Taryn. And my wife needs me."

"But you said *I'm* the one you want."

"I never said that. I never would have said that. Anyway, everything has changed."

"Just because she's pregnant? How does that change anything?"

"It changes everything. Can't you understand that?"

"But I love you. And you want me. I know you do." Desperately she reached out to him, but he took hold of her wrists, trapping them.

"I will always care about you, but we have to move on. You have your whole life to look forward to. You'll be going to grad school. You'll be working with Dr. Vogel, collaborating on that paper —"

"I don't give a fuck about that paper. I only care about us!"

"There is no 'us.' From now on, we are teacher and student, nothing more. You have to accept this."

She yanked free of his grasp. "Accept that I'm just a fling? That you're going to just fuck me and forget me?"

"I'll never forget you."

"But I'm not good enough for you to love, am I? *Am I?*"

He flinched at the rage in her voice. For a moment he just stared at her, as if she'd transformed into someone, something he'd never encountered before. When at last he spoke, his voice was both quiet and desperate. "You are beautiful and talented, and someday you'll meet a man who'll give you all the love you deserve."

"But that man won't be you."

"It can't be."

"Didn't I . . . ." She choked back a sob. "Didn't I make you happy?"

"This has nothing to do with being happy. It's about what needs to happen now. What I did was wrong."

"I wanted it too!"

"But I'm the one who's married. And I'm your teacher, which makes it even more wrong. I need to end this before it gets any more difficult than it already is."

"Difficult for you, you mean."

"For both of us."

"You don't care about me. You used me, Jack. You're just like those so-called heroes you talk about in class. Jason and Abelard and that fucking Aeneas."

"Please, Taryn. Let's not have it end this way."

"Which way?"

"With you angry. Let's be reasonable about this."

"Oh, I can be reasonable." She rose to her feet, but he did not stand up. He remained seated on that ice-cold bench, staring up at her. She glimpsed fear in his eyes, and at that moment she realized who was actually in control. Who held all the power. This time when she spoke, she was chillingly calm. "You're about to find out just how reasonable I can be."

As she walked away, he didn't call after her, didn't follow her. She could feel his gaze on her back as she crossed the road, as she kept walking, back to campus. She wouldn't give him the satisfaction of seeing her glance at him one last time. She refused to look backward at all, only forward, to what came next.

By the time she reached the university library, she knew what she was going to do. She would not be like tragic Queen Dido, falling on a sword, or Heloise, locked away to wither and rot in a convent. She sat down at one of the library computers and pulled up the website she'd looked at only a few weeks ago: Mount Auburn Hospital, in Cambridge.

She pulled out her cell phone and dialed.

CHAPTER 30
TARYN

The clinic waiting room was filled with old people. On her left was a silver-haired man with a rattling cough; on her right was a woman with hands so gnarled by arthritis she could barely zip up her purse. Taryn was the youngest person in the room, and as she dutifully filled out the health questionnaire, marking no to every question, she noticed glances from the other patients, who were no doubt wondering why someone so obviously healthy was here to see the doctor.

She signed the completed form, handed it to the receptionist, and sat down to wait.

The old man with the cough went in first, then a man with a cane, then the woman with the gnarled hands. By the time the nurse finally emerged and called out, "Taryn?" she was the last patient in the waiting room. The nurse led her down a short hall into the exam room and handed her a paper gown. "Everything off except your underwear," she said.

Taryn would rather not meet her rival while half-naked, but she undressed as instructed and once again sat down to wait. On the wall hung a framed diploma from Boston University School of Medicine and, beneath it, a certificate from the American Board of Internal Medicine, proof that Margaret Dorian was a woman to be reckoned with.

But Taryn was the one her husband lusted after.

There was a knock on the door, and Dr. Dorian stepped in, carrying a clipboard with Taryn's patient questionnaire. Even though it was nearly five in the afternoon and she had probably been seeing patients all day, she looked relaxed and unhurried, her hair neatly swept back in a ponytail, a stethoscope casually draped around her neck.

She greeted her patient with a smile. "Hello, Taryn. I'm Dr. Dorian. You're here for a physical?"

"Yes, ma'am."

She turned to the sink and washed her hands. "Is this for a job?"

"For school. I'm hoping to start a graduate program this fall. English lit."

"Good for you." She dried her hands and

glanced at the clipboard with the questionnaire. "From what I see here, it looks like you're pretty healthy. Any current medical problems? Complaints?"

Taryn shrugged. "I'm a little stressed. You know, senior year."

She smiled. "Take the time to enjoy it. I guarantee, when you get older, you'll look back at this year with nostalgia."

As Dr. Dorian leaned in close to peer into her eyes and ears and palpate her neck, Taryn took a close look at her, noting the strands of silver streaking her red hair and the laugh lines creasing the corners of her eyes. Though she was somewhere in her late thirties, she was still pretty; in her twenties, she must have been stunning. If she really was pregnant, as Jack claimed, it didn't yet show. Had he lied to her? Was it merely an excuse he'd invented to break things off between them?

Dr. Dorian pressed the stethoscope to Taryn's chest. "Take a deep breath."

Taryn inhaled the other woman's scent of soap and disinfectant. Certainly it was not a scent to inspire passion. So this was what Jack went home to every night, the smell of sterility and exam rooms. To a woman who spent her day pressing aging flesh and peering into orifices. Why would he choose this over what Taryn could offer him?

She stretched out on the table so the doctor could examine her abdomen. As she felt the doctor's warm hands press against her belly, Taryn thought of the baby now growing in Margaret Dorian's abdomen. Jack's baby. Neither Jack nor his wife was young, and Taryn wondered why they hadn't had children up till now. Because they couldn't, or because they'd chosen not to? That baby was the reason Jack had left her, and even though it was now just a ball of cells that was probably no bigger than her thumb, she hated it. As Dr. Dorian felt for her liver and spleen, Taryn stared at the other woman's belly, willing the baby inside her to shrivel up and die. If it did not exist, Jack would still be with her.

"Everything seems normal," Dr. Dorian said, straightening. "You're a perfectly healthy twenty-two-year-old. Now it's up to you to stay that way. Do you smoke cigarettes or use drugs? Alcohol?"

"I have a drink now and then."

"Unprotected sex?"

If only you knew.

"I try to be careful," Taryn replied. "But sometimes, you know how it is. You get carried away."

"I can order a pregnancy test. If you think

299

you need one."

That was something Taryn had not even considered. "No," she finally said. "I don't need one."

"Well, just keep being careful," Dr. Dorian said and gave Taryn's shoulder a squeeze. She was not yet a mother, but already maternal gestures seemed natural to her. "Now, do you have any school forms for me to fill out?"

"I'll mail them to you."

"Certainly." She jotted a note in the chart. "Which grad school will you be attending?"

"Commonwealth."

She glanced up. "Oh? My husband's on the faculty there."

"Yes, I know. I took one of his seminars. It's called Star-Crossed Lovers."

"What a small world!"

"Yes, isn't it?"

"So what will you be studying in grad school?"

"English lit. I never would have gotten into the program without your husband's help. He wrote me the best recommendation letters, and that made all the difference."

Dr. Dorian smiled. It was not a fake smile just to be polite; no, this was a smile of genuine delight about her husband's good deed. "He loves it when he finds a student who really shines."

"When I was looking for a doctor, I noticed your name was Dorian. That's kind of the reason I picked you."

"Really? I'll have to thank him for the referral!"

"Be sure to tell him I said hello. Tell him I'll never forget all the lessons he taught me."

"I certainly will." She gave a breezy wave as she headed for the door. "Good luck in grad school, Taryn. In case I don't see you again."

Oh, you'll be seeing me. Sooner than you think.

Chapter 31
Jack

It was hard to believe that Charlie was dying when he showed up at their house looking almost as hale as he had before his diagnosis. His glacier-blue eyes still flashed the chilly sharpness that could bring criminals to their knees. He might have lost some weight from the radiation therapy, but years of regular workouts at Gold's Gym had built a sturdy frame, thick with muscles, and he did not project the shrunken look Jack had seen in other cancer patients.

And tonight, he'd arrived in high spirits and waving a bottle of sixteen-year-old Lagavulin whiskey — his favorite brand, which made it Jack's favorite as well.

As rib eye steaks broiled in the kitchen, Charlie poured the whiskey and handed glasses to Maggie and Jack. "No better time than the present to celebrate being alive," he said. "And from now on, only the expensive stuff will do!"

Both Charlie and Jack gulped down the whiskey, but Maggie quietly set hers down untouched, a detail Charlie — observant as always — did not miss.

"Not going to join our toast, darling?" he asked.

"Actually, Dad, I have a good reason not to. Jack and I have some news."

"It's something big," Jack said, grinning. "*Really* big."

"Well, I hope it won't be *that* big," Maggie said, laughing. She went to stand face to face with her father. "Dad, we're going to have a baby."

Slowly Charlie put down his glass. For a moment he could not speak; he simply stared at his daughter, his beautiful daughter.

"It's going to happen in October. My doctor says the pregnancy looks good, and I'm feeling great. Dad, aren't you going to say anything?"

"Oh dear God. My Maggie. Is this real?"

"It is." Laughing and sobbing at the same time, she took Charlie's hands in hers. "It is, it is! You're finally going to be a grandpa!"

In all the years that Jack had known him, he had seen Charlie cry only once, at the funeral of Maggie's mother, Annie. But at that moment his face crumpled, and suddenly all three of them were hugging and weeping. They wept for joy. They wept in gratitude for this chance at a family again. They wept in hope that this time he and Maggie would have a baby to love, even as Charlie was facing the end of his own life. Jack also knew that part of his own reaction rose from the stress of the whole Taryn affair — from the annihilating guilt of cheating on Maggie, from the lies and deception, from not stopping himself from using Taryn and adding to the scar tissue of men who had abandoned her. And from the prowling fear of it all coming out.

To give them some privacy, Jack retreated to the kitchen. He pulled the steaks out of the broiler, tossed the salad, and opened a bottle of wine. Charlie's heart-healthy diet was now out the window; in the months left to him, he'd eat all the steak he damn well wanted. When Jack returned to the living room, father and daughter were sitting on the sofa, Charlie's arm slung over her shoulder, his cheeks flushed with happiness.

"You've got so much to think about now, eh, Jack?" Charlie said.

"It's just starting to sink in, all the things we'll need to do. New paint and curtains in the spare room. Furniture, baby clothes. Heck, I've never even held a baby. The whole thing's a little scary to me."

"If only my Annie were still here, she'd set you straight on everything. Burping, swaddling, feeding schedules. Look at the fine job she did with our Maggie here. She must be smiling down at us right now."

Maggie leaned her head on Charlie's shoulder. "I know she is, Dad."

"So what're you going to name him? I hope you're not thinking of fancy names for the kid like Ethan or Oliver."

"What's wrong with Ethan or Oliver?" Jack said.

"Better to choose a good solid name for a good solid lad. There's nothing wrong with Joe or Sam."

"What if it's a girl?"

Charlie shook his head. "No, it's going to be a boy. I have a very strong feeling about this." Gently he placed a palm against Maggie's abdomen. "And I'll make damn sure I live long enough to see him come into the world."

"Nothing would make us happier," Maggie said.

"Now, you know what'd also make me happy?" Charlie looked at Jack. "Getting some food into my girl here. She's eating for two now, so let's make sure she and my grandbaby are properly fed."

Jack bowed, gesturing toward the dining room. "My lord and lady, medium-rare steaks await you both."

Charlie walked his daughter to the table, treating her as if she were the fragile member of the family, not him. In truth, the news of the baby seemed to have breathed fresh vigor into Charlie, and his laugh was louder, his appetite heartier, than Jack could remember. By the time Jack finished pouring wine and dishing out salads for everyone, Charlie had already devoured a third of his rib eye and had added so much butter to his baked potato that it was swimming in a melted puddle of it.

Maggie shot her husband a joyful glance. Tonight it seemed impossible that Charlie was sick. *If only this moment could last forever,* Jack thought. *All of us alive and happy. Everything right with our world.*

He sliced into his steak. Even that was perfect.

"Oh, Jack, I almost forgot to tell you," said Maggie. "One of your students dropped by to see me at the clinic today."

"Oh? Who?"

"A girl named Taryn Moore."

Jack sucked in a gasp, inhaling wine. For a stinging moment he couldn't breathe, couldn't speak.

306

"Are you okay?" said Maggie.

He shook his head and gestured that the drink had gone up his nose. His sinuses felt as if they'd been cauterized, and he tried to swallow but instead coughed and gagged at the same time.

As tears ran down his face, he waved her away.

"Jack, breathe. Breathe."

He finally managed to suck in a breath. "Went down the wrong pipe," he gasped and sank back, wiping his face with a napkin. "Hate it when that happens."

Charlie pushed a water glass to him. As Jack reached for it, he saw Charlie watching him, those ice-blue eyes fixed on his.

Jack took a sip of water and felt the spasms in his throat ease. "Sorry."

"You scared me," said Maggie. "The good news is it was only wine you inhaled and not steak."

Yeah, great news. Taryn Moore is stalking my wife.

He settled back in his chair and picked up the steak knife, but he'd lost his appetite. He wanted only to slink away from the table, away from Charlie's watchful gaze.

"So what's that you were saying, Maggie?" Charlie asked, slicing off another bite of steak. "About Jack's student?"

307

"Oh, right. Taryn Moore. She asked me to say hello. Do you remember her, Jack?"

He nodded, trying to appear calm. Taryn hadn't just randomly chosen his wife as her doctor. She'd specifically chosen Maggie just to let him know she was not finished with him. That more trouble was coming.

He sipped his water. "Yeah. I think she's in my seminar."

"You think? You have only fifteen students in that seminar."

"Yeah, Taryn . . . uh . . . Moore. I know which one she is."

"I should think you'd remember. She's hard to miss. She's fashion-model gorgeous."

"Is she, now?" said Charlie. His gaze was still on Jack.

Jack made a noncommittal shrug. "I suppose she's not bad looking. Kind of quiet." He downed more water.

"Really? She didn't strike me that way at all," said Maggie. "In fact, she seemed pretty high spirited. And you'll be happy to hear she thinks you're the best professor she's ever had."

As he reached for his glass of wine, he had a terrible thought. "She's not going to be your regular patient, is she?"

"No. She only came by for a physical. She

308

said she needed it for grad school."

As far as Jack knew, the university did not require a physical exam to apply to graduate school, so there was no good reason for her to visit Maggie. *Her only reason is me. She's tormenting me.*

"Speaking of names for the baby, don't you think Taryn's a beautiful name, for either a girl or a boy? I looked it up, and it's Welsh for *thunder.*" She pressed a hand to her belly. "Maybe what we have here is a baby Taryn. What do you think?"

Yeah, great!

"I'm not crazy about the name," Jack said. In fact, it would be a lifelong punishment: having his child named after his mistress. It suddenly occurred to him that although he and Taryn had been as intimate as two bodies could be, he actually knew very little about her. She could be insane. She could be dangerous.

This much he did know: if she wanted to, she could destroy him.

CHAPTER 32
JACK

"Professor Dorian?" said the voice on the phone.

"Yes?"

"This is Elizabeth Sacco from the Title Nine Office. I'm wondering if we might talk again soon."

"Again?" He could not keep his voice from leaping an octave higher. "What is this about?"

"I'm afraid there's been another complaint against you. Do you have some free time today or tomorrow so we can discuss the matter?"

He felt his face flush in panic. "What kind of complaint?"

"I think it's better if we have this conversation in person."

It's Taryn. It has to be her.

It was eight thirty, and his office was just a few buildings away from Sacco's office, but he needed time to absorb this fresh blow and prepare himself for the possibilities. "I'm free today. I can be there around ten. Would that work?"

"That would be fine. This shouldn't take long."

Yeah, he thought. It didn't take long to say *you're fired.*

At five minutes to ten o'clock, and for the second time that semester, he stood at the door through which he'd hoped never to pass again:

OFFICE FOR UNIVERSITY EQUITY AND COMPLIANCE, DR. ELIZABETH SACCO, TITLE IX COORDINATOR.

He strolled in, trying to look casual, but his nerves were sizzling. The same female receptionist greeted him with her quietly damning smile and led him into Elizabeth Sacco's inner office. Sacco shook his hand and sat down at her desk as he took the seat across from her. No exchange of niceties, nothing about the latest snowstorm or how great the Celtics were doing.

"I realize this is probably getting old," she said. "Meeting like this."

"No problem," he said, trying to feign nonchalance. "You said there was another complaint?"

311

"Yes. I just want to run it by you, to get your response." She sounded so reasonable, so nonconfrontational. Was she putting him at ease, merely to lay a trap?

"Okay."

"We received an anonymous call yesterday. The caller claimed you're involved in a sexual relationship with a student."

He felt as if a grenade had gone off in his chest. He managed to keep his voice steady as he said, "Wow. That's a pretty serious charge. Did the caller give any specifics?"

"I have no other details, only what the caller said." She checked her notes. "Quote: 'I think Professor Dorian is having an affair with an undergraduate female student.' That's the full statement. Nothing else, no details, no names, no places. After making that statement, the person hung up."

"And how am I supposed to respond to something like that?"

"Yet it's not a complaint I can ignore. To tell you the truth, I wasn't sure what to do with this."

"Then maybe it should be ignored."

"Still, I have to document your response."

"You said it was anonymous?"

"Yes. We get anonymous complaints every so often, from callers who are afraid to identify themselves. And we have no choice but to follow protocol and inform the accused. So tell me, Professor, is there any truth at all to this complaint?"

His mouth went dry. The last time he'd sat here, the accusation against him had been blatantly false and easily refuted. Not this time. This time he was guilty as hell, and the consequence of a sexual relationship with a student would be immediate termination.

"Professor Dorian?"

"I'm guessing this must be some disgruntled student trying to get back at me again. Maybe someone I gave a bad grade to. And this is how she's retaliating."

For a long moment Dr. Sacco studied him, searching for any tics or microexpressions that might betray him.

"So that's your response," she said.

"Yes." He hated having to lie. Hated that he had plunged blindly into that damn affair with Taryn. He hated the day he'd met her, hated the fact he wasn't a better man than what he'd become. Hated that he was not the good husband Maggie deserved. The last time he'd sat in this chair, he'd been charged with defending a fictitious teacher having an affair with a fictitious student. It had been like a preview of coming attractions. His life had imitated art in all its tragically stupid glory.

"Then unless some other evidence develops, that's all for now," she said. "I'm sorry for any inconvenience."

Unless some other evidence develops.

Which meant she'd be watching him. Which meant he would always be under this shadow of doubt and could never slip up, never let down his guard.

He stood up to leave, but at the door he paused. "You said it was an anonymous caller on the phone. Did she give you *any* clue who she was?" he asked.

Her eyes narrowed, and suddenly he regretted the question. "Why would you want to know that?" she asked.

"If I'm going to be accused of something this serious, I'd like some idea of who she is."

"I suppose I can tell you it wasn't a she."

This startled him. "The caller was *male*?"

"Yes."

He knew at once who had made the call: Cody Atwood, the boy who always trailed in Taryn's wake. The boy who clearly worshipped her, who seemed to have no other friends. For him, Taryn must seem like a dazzlingly brilliant sun around which he revolved.

Taryn had put him up to this. What other torments did she have in store?

CHAPTER 33
JACK

It was probably paranoia, but as he walked across campus the next day, he felt as if everybody who saw him knew his secret. As if scored on his forehead was the bright-red letter *A*. Hester Prynne, meet Jack Dorian.

Every other morning when he walked into his seminar, he'd hear the buzz of conversation and greetings of "Hey, Professor." But that morning, a strangely conspiratorial silence hung over the room. Where Taryn usually sat, there was an empty chair, like a black hole sucking in all the light. Cody was present, though, and when Jack looked at him, Cody could not hold Jack's gaze.

So it *was* Cody who'd called the Title IX office. Had the son of a bitch blabbed to the whole class? Was that why they were all staring at him?

Jack refused to let them know how rattled he was. He bid them all his usual "good morning" and took out his notes. He was

316

damn well going to conduct this class as he always did, despite the anxiety gnawing like a rodent in his stomach. At least he didn't have to deal with Taryn's presence. He hoped she'd drop out of the course, just to avoid the discomfort of their facing each other across the table for these final weeks of the semester. Perhaps that noose around his neck was loosening, just a bit. Just enough for him to breathe again.

But that afternoon, while he sat in Dunkin' in Garrison Hall, the noose snapped tighter than ever.

He was having coffee and reviewing his notes on *The Human Stain* for his Modern American Novel course when he looked up to see Taryn descending on him like a hawk. Without a word, she scraped a chair across to his table. She was dressed all in black today, the color of doom, her face so rigid it might have been chipped from granite.

"Taryn," he said, "I was wondering why you didn't show up for —"

"I'm going to do the talking," she snapped. "And you're going to listen." She dropped into the chair and leaned toward him with a predatory lurch.

He glanced at the students sitting a few tables away, worried that others would hear, but no one seemed to be paying attention.

They were all in their own little bubbles, unaware of the nasty little drama unfolding just a few feet away.

"Can we do this outside?" he asked.

"No. Right here."

"Then please can you keep it down? Let's not make a scene."

"I don't care if we do make a scene, Jack. All things considered, I think I'm being pretty fucking calm about this."

He shot another glance around the room. Said quietly: "What do you want? Just tell me what you want."

"Let me lay it out for you, bullet point by bullet point. One, I won't be returning to your seminar. I know you're probably relieved as hell not to see me in class anymore, but it doesn't mean I'm dropping out. Oh no, I'm enrolled till the end.

"Two, you're going to give me an A because I deserve it. And because of all the pain and suffering you put me through.

"Three, you are going to pull every string you can and get me whatever I want. For a start, I'll need a paid position as a teaching assistant, and you're going to write me a recommendation worthy of Heloise d'Argenteuil. And if you don't, I'm going straight to Elizabeth Sacco and telling her how you fucked my brains out."

"It's your word against mine, Taryn. How are you going to prove —"

"I'll tell you how I'm going to prove it. You left behind a little souvenir at my apartment." She whipped out her cell phone and thrust it at him.

He stared at the photo on her phone, a photo that made no sense. All he saw was a close-up of dark-green fabric. "What is this?"

"Don't you recognize it? It's the sofa in my apartment."

"What does this have to do with anything?"

"Have you forgotten what we did there? Maybe you can't see the little white stain you left behind. But it's still there, on the fabric."

His stomach clenched. *Semen. She's talking about semen.*

"I'd call that pretty good proof," she said, shoving her phone back in her pocket. "I've also got a witness in Dr. Hannah Greenwald. She saw us together at the conference hotel. At breakfast, remember? And I've also saved all those texts you sent me. Even if you've deleted them from your phone, I've still got them. I've got proof, Jack. *So* much proof."

Yes, he *had* sent her texts, but he couldn't

recall what he'd written or if there'd been anything incriminating in them. He'd since deleted them, but she already had more than enough evidence to destroy his job, his marriage, his life. And nothing in her face, cold with purpose, made him doubt that she was ruthless enough to do it.

"This is blackmail," he said.

"Call it what you want. I'm just collecting what I'm due."

"All right. All right." He tried to steady his breaths, tried to think past his panic. "If I give you the A, if I do everything you want, what happens then? Can we just end this? Can we get on with our lives?"

"I haven't decided."

"Haven't decided *what*?" His voice rose, and suddenly he felt the collective lines of awareness from others in the café converging on them. At least there was no one here whom he recognized.

"I haven't decided what else I want from you," she said. She scraped back her chair and stood up. "But when it's time for me to collect, I'll be in touch."

"But stay away from my wife."

"What?"

"You visited her at her office, and it wasn't for a physical. I don't want you to ever get near her again."

"Or what?"

"Just don't."

She snapped on dark glasses and walked away.

He watched her push through the door and exit into a cold gray drizzle. And he thought about the metaphor at the core of Philip Roth's novel, the universal *human stain* — that messy moral complex of imperfections that pollutes everything a person touches.

And we all end up paying for it.

CHAPTER 34
JACK

"Your girl's officially in the program!" announced Ray McGuire. He stood grinning in Jack's doorway, his head bent at a rakish tilt. "I just signed the acceptance letter. It'll go out in today's mail. That should make her pretty damn happy. A teaching assistantship is still pending the fall budget. But she's in."

"She certainly earned it," said Jack. *In more ways than one.*

"The grad committee had it narrowed down to two final candidates. It was your recommendation letter that nudged her over the finish line. We're expecting great things from her, Jack. Must make you proud, eh?"

Relieved was what Jack really felt. Relieved that he'd delivered the goods as promised. This should be the end of it, because Taryn couldn't afford to expose him now; it would nullify his recommendation letters and jeopardize her future at the university.

They'd been partners in sin, and now they were partners in deception. However much they despised each other, they were now forever chained to each other, and Taryn was clever enough to understand this.

This was absolutely the end of it.

When another week went by with no word from her, he allowed himself to breathe again. He could even laugh again when Charlie showed up for dinner at their house. Charlie had brought along his laundry so they could wash it for him, sparing him the chore. As Jack carried the laundry basket into the house, Charlie followed, holding aloft a bottle of his favorite Lagavulin in one hand and a carton of organic whole milk in the other.

"One drink for us fellas, one drink for the mommy-to-be," he said.

"Oh, Dad, you know I've never been crazy about milk," said Maggie.

"Better learn to like it, darlin'. That little bump's counting on the calcium."

Little Bump was what Charlie had started calling the baby, a far better name than Maggie's first choice, Taryn. Whether it was a boy or a girl, that was the name she kept returning to, a name straight out of Jack's nightmares.

"What Little Bump really needs is for

Mommy to sit down and take it easy," Jack said. "Daddy's got everything under control."

He was, in fact, happy to leave the two of them alone in the living room. He brought Charlie's laundry down to the cellar, loaded it into the washing machine, and headed back upstairs to finish cooking dinner. After all, how many months did Maggie have left with her father? They were all painfully aware of the passage of time. As the metastases spread through Charlie's body, it was a race between the pregnancy and how fast cancer would take him down. But Charlie had always been a fighter, and now he had something to really fight for: a glimpse of his very first grandchild.

That evening, looking at his ruddy, laughing face over the dinner table, Jack had little doubt Charlie would win that fight. He piled pasta onto his plate, poured himself another glass of whiskey, and dived into his meal like a man starved for life. Jack and Maggie exchanged smiles because, at that moment, everything was as right with their world as it could be. Her father might be dying, but a new life was on the way. And they had each other, a blessing that he would never again put at risk.

From the cellar came the buzz of the

dryer. Jack stood up. "I'd better get down-stairs before everything gets wrinkled."

"You'll make someone a very good wife, Jack," Charlie said.

"Well, you can't have him, Dad," said Maggie. "He's mine."

All yours, thought Jack as he headed down to the cellar. *And I'll never forget it.* While he pulled Charlie's laundry out of the dryer, he could hear Maggie upstairs in the kitchen, grinding coffee beans and loading the dishwasher. Everyday domestic sounds he'd once taken for granted. He'd come far too close to losing it all. Now, just the act of folding Charlie's sheets, still warm from the dryer, made him happy. Soon there'd be baby clothes and crib sheets to wash as well, and diapers to change and baby bottles to warm. He looked forward to it all — yes, even the diapers.

He carried the basket of folded laundry upstairs to the kitchen, where Maggie was arranging coffee cups and saucers on a tray. She didn't hear him and gave a little squeal as he ambushed her from behind, hugging her close.

"Hey, you," she laughed.

"You smell good."

"Probably like cheese and tomato sauce."

"I like cheese and tomato sauce."

Maggie turned around to face him. "God, I wish we could hold on to this moment. You and me and Dad. I wish we could just freeze it as it is now, before —"

The sound of a throat being cleared made them turn. Charlie stood in the doorway, looking a little sheepish that he'd caught them embracing.

"Everything okay, Dad?" said Maggie.

"It's starting to rain. I think maybe I should call it a night, before the weather gets worse."

"You don't want to stay for coffee and ice cream?"

"I couldn't eat another bite, anyway. I'll leave you two lovebirds to have at it." He picked up the laundry basket from the kitchen table. "Thanks for washing my sheets, Jack. I never could get the hang of folding 'em as nice as you."

"Your daughter taught me well!" Jack called out as Maggie walked her father to the front door.

When she came back, she looked worried.

"What?" he asked.

"It's really starting to pour. Maybe we should have driven him home."

"He's not an invalid, Maggie."

"Not yet. I'm dreading the day when that happens."

"But you saw him go through dinner. It's hard to believe he's sick."

"We can always hope for a miracle." She turned to the tray of coffee cups.

"Let me carry those. How about you dish out some ice cream?"

Jack brought the tray into the dining room. Just as he set it down, his cell phone rang. He picked it up from the windowsill, where he'd left it earlier, and glanced at the caller ID on the screen: *Spam likely.*

Of course. Half the damn calls he got at dinnertime were spam. He declined the call and was about to put down the phone again when he saw the text message. It was from Taryn, and it was only two words long.

I'm pregnant.

For a moment he could not move, could not even breathe. His legs suddenly unsteady, he sank into a chair. He was still sitting there when Maggie walked into the dining room carrying dishes of ice cream. She sat down across from him, but he could not bear to look at her. Instead he stared off into the living room, focusing on the fire crackling in the hearth. At that instant he wanted to leap into those flames, let them consume him. It was what he deserved.

"Don't you want your ice cream?" Maggie said.

"I — I'll be right back." He grabbed his phone and lurched to his feet.

"Are you okay?"

"Just a little, uh, stomach thing."

He bolted upstairs to the bathroom and suddenly felt so light headed he had to steady himself against the sink. He looked at the text message again: I'm pregnant.

He deleted it.

She couldn't be pregnant. This had to be a lie and one more way of torturing him. Frantic, he thought back to the two times they'd had sex. Neither time had he been wearing a condom. What a fucking idiot he'd been. He'd simply assumed she was on the pill, but what if she hadn't been? He counted back the weeks and realized that, yes, it had been long enough ago for her to now test positive on a home pregnancy test.

God, it was possible. Very possible.

He dropped to his knees, hung his head over the toilet bowl, and threw up. He flushed away the contents but stayed huddled there, waiting as the nausea passed. But this nightmare would not pass. He was living it, trapped in it. He longed for the coward's way out: a convenient heart attack that would take him down here, now, before

Maggie learned the truth.

I need to find a way out of this, he thought. *There has to be a way.*

Chapter 35
Taryn

The face of Medea glared up at her from the cover of the textbook, the eyes alight with fury, her hair crowned in flames. It was the face of a woman who had been betrayed by the man she loved, a woman who was about to exact a price for that betrayal. Unlike the pitiful Queen Dido, Medea did not ascend her own funeral pyre and plunge a sword into her breast. She did not allow herself to be crushed and defeated when her husband, Jason, abandoned her for another woman. No, Medea embraced her rage. She reveled in it.

She acted upon it.

Taryn set the textbook down on her kitchen counter, where Medea's fierce image would remind her to stay strong and fight for what should be hers. Tonight she would need that strength, but already she felt her resolve wavering. For an instant the kitchen seemed to tilt, and she reached out to steady herself against the counter. She'd had a glass of Zinfandel, and now her stomach felt unsettled. That was why she was dizzy, of course; alcohol tossed into an empty stomach. She knew she shouldn't be drinking at all, but tonight she'd needed something to calm her nerves.

She opened the freezer, removed a carton of macaroni and cheese, and put it in the microwave. While it heated up, she thought about what she would say to him when he arrived. She would remind him of all the reasons they belonged together, all the reasons he'd forever regret it if he did not choose her. This was *his* child growing inside her, and even though it was still too small for her to feel it move, when she pressed her hand to her abdomen, she could almost believe a tiny hand was pressing back, reaching for her. For its mother. She thought of Maggie Dorian, thirty-eight years old and pregnant as well. When a woman was that old, her pregnancy could go wrong. How much simpler it would be for everyone involved if it did. The baby could die. Maggie could die. It happened to other women, didn't it, so why couldn't it happen to her? Taryn didn't hate her, but that wife was the one thing standing between Taryn and her happiness. The one thing that was pulling Jack away from her. The one thing that was making him abandon her, just as her father did. Just as every man in her life did.

Tonight he had to choose. And she was determined he would choose her.

The microwave timer dinged, but she was still nauseated from the wine, and she couldn't bear the thought of eating anything. She left the mac and cheese in the microwave and paced into the living room, then back into the kitchen. All this waiting was unbearable. It seemed all her life she'd been waiting for something. For love. For success. For someone, anyone, to *see* her. Instead of pacing, fretting, she should be at work on her new paper, the one due in a week: "Hell Hath No Fury: Violence and the Scorned Woman." She stopped at her desk and glanced down at the printed manuscript, where she'd scribbled revisions in the margins. Oh yes, she could write entire books about scorned women. About men and their casual cruelty, about the women who loved them, the women they betrayed. Women who chose to fight back.

Women like her.

Suddenly the room felt stifling. She crossed the living room and opened the balcony door. Rain-swept wind blasted her in the face as she stepped outside to scan the street below. At this hour, in this storm, there were no passing cars, not a single soul walking below. A driving rain was falling in sheets beyond her balcony overhang, rain mingled with sleet, but she lingered outside, watching. Waiting. Lately, she could not abide overheated rooms, and only now, standing in the cold, did she finally feel she could breathe.

As she gazed down at the unforgiving concrete far below, she suddenly wondered what it would be like to climb over this railing and to dive off. To plummet through the darkness, the wind rushing past her face and clawing at her hair. A few seconds of terror, ending in nothing at all. But if she died, it would not be as another Queen Dido, meekly surrendering to grief. No, she would make her death matter. It would not be a surrender but the start of a slow and inexorable tightening of screws that would eventually crush Jack Dorian. She would die victorious, knowing that by ending her own life, she would forever ruin his.

Oh yes. She'd make certain of that.

■ ■ ■ ■

AFTER

■ ■ ■ ■

CHAPTER 36
JACK

To All Members of the Commonwealth Community:

With deep sadness I write to share the news of the untimely death this past weekend of one of our students, Taryn E. Moore. Taryn was a senior English major who had excelled in her studies and who was planning to enter our English doctoral program this coming fall. We send our heartfelt sympathies to Taryn's family and friends and we want everyone to know that the Center for Spirituality is open for those who need counseling about this terrible loss.

The email had been sent at 6:10 a.m. that Monday from the president of Commonwealth University. It was buried among the dozens of other emails that daily streamed into Jack's inbox, and he might have skipped right past it were it not for the name on the subject line.

Taryn Moore.

With a feeling of dread, he'd opened the email, bracing himself for the worst. An accusation, a demand that he resign, or even worse. Instead, what he'd found was a mass email, sent to the entire university community. There was no mention of the circumstances of her death, no speculation about why she had died.

He clicked onto the *Boston Globe* site and typed her name into the search box. A short article appeared.

Boston police are investigating the death of a Commonwealth University student who was found dead in Boston early Saturday morning. The body of Taryn E. Moore, age 22, of Hobart, Maine, was discovered lying on the sidewalk outside her apartment building at 325 Ashford Street. Police believe she died after a fall from an upper-level balcony.

Taryn's apartment was on the fifth floor.

He tried not to think about the damage that a fall from that height onto concrete could do to a body. That body, once so warm and alive as it had writhed under his own, was now cold and lifeless flesh.

Thank God Maggie had already left for work, so he could sit and process this information while alone. He'd woken up an hour ago with his head still thick from an Ativan fog, dreading the day to come. The consequences of his actions were fast closing in on him, and he'd felt certain this was the day that life as he knew it would be over.

But this news changed everything.

He clicked onto other online news sites but could find no other mention of her death. On Facebook, however, he found a photograph of Taryn wearing a brilliant smile, accompanied by the caption: *My heart is broken.* It was posted by Cody Atwood. Jack stared at the image, torn between gnawing guilt and a perverse sense of relief. And sadness; how could he not feel sad about the loss of a young and vibrant life? Yet he couldn't deny that he had hoped for some sort of divine intervention, and this was exactly what had been delivered.

No one could argue that jumping off a balcony wasn't her decision and hers alone. As horrible as that was, Jack could not be held responsible, even if their affair was what had made her do it.

An affair that no one would ever have to know about.

He drove to school in a daze, wishing he did not have to face his seminar students today, but this was the final week of the semester, and he had no good excuse to cancel class. The president's email had gone out to the entire university, so by now, Jack's students would know about Taryn's death. He would have to address the issue and allow them to express their grief. Even though she was not the most popular member of the seminar, she was their classmate, and for him to ignore her passing would be insensitive.

It would also make them wonder.

When he walked into the classroom, he expected to see somber faces. Instead, his students seemed no different than on any other day. There was Jason, slouched in his chair and staring at his smartphone as usual. There was Beth, laptop open, ready to take notes. There were Jessica and Caitlin, heads once again bent together in conspiratorial whispers.

But Cody was absent. The two chairs where Cody and Taryn had sat much of the semester were now a gaping hole, glaring at Jack from the end of the table.

He tried not to look at the vacant chairs and instead focused on the thirteen students who were there. "I assume you've all heard the news by now. About Taryn," he said.

There were nods all around the table. And finally, a few appropriately solemn expressions.

Beth said, "It's so hard to understand why she did it. It seemed like she had it all."

"No one ever has it all, Beth," Jack said gently.

"But she was so smart. And pretty." Beth looked at the empty chairs and shook her head. "God, this has got to be horrible for Cody."

"Has anyone seen him? Spoken to him?" Jack asked.

Shrugs all around the table.

"Didn't know him all that well," admitted Jason.

Of course he didn't, because he'd never wanted to. That was the nature of popularity; everyone avoided the homely kid, lest their stain rub off on them. But Taryn, to her credit, had not.

"Do *you* know why she killed herself, Professor?" asked Jessica.

Jack stiffened at the question. "Why would I?"

"I don't know. I just thought you might."

He stared at her, wondering what was behind the question. What did she know? What game was she playing? Thirteen pairs of eyes watched him, waiting for his answer.

Or maybe for his confession.

"I have no idea why she did it, Jessica," he finally said. "And I don't think anyone ever will."

CHAPTER 37
FRANKIE

Although she graduated from college three decades earlier, Frankie still feels a freshman's twinge of anxiety, sitting across the desk from a university professor. Jack Dorian's bookcase is crammed with intimidatingly fat textbooks, some of which bear his name as the author. On the desk is a stack of student papers, the top one bearing an ugly C-minus. Frankie can imagine what it's like for a student to sit in this chair and face the man with the power to flunk them — or help launch their career.

But today, the balance of power is tilted toward Frankie's side of the desk. Though he may not realize it, Jack Dorian is the one with everything to lose.

At the moment, Dorian appears unruffled, his hands relaxed on the desktop, his attention focused on Mac. Male subjects always assume their most formidable opponent is another man, and too often they regard

Frankie as merely an appendage, scarcely worth a glance. There are advantages to being overlooked; it gives Frankie the chance to observe without being noticed, to focus on body language and nonverbal cues. She notes that Dorian is still lean and fit at forty-one, that the hair at his temples is just beginning to show flattering glints of silver. He is certainly attractive enough to deserve the four chili peppers he's been awarded on RateMyProfessors.com.

"Taryn's death is a loss not just to her friends and family but also to the academic community," says Dorian. "She was a brilliant student and an exceptionally gifted writer. I can show you the most recent paper she wrote for my class. You'll see for yourself how promising she was. We were all shocked when we heard about her suicide."

He does not yet know this is now a homicide investigation, and that is to their advantage. They don't want to rattle him. They want him relaxed and talkative, and Mac is wearing his most congenial smile.

"You said you were Taryn's faculty adviser," says Mac. It's an easy question, non-confrontational. Nothing to alarm him.

"Yes. I was advising her on her senior project."

"What sort of project?"

"She was writing a paper about how women are viewed in classical literature."

"Would that be, um . . ." Mac glances at his notes. " 'Hell Hath No Fury: Violence and the Scorned Woman'?"

Dorian blinks in surprise. "Why, yes, as a matter of fact. How did you know?"

"We saw a draft of the paper in her apartment."

"I see."

"How well did you know her? As her senior faculty adviser and all."

There is a three-second pause before Dorian answers. "I get to know all the students I advise. Taryn dreamed of a career in academia but she started off at a disadvantage. I know she was anxious to rise above that."

"What sort of disadvantage?"

"Her father abandoned the family when Taryn was just a child. She was raised by a single mom, and I gathered it was something of a struggle to pay the bills."

"Have you spoken to her mother?"

Dorian winces. "I know I *should* call her. But it's, well, a painful conversation. I don't know what I can say to make it easier for her."

"Taryn's mother is desperate to find out why her daughter killed herself, and we don't have any answers. Do you?"

Dorian shifts in his chair, and the squeak of leather seems startlingly loud. "I'm not sure I do."

"You deal with kids her age as part of your job, so you must have some insight into how their minds work. She was a pretty girl, and she was looking forward to starting grad school. She had her whole life ahead of her. So what went wrong?"

Dorian's gaze drifts toward the window, where the wintry light casts his face in a chilly shade of gray. "Who knows what goes on in the heads of kids her age? I've worked with enough of them to know they're on emotional roller coasters. One minute they're deliriously happy, and the next, their whole life's a catastrophe."

"Why would she take her life?" asks Mac.

"That's a question for a psychiatrist, not an English professor."

"Even a professor who knew her well?"

Again a pause, but this one is longer. Frankie sees the muscles of his face twitch, and the fingers of his left hand are suddenly pressed flat against the desktop. "I have no idea why she did it."

Frankie at last enters the conversation. "Did she ever mention her boyfriend?"

He frowns, as if suddenly aware of her

presence. "The boy from Maine? Is that who you mean?"

"So you've heard about him."

"Yes. His name was Liam something."

"Liam Reilly. Taryn's mother said he dated her all through high school."

"He could certainly be the reason for her suicide, then. When they broke up, she was distraught about it."

"You didn't think that detail was worth mentioning?"

"You've just reminded me about it."

"Tell us about this breakup."

He shrugs. "For a week, she didn't show up for class. Then she came to my office and told me she wanted to apply to grad school. I think it was to prove to herself, and to him, that she was worthwhile."

"Did she seem suicidal at the time?"

"No, just . . . determined."

"Did she mention having any other boyfriends? Anyone new she was seeing?"

Dorian's gaze veers back to the window. "I don't recall her saying anything like that."

"You're certain?"

"I was her academic adviser, not her therapist. Maybe her mother can answer that question."

"She can't. But parents are often the last to know."

347

Mac says: "Do you know anyone who might have hurt Taryn?"

Dorian's gaze snaps back to Mac, and Frankie catches the flash of alarm in his eyes. "*Hurt* her? I thought it was a suicide."

"We're exploring all possibilities. That's why we're here, to be certain we don't overlook anything."

Dorian swallows. "Of course. I wish I could help you, but that's all I know. If I think of anything, I'll give you a call."

"Then that should do it." Mac closes his notepad and smiles. That smile is not benign; it is more like a glimpse of a shark's jaws about to clamp down.

And Frankie is the jaws.

Dorian is already rising to his feet when she asks him: "Are you acquainted with a student named Cody Atwood?"

Slowly Dorian settles back in his chair. "Yes. From my seminar."

"Which seminar?"

"Star-Crossed Lovers. About tragic love stories from mythology and classical literature."

"Was Taryn Moore also in that seminar?"

"She was. Why are you asking about Cody?"

"Because he's been talking a lot about Taryn. And about you, Professor."

Dorian says nothing. He doesn't need to; his pallor tells Frankie what she needs to know.

"Cody said that Taryn had a very big crush on you."

"It's possible," he admits.

"Were you aware of it?"

"She may have, um, flirted with me. That's not unusual for female students."

"Is it also not unusual for you and a female student to travel out of town together?"

He stiffens. "You're talking about Amherst? The Annual Conference on Comparative Literature?"

"Where you stayed in the same hotel."

"It was the official conference hotel. Most of the attendees stayed there."

His attention has shifted from Mac and is now fully riveted on Frankie. Only now does it dawn on him who is really in charge. *Yes, Professor, I've been here the whole time, watching. Observing. But you didn't pay attention to this middle-aged gal in the size-fourteen blue pantsuit.*

"Cody Atwood was so concerned about you and Taryn that he called the university's Title Nine office to complain," says Frankie.

"I was cleared of any accusations."

"Yes, we spoke to Dr. Sacco. She said you

denied it."

"That's right. That should have been the end of it."

"Still, we have to ask. Is there anything you haven't told us about your relationship with Taryn?"

Four beats of silence pass. He straightens and looks Frankie in the eye. "I don't have anything else to tell you."

She stands to leave, but at the door she stops. "I almost forgot to ask. Did Taryn ever mention losing her cell phone?"

"Her cell phone? No. Why?"

"We searched her apartment, but we haven't found it. It seems to have disappeared."

He shakes his head. "I'm sorry. I have no idea where it might be."

"Oh. One final question."

She sees the flash of irritation in his eyes. He is so anxious to get them out of his office that he barely manages a tight smile. "Certainly."

"Where were you Friday night?"

"Friday? You mean . . ."

"The night Taryn died."

"You're asking *me*? Seriously?"

"It's just a routine question. We're asking everyone who knew her."

"I was home all night," he says. "With my wife."

Frankie and Mac sit in her parked car, sleet ticking their windshield, and watch a leggy young woman in a miniskirt walk by, hugging herself in the cold.

"What the hell's wrong with girls these days?" Mac says. "Look at that getup she's wearing. Gonna get frostbite up in her you-know-where."

Frankie thinks of her own twins and their sometimes-reckless choices of wardrobe. The see-through blouses, the minidresses on subzero nights, the skirts with thigh-high slits. How do parents protect them, she wonders, when kids are biologically programmed to take risks? *Stay alive, stay safe* is every mother's prayer, the same prayer that runs through her own head late at night whenever her twins are out on the town. *Stay alive, stay safe.*

A prayer that failed Taryn Moore's mother.

"So what do you think about the professor?" Mac asks.

"He's hiding something."

"No shit."

"Maybe murder. Or maybe just an affair."

"She *was* an adult. Even if he was boink-

351

ing her, it's not a crime."

"But it is a motive. An affair with a student would wreck his career, not to mention his marriage." She looks at Mac. "You get a look at his wife's photo on the desk? She's a good-looking woman, but a hot young student's got to be a temptation."

"Okay, so he's got a motive. But that's a long way from proving he killed her."

Frankie starts the car. "We're just getting started."

CHAPTER 38
JACK

Is there anything you haven't told us about your relationship with Taryn?

As he lay in bed, Loomis's words were on a Möbius strip, continuously running through Jack's brain. The only other time he'd been interrogated by the police was when he was twelve years old and had shoplifted a cheap bracelet at the mall for a Mother's Day gift. After a stern warning, the police officer had let him go. He had been terrified by the encounter and had never again shoplifted.

He was three decades older now and still every bit as terrified by the police.

Thanks to Cody Atwood, they knew Taryn was in love with him. They knew about the Amherst conference. It wasn't so much the questions they'd asked that rattled him as the damning blankness of their expressions. He'd seen Charlie wear that same look, an unforgiving poker-player's face that could make any suspect squirm. A dead-eyed stare that seemed to cut straight to your soul. With her intimidating stare, Detective Loomis had telegraphed that same authority.

Is there anything you haven't told us about your relationship with Taryn?

Loomis had said they were "exploring all possibilities," and one of those possibilities was murder. That was why they were in his office. They were there to scare him into confessing to a crime he'd never committed.

Or had he?

That terrible possibility struck him as he lay in bed. What if he *had* done it? The night Taryn had died, he'd gulped down wine and chased it with Ativan to help him sleep. Ever since the Christmas when that same combination had caused him to take a midnight drive that he'd never remembered, he had avoided mixing the two. But that night, after Taryn had texted him she was pregnant, he'd been desperate for sleep. Had he taken another late-night drive without remembering it? Was he, deep in some reptilian part of his brain, capable of murder?

As soon as Maggie went downstairs to make coffee the next morning, he grabbed his iPad from the nightstand. Quickly he scanned local sites for any updates on the investigation.

The headlines still covered Taryn's death as a probable suicide, buttressing the story with articles about the growing number of young people who killed themselves and how one in five college students was so stressed out that they considered ending their life. One piece listed the possible causes: academic pressures, physical and mental health problems, failed relationships, loneliness.

They'd neglected to include one more cause: impregnated and abandoned by one's professor.

He was relieved to read that Taryn's phone had not been located, but it was only a matter of time before the police subpoenaed her mobile carrier and gained access to her text messages — and his.

He glanced at the night table, where the bottle of Ativan was still sitting. How many had he taken that night? He couldn't remember.

He googled *Ativan* and clicked on a drug-advice website.

Ativan (lorazepam) is an antianxiety agent (benzodiazepines, tranquilizer) used for the relief of anxiety, agitation and irritability, and insomnia and to calm people with mania,

schizophrenia, obsessive-compulsive disor-
der . . .

Adverse Reactions: Ativan may cause the following reactions: clumsiness, dizziness, sleepiness, unsteadiness, agitation, disorientation, depression, parasomnia, amnesia . . .

Parasomnia. Sleepwalking. Taking nocturnal trips without awareness or recall.

The night Taryn had died, he'd sat alone in the dark living room, sipping pinot grigio just to calm his nerves. By the time he'd finally climbed the stairs to bed, that wine bottle had been empty. Even then, he couldn't fall asleep and had reached for the Ativan to knock him out. The next morning he'd awakened alone with a megaton hangover and Maggie already off to work.

He scrolled down the page and clicked on another link about Ativan. It was a site featuring true-crime cases, and what he read there drove an icicle through his heart.

. . . the defendant had no memory of the hours before the killing. He recalled that he took ten milligrams of Ativan, was unable to sleep, and took an additional pill. "The next thing I remember," he testified, "was awakening with handcuffs on my wrists."

He had stabbed his wife more than twenty times.

■ ■ ■ ■

Maggie was sitting at the kitchen counter, watching TV, when he came downstairs. She looked up and frowned at him.

"You look exhausted."

"I had a bad night — couldn't get to sleep." He poured a cup of coffee and took a shaky gulp. "What are you watching?"

"The news. It's about your student, Taryn Moore. The one who came to see me for a physical."

He took another nervous sip of coffee and tried to keep his voice steady. "What're they saying?"

"They still don't know why she killed herself. They said she'd been accepted into the doctoral program and was looking forward to that. You must have helped her with the application. I mean, you were her adviser, right?"

"Yeah."

"So you would have known her pretty well."

His chest tightened. "Meaning what?"

"Did you see any warning signs? She must have confided something about her personal life. They said she'd recently broken up with a boyfriend. Did you have any clue how

357

distraught she was?"

"She, uh, may have mentioned the breakup. But it seemed to me she was moving on with her life. Going to grad school and all."

Maggie said, "She was in perfect health. Smart, gorgeous, her whole life ahead of her. It's just so hard to understand."

Casually, he crossed to the coffeepot to refill his cup. "What do the police say?"

"The reporter said they haven't ruled out the possibility of foul play."

"Foul play? They said that?"

With the remote, Maggie flicked through the channels and stopped at NECN, where the story was now being aired. He felt a small shock at the photo of Taryn smiling radiantly, her eyes bright and daring, her hair lit by the sun. The shot shifted to Detective Frances Loomis as a reporter asked her: "So this is still an active investigation? Could it be something other than suicide?"

"The manner of death is still to be determined by the medical examiner," Loomis answered.

Maggie muted the television. "Did you know the girl's boyfriend? The one she broke up with?"

"No. I mean, she did tell me they'd broken up."

"What did she say about him?"

"Why does it matter?"

She glanced at him. "Why are you so jumpy?"

"Look, this whole thing is kind of upsetting to me. Can we not talk about it?" He looked at his phone, scanning the latest emails, but saw nothing out of the ordinary. No new accusations, no anonymous threats.

The TV screen again filled with the image of Detective Loomis's poker-player face. Maggie turned up the volume just as the reporter asked: "Is there any indication this isn't a suicide?"

"I have no further comment at this time."

Maggie shut off the TV and looked at him. "That detective is being weirdly noncommittal, don't you think? *Could* it have been murder?"

"What makes you even think that?"

"It's just the way she answered the question. Very cagey. Oh well." Maggie took her coffee cup to the sink and rinsed it. "I'm sure the police are checking out the big three."

"The big three?"

"Like they talk about on true-crime shows. It's the three pillars of guilt that police always look for in a murder investigation: motive, means, and opportunity."

Motive, means, and opportunity. Jack was already at one and climbing.

CHAPTER 39
FRANKIE

The twins are once again going out for the night, and from the kitchen, where Frankie sits with her laptop and papers, she can hear her daughters chattering in their bedroom about which skirt and which shoes to wear, and should the lipstick be red or pink? At eighteen, the twins are old enough to choose their own clothes and their own boyfriends, and even if Frankie doesn't approve of their choices, she tries to keep her objections to herself. Forbidden fruit is the sweetest of all; the travails of the Capulets and Montagues taught every parent that much. Frankie blocks out the twins' inane debate of hair up or hair down. Instead she focuses on the typed pages spread out across her kitchen table. Here is the essay that Taryn Moore wrote in the weeks before her death. Might it contain clues to the turmoil in her own life? The document is still just a draft, with Taryn's handwritten corrections scratched in the margins.

HELL HATH NO FURY: VIOLENCE AND THE SCORNED WOMAN

Stories about women betrayed by men abound in both Greek mythology and classical literature (Ariadne, Queen Dido), commonly ending in death for the women, often by their own hands in piteous acts of self-destruction. Some, however, like Medea, choose an alternate path: vengeance . . .

Medea. Frankie remembers the textbook she saw on Taryn's kitchen countertop with a woman's face on the cover, her mouth open in a fearsome roar, her hair an angry corona of flames. She cannot remember the details of the myth or what drove Medea to vengeance; she knows only that the name itself carries echoes of violence.

She types the name *Medea* into Google and clicks on the first link. What appears is not the monstrous face from Taryn's textbook. This Medea is a golden-haired beauty in a flowing gown.

Medea, depicted in many stories as a sorceress, is a prominent figure in the myth of Jason and the Argonauts.

"Hey, Mom, we're heading out now."

Frankie turns to look at her daughter Gabby and frowns at the short skirt and daringly low-cut blouse. "Are you really going out looking like that?"

"I swear, you say that every single time."

"Because you're dressed like *that* every single time."

"And nothing bad has ever happened to us."

"Yet."

Gabby laughs. "You never take off the badge, do you?" She gives her mom a wave. "We'll be fine. Don't wait up."

"You know, I've seen what happens to girls who get careless."

"There are two of us, Mom."

"There are two boys too."

"We always look out for each other. And we know all those cool self-defense moves you taught us, remember?" Gabby gives the air a vicious karate chop. "Don't worry, these guys are okay."

Frankie sighs and takes off her glasses. "How do you know they are?"

"You've gotta stop ragging on about musicians. They're totally focused on their careers, and you should see the great gigs they've already lined up this year."

"Oh, honey. You could both do so much better than those boys."

"Ha! I bet Granny said the same thing to you about Daddy."

If only she did, thinks Frankie. If only

someone *had* warned her about the man she was about to marry. Frankie has never told her daughters the truth about their father, and she never will. Let them go on believing in the daddy they loved, the daddy whose stature has only grown in their memories since his death three years ago. As much as Frankie wants to grab her girls by their shoulders and warn them, *Don't make my mistake — don't fall for a man who'll break your heart,* the truth about their father will only hurt them.

The laptop screen catches Gabby's eye, and she asks: "Why are you reading about Medea?"

"It's for a case I'm investigating."

"I hope it's nothing like what Medea did."

Frankie looks at her daughter in surprise. "You know the myth?"

"Oh, sure. We read the play in Honors English, and it stuck with me, you know? How far a woman will go to get her revenge."

"What happens?"

"You know the story of Jason and the Argonauts? Well, Medea falls in love with Jason and helps him steal the Golden Fleece. She even kills her own brother so that Jason can make his escape. They sail off together, get married, and have kids. But then Jason turns into a real dick. He deserts her and marries another woman. Medea's so pissed off she murders his new bride. Then to *really* get back at Jason, she stabs their own kids to death."

"Hey, Gabby?" Sibyl calls out from the foyer. "Come on, we're gonna be late."

"Yeah, I'm coming."

"Wait," says Frankie. "What happens to Medea?"

"Nothing."

"Nothing?"

Gabby pauses in the doorway and looks back at her mother. "Some god takes her up in his magic chariot and whisks her off to safety." She waves. "Night, Mom."

Frankie hears her daughters clack out of the house in their high heels, and the front door thumps shut. She looks once again at the laptop screen, where the image of golden-haired Medea glows, a beauty in a flowing gown. Only then does she notice what is clutched in Medea's hand.

A knife, dripping with the blood of her own children.

The ringing of her cell phone makes her jump. She glances down at the caller ID and answers: "Hey, Mac."

"You ready for some good news?"

"Always."

"Verizon just delivered. They can't locate Taryn Moore's phone, which means it's either been destroyed or it's turned off. But they did give us her call log, her text messages. Everything."

"And?"

"You're gonna *love* who shows up on that log."

CHAPTER 40
FRANKIE

Professor Jack Dorian is wearing a game face, but Frankie can see the man is nervous, as well he should be. If he knew what they knew, he'd be halfway to Mexico by now. With a tight smile, he ushers the two detectives into his office and closes the door.

"I'm surprised you're back to see me so soon," he says. "I thought you'd completed the investigation."

"As it turns out, we're just getting started," says Frankie as she and Mac sit down.

"Oh?" Dorian's fingers briefly twitch into a claw on the desk. It is just a split-second spasm, but it's a clue she doesn't miss.

"New evidence has come up that points in a different direction." Frankie is enjoying this. Enjoying the pleasure of turning the screws on him and seeing the glint of fear in his eyes.

"New evidence?" he finally manages to ask.

"We didn't tell you what turned up at her autopsy. A little surprise. Taryn Moore was pregnant."

He doesn't respond, but the color of his face says it all. It is the ashen gray of panic.

"Did you know she was pregnant, Professor Dorian?"

He gives a stunned shake of the head. "Why would I?"

"We thought you might, since you were her adviser. And according to Cody Atwood, you and Taryn had a *very* close relationship."

"An academic relationship. It doesn't mean she shared details of her personal life with me. Kids have their own circle of friends. Most of the time, we adults are peripheral to their worlds. They hardly register what we do or say or think."

He is rambling, filling the silence to disguise his fear, but she sees the faint sheen of sweat on his forehead, hears the rising pitch of his voice. She says, "We're trying to find out who the father is. DNA is still pending, but we'll learn the answer eventually."

"She, uh, did have that boyfriend."

"Liam Reilly insists the baby isn't his."

"Can you be sure he's telling the truth?"

"He said they broke up months ago, before this pregnancy would have been conceived." She lets the silence stretch on, lets him twist in the wind for a moment. "Do you have any idea who the father might be?"

Dorian gives a helpless shrug. "I don't understand why you're asking me."

"Because her pregnancy may be relevant to the investigation."

"Last week, you seemed to believe it was suicide."

"Last week, we didn't have a record of her text messages." She pauses to let that sink in, and she sees his face snap taut. He doesn't say a word; he is paralyzed, unable to stop this freight train that is now barreling straight toward him.

"We know about your affair with Taryn Moore," she says.

The breath whooshes out of him. He slumps forward and drops his head in his hands, his fingers buried like claws in his hair. For a moment Frankie worries that he might drop dead of a heart attack right before their eyes.

"Professor Dorian?" she says.

"It was a mistake," he groans. "A huge, horrible mistake."

"I would have to agree."

"I swear to you, this never happened with any other student. She was the only one. I just couldn't help myself."

"Are you saying she seduced you? That it's her fault?"

"No. No, I have no excuse at all, except . . ." He raises his head and meets her gaze with a look of abject misery. "She needed *someone* to care about her, someone who'd value her. I was the person she turned to. She was brilliant. And beautiful. And so desperately hungry for love." He pauses. "I guess I needed someone too."

"And your wife? How does she fit into the equation?"

Pain contorts his face. "Maggie doesn't deserve this. It's my fault, all mine."

"So you admit having the affair."

"Yes."

"And are you the father of Taryn's child?"

He sighs. "Yes, it could be mine."

"DNA will prove it, one way or another. Just as it will prove you were in the victim's apartment, where you had sexual relations." At his puzzled look, she says: "We found semen on her sofa. Yours, I assume?"

He winces but does not deny it.

Satisfied, Frankie looks at Mac. *You can take it from here.*

370

"Where were you last Friday night, Professor Dorian?" he asks.

"Friday night . . ."

"The night Taryn Moore died."

In an instant, the conversation has shifted, and not just because Mac is now the one asking the questions. Dorian's head jerks up. He knows that things are about to get worse for him. Much worse.

"I've already answered that question. I told you, I was home that night."

"What did you do that night?"

"We had Maggie's father over for dinner."

"Do you remember what you ate?"

"Yes, because I cooked it. We had pasta with a veal sauce."

"And after dinner? What did you do?"

"After Charlie left, I went to bed early, because I was exhausted. And I, uh, had an upset stomach."

"Did you stay in bed?"

"Yes," he says without hesitation.

"All night?"

"Yes."

"Or did you get up sometime that night while your wife was sleeping? Did you slip out of the house and drive to Taryn Moore's apartment?"

"What? No —"

"But you did have plans to meet her that

371

night, at her apartment. That's why she waited up for you. She let you into her building."

"This is crazy. I never left my house that night."

"What about this text message you wrote?" Mac pulls a folded printout from his pocket and opens it up to read aloud. "On Friday, at six thirty p.m., Taryn sent you this text: 'I'm pregnant.' Two minutes later she sends you another one: 'You know it's yours.'"

Dorian stares back, silent. Stunned.

"And then three minutes later she texts you a third time," Mac continues, relentless. "At six thirty-five she writes: 'I'm going to tell Maggie.' And that's when you finally respond."

"No, that's not true. I didn't answer her! I never responded at all."

"It's right here in black and white, Professor. What you wrote to Taryn. Six thirty-seven p.m., you texted: 'Tonite, your place. Wait for me.'" Mac looks at Dorian. "Friday night, as you promised, you drove to her apartment, didn't you? And you took care of the problem."

To Frankie's surprise, Dorian suddenly bolts forward in his chair, his face florid with outrage. "This is bullshit! You're *lying.*

Is this how you get innocent people to confess? You make up crap like this and expect us to sign whatever statement you put in front of us?"

"You can't argue with your own text message."

"I never wrote any such text."

"It was sent from your cell phone."

"This isn't going to work, what you're doing." Dorian's voice is now rock steady, his gaze unflinching. He reaches into his desk, pulls out his phone, and slides it across to Mac. "See for yourself. There's no such message on my phone."

Mac scrolls through the texts and gives a snort. "It's not here because you've deleted the entire conversation. But you know it never really goes away, don't you? You may have erased it, but those messages are still on the server." He slides the phone back to Dorian. "Now tell us where you were last Friday night."

"At home. In bed with my wife."

"You keep saying that."

"Because it's true. Ask Maggie. She has no reason to lie."

"Does she know about your affair?"

The question seems to knock the wind out of him. Defeated, Dorian slumps back in his chair. "No," he says softly.

"When she finds out, I doubt she'll be in any mood to vouch for you. So you might as well tell us the truth."

"I *have* told you the truth." He stares straight at Mac. "I didn't write that text. And I sure as hell didn't hurt Taryn."

Frankie knows that her partner is ready to clap on the handcuffs, but she is feeling the first stirring of doubt. She sits studying Dorian, bothered by his responses to their questions. How can anyone deny something as undeniable as a text message? With all the evidence they have, he must know it is futile for him to lie.

If he is lying.

She stands up. "We'll be speaking with you again, Professor."

Mac shoots her an astonished look. After a few grudging seconds he, too, rises to his feet. He is silent as they walk out of Dorian's office, still silent as they head down the stairwell. Only when they push outside the building does Mac finally blurt: "What the hell, Frankie, we *have* him. We've got enough."

"I'm not sure we do."

"You really believe his bullshit? 'I didn't write that text!' Yeah, and the dog ate his homework."

"His cell phone never pinged near Taryn

Moore's apartment that night. We can't prove he was in the area."

"He's not stupid. He left his phone at home when he killed her."

"No, I think he's very smart." They climb into the car, where she sits thinking for a moment.

"What's it going to take to convince you?" says Mac.

She starts the engine. "Let's go talk to the wife."

CHAPTER 41
JACK

Pick up, Maggie. Please pick up.

He sat at his desk, his heart racing as he listened to Maggie's cell phone ring. Three times. Four.

Then she answered. "Hey, I was just about to call you."

Had she already heard from the police? Was that why she was going to call him? He couldn't suppress the squeak of panic in his voice when he said, "Maggie, I need to tell you something."

"Why don't you tell me over dinner? I feel like going out tonight anyway. Someplace nice. What do you think?"

She sounded so cheerful and warm, wanting to meet for dinner. So husband-and-wife normal. After tonight, nothing would ever be normal again.

"Listen, Maggie. There are two detectives coming to see you right now. They're going to ask you —"

"Detectives? Jack, are you okay?"

"I'm fine. I'm at the office. They were just here, and now they're heading to the clinic to talk to you."

"Why? What's going on?"

"They're going to ask you about last Friday night. Where I was, where you were."

"Last Friday? I'm not following you. What happened?"

He paused to steady his breathing. "You know that student who died last week, Taryn Moore? The police don't think it was a suicide. They think she was murdered."

"Oh my God."

"And they're talking to people who knew her. Asking everyone to account for where they were the night she died."

"Why are they coming to see me? I hardly knew her."

"Look, let's meet. I don't want to do this over the phone."

"Why do they want to talk to *me*?"

"Because I *did* know her, and they want to confirm where *I* was. So when they ask you about Friday night, just tell them the truth. Tell them exactly what we did, that we had dinner with your dad and then we went to bed. They need to know we were together that night. *All* night."

"Last Friday? But we weren't together all night."

He paused. In the silence, he could hear his blood roaring in his ears. "What? But we were."

"Around midnight, I got called into the hospital for a patient who had chest pains. I didn't get home until around four in the morning. Didn't you hear me climb back into bed?"

"No." Because he was zonked out on Ativan.

"Then you must have slept through the whole thing."

Midnight till four a.m. That was a four-hour window he couldn't account for. Four hours during which he *could* have gotten dressed, *could* have driven into the city. It was more than enough time for him to have killed Taryn, gone back home, and jumped back into bed.

"The police don't have to know that," he said. "You don't even have to mention it."

"Why wouldn't I tell them the truth?"

"It will just complicate things."

"Jack, all they have to do is look in my patient's hospital chart to know I was there. They'll see that I wrote a note around three in the morning."

He tried to steady his voice, but panic was

making his breaths come fast. Any minute now, the police would be knocking at her office door. And they'd almost certainly tell her about Taryn and him. About how he had betrayed his wife.

She cannot hear it from them.

"Maggie, I need you to drop whatever you're doing. Leave the clinic *right now.* Meet me at . . ."

They couldn't meet at home or any other place the police would certainly look. They had already subpoenaed Taryn's phone records; what if they were listening to this call right now?

"Maggie," he said. "My phone may be tapped."

"Why?"

"I'll explain everything. But I need to talk to you before they do."

A long pause followed as she processed his words. "Jack, you're scaring me."

"Just do this for me. Please. Meet me at . . ." He thought about it for a moment. "Meet me at the spot where I proposed to you. And leave *now.*"

He hung up. He had no words of re-assurance to offer her, no promise that everything would turn out fine, because everything was *not* fine.

And it was about to get a lot worse.

■ ■ ■ ■

As he stood before Renoir's *Dance at Bougival,* he wished he had chosen some other place to meet, but this was the only locale that had popped into his head during the phone call. Twelve years ago, this gallery in the MFA was where he had dropped to his knees and presented Maggie with a diamond engagement ring. This was where they had kissed and promised that they would spend the rest of their lives together. Now he stared at the Renoir and prayed this wouldn't be the end of them. That Maggie wouldn't throw him out and divorce him. That their baby wouldn't come into the world without him at Maggie's side. Despite what he was about to confess to her, there had to be some way to keep them all together.

He just couldn't think of what he could say to make that happen.

Twenty minutes later, Maggie walked into the gallery, bundled in her shearling coat and cashmere scarf. "What are we doing here, Jack?" she asked.

Without a word, he took her by the arm and led her toward a quieter spot, past the poster of Abelard and Heloise locked in a passionate kiss. It was a damning reminder of how he had landed in this personal hell; a Hieronymus Bosch painting would have been more appropriate. He took her to a viewing bench at the far end of the gallery, and they both sat down.

Maggie's face was pale from the cold, and he could feel the evening's chill lifting off her clothes. "What's going on?" she whispered. "Why do the police want to see me?"

He paused as a security guard strolled in. The guard eyed them, then moved on into the next gallery. When he was out of earshot, Jack said: "I have something to tell you. This isn't going to be easy. In fact, it's the hardest thing I've ever had to say."

"You're scaring me. Just say it."

He took a deep breath. "That student, Taryn Moore. You know I was her faculty adviser. I helped her get into the doctoral program."

"Yes, I know."

"She was extremely bright. An excellent student. But after her boyfriend broke up with her, she was an emotional wreck. She had no one else to confide in, and we . . . we got close."

"How close?" Maggie leaned toward him, her gaze fixed on his. "Do you have something to confess?"

He sighed. "I do." *I do.* It was an echo of his wedding vows, the vows that, in a mania of lust, he had briefly forsaken. "I slept with her, Maggie. I'm sorry. I'm truly, deeply sorry."

She stared at him as if she had not understood a word.

"It meant nothing. I never loved her," he said. "I only ever loved *you.*"

"How long did it go on?" Maggie's voice was strangely, frighteningly calm.

"It was over as soon as it happened. Just once." *Twice* was the truth, but he couldn't say it. And it made no difference anyway. Not now. "I'm sorry."

"Where did it happen? This momentary little affair?"

"Amherst. The conference. I had too much to drink, and one thing led to another . . ."

"Oh my God." She pressed her hand to her mouth. "I don't believe this."

"I'm sorry."

"Stop saying that."

Over the museum PA system, a voice announced that the museum would close in thirty minutes.

"But I am," he said. "I *am* sorry."

"And now that girl is dead. The girl you had sex with."

"It's probably a suicide. But just to be sure, the police are questioning everyone who knew her."

"And you need an alibi for that night."

"Yes," he whispered. "I'm sorry."

"If you say that one more time, I'm going to fucking scream." She shot to her feet and started to walk away, then paced back to stand over him. "We've been married twelve years. We have a child coming. And you go and fuck a *student*?"

The guard had walked back into the gallery, drawn by the sound of their voices, and he stood watching them from the far end of the room.

"Please, Maggie. They'll hear us."

"I don't care. Why are you a suspect? Why are the police even looking at you?"

Jack rubbed his face, then looked up at her. "Because she was pregnant," he murmured.

An involuntary gasp rose in Maggie's throat. "I can't believe this."

"She'd just broken up with her boyfriend. It's probably his."

"Or it could be yours. Jesus." She closed her eyes to regain her center. "Do the police know you had an affair with her?"

"They know we were involved."

"How do they know that?"

383

"There were text messages. Between us."

She nodded, her face tight with disgust. "And where exactly were you the night she died?"

"I told you. I was home, asleep."

"And you want me to tell the police I was with you all night."

"Yes."

"But I wasn't. I told you, I had to go to the hospital to see a patient." She paused as a thought occurred to her. Quietly she asked: "*Did* you do it, Jack?"

"Did I do what?"

"Did you kill her?"

"No! I can't believe you'd even ask that."

"But you did have a motive."

And I'd swallowed a killer combo of wine and Ativan.

Without another word, Maggie spun around to leave.

He jumped up and grabbed her arm. "Maggie, please."

She yanked herself free. He didn't want to cause more of a disturbance by chasing after her, so he sat back down and stared dully at the Abelard-and-Heloise banner hanging on the opposite wall.

"Sir? The museum is closing."

Jack looked up to see the security guard standing in front of him.

384

"Rough day?" the guard asked.

With a sigh, Jack rose to his feet. "You have no idea."

"People don't," the guard asked.

"—" he said, jack rose to his feet. "You
...no...son."

CHAPTER 42
FRANKIE

"What if the wife backs up his alibi?" says Mac, as they pull into a stall in the clinic parking lot.

Frankie turns off the engine and looks at Mac. "If your wife killed her lover, would you give *her* an alibi?"

"It depends."

"Come on, Mac. Put yourself in Maggie Dorian's position. When she finds out her husband's cheating on her, she's not going to be in any mood to protect him."

"You're assuming she doesn't already know about the affair. Maybe she does know. Maybe she's still willing to protect him."

"Protect a husband who's cheating on you?"

"I don't know. Women put up with all sorts of crazy shit. Why do they stick with men who smack 'em around? Being in love makes people stupid. Or blind."

386

Frankie sits for a moment, staring at the clinic entrance, thinking about her own marriage, her own blindness. She thinks about the day her husband, Joe, was found dead of a heart attack in the stairwell of his mistress's apartment building, the building that Frankie cannot seem to stay away from. The building she obsessively visits. Joe was fifty-nine years old, and the emotional strain of the affair must have been too hard on his heart. Or maybe it was the three-flight climb to his girlfriend's apartment, along with his sky-high cholesterol and the extra thirty pounds he hauled around like a sandbag on his belly.

Two days after he died, she visited that stairwell. It was a grim pilgrimage that Mac had pleaded with her not to make, but she needed to see the place where Joe had collapsed. Maybe it was the cop in her, wanting to visit the scene, wanting to understand how it all went down. She felt oddly detached, almost clinical, as she looked at the concrete steps, at the dented stairwell door and the smudged walls. By then she already knew about the mistress; Mac had reluctantly broken the news to her after she'd demanded to know why Joe had died in *that* stairwell, in *that* building, when he was supposed to be on a business trip in Philadelphia. Rather than anger or grief or any of the normal emotions she should have felt that day, what she felt instead was bewilderment that she had missed all the signs of his infidelity. She was a homicide detective; how could she not have known about the other woman?

Only later, weeks later, did rage finally boil up inside her, but then she could do nothing about it because Joe was already dead. There is no point in screaming at a corpse.

She can feel that same anger bubbling up inside her now, on Dr. Maggie Dorian's behalf. Anger against Jack Dorian for betraying his wife. Anger about his likely role in Taryn Moore's death.

Oh yes, Frankie is ready to take the man down. She just has to prove he is guilty.

As she and Mac walk into the clinic's crowded waiting room, she is already rehearsing how to break the news to Maggie Dorian. Dr. Dorian is the innocent in all this, the clueless wife whose life and marriage are about to be demolished. There is no easy way to tell a woman her husband has betrayed her, and Frankie is bracing herself for the woman's reaction. She also hopes they can use it to their advantage. An angry wife might be their most powerful ally.

The clinic receptionist slides open the

glass partition and smiles at them. "Can I help you?"

"We're here to see Dr. Dorian."

"Did you have an appointment?"

"No, ma'am."

"I'm sorry, but this clinic doesn't take walk-ins. I can schedule an appointment with one of our other doctors for a few weeks from now."

Mindful of the patients sitting nearby, Frankie slides her badge across to the receptionist and says quietly: "Boston PD. We need to speak to Dr. Dorian."

The receptionist stares at the badge. "Oh. I'm afraid she's not here."

"When will she return?"

"I'm not really sure when she'll be back. Maybe tomorrow? She asked me to cancel the rest of her appointments for the day. She had to leave for a family emergency."

Frankie glances at Mac and sees, in his face, the same sense of alarm she is feeling. She keeps her voice steady, her expression neutral, as she asks the receptionist: "What time did Dr. Dorian leave the clinic?"

"It was about half an hour ago. I've been trying to reschedule all her patients. Any minute now, they'll start showing up here, expecting —"

"Do you know what the family emergency is?"

"No. She got a phone call, and a few minutes later, she ran out."

"Where did she go?" Mac snaps.

The woman glances at the patients in the waiting area, where everyone is now tuned in to the conversation and staring at them. "I don't know. She wouldn't tell me."

CHAPTER 43
JACK

As he walked to the university parking garage where he'd left his Audi, he called Maggie twice. She didn't answer, and Jack couldn't blame her. Classes were over for the day, and the frigid wind that swept the deserted campus sliced straight through his coat. He had not eaten since breakfast, and he yearned to simply collapse into a coma and never wake up. He'd heard that hypothermia was not a bad way to die. It was simply a matter of falling asleep as your body temperature plummeted and your organs shut down. A merciful end that he did not deserve. No, he was condemned to suffer through the consequences of his actions. A divorce. The loss of his job. Maybe even prison.

As he approached his car, he barely registered the sound of another vehicle's engine rumbling to life.

He was just a dozen feet from his Audi

when he looked up and saw a black SUV roaring toward him, its headlights blinding. Jack stumbled backward, flattening himself against the grille of his car, but instead of swerving onto the down ramp, the SUV kept rolling straight toward Jack, so close that he could hear the squeal of the proximity sensors. It did not screech to a stop until it had him pinned against his Audi.

"Hey!" Jack yelled.

No one answered.

Through the tinted windshield, he could just make out the silhouette of the driver: a man wearing a baseball cap. Affixed to the windshield was a student-parking sticker.

"Cody!" Jack yelled. "What the hell are you doing?"

Still no answer.

"Cody, back up!"

The SUV only revved louder, the fumes stinging Jack's eyes. He tried to squeeze free, but Cody took his foot off the brake, and the SUV inched forward, pinning him even tighter.

"Please don't do this!" Jack said. "Cody?"

Through the windshield, he saw Cody's hand move to his face. He was crying. So this was how Jack would pay for his sins, crushed to death by a lovelorn kid who was too grief stricken to see reason or to care about the consequences. One tap on the accelerator pedal, and three thousand pounds of metal would crush his pelvis. Even if he screamed for help, at this hour in this nearly empty garage, who would hear him?

I will never see Maggie again. Or our child.

"This isn't who you are, Cody! You aren't a killer!" Jack pleaded.

The door swung open, and Cody stepped out, face red and wet. He stared at Jack over the door. "You never even loved her," he said. "You used her. Then you kicked her away. *You* killed her."

"I didn't do anything like that."

"I'm the one who loved her." He thumped his chest. "I was the *only* one. Not you and not Liam. Not even her own father."

"Cody, I did not kill her. I wasn't anywhere near her place when she died. I was home in bed."

"Nobody else wanted her dead, only you. Nobody else had a reason."

"What about you, Cody? Didn't you have a reason?"

"What?"

"You loved her, but did she ever love *you*?"

This was a dangerous move Jack was making, but he didn't know what else to do or any other way to appeal to Cody. Turn the blame on Taryn. Make *her* the one responsible for his heartbreak. She had used him, abused him. Cared nothing about him.

"Maybe *you're* the one who killed her," Jack said.

Just as he started to sputter an answer, headlights flickered toward them. Jack heard the sound of a vehicle approaching from the lower ramp, and a yellow utility vehicle rounded the curve.

Cody jumped back into his vehicle and threw it into reverse. Suddenly freed, Jack stumbled forward, his legs numb and wobbly, as Cody's car shot past the utility vehicle and screeched away down the ramp.

"Hey, Professor. You okay?" called out the driver. Jack recognized him; it was Larry Walsh, one of the university's Buildings and Grounds employees.

Jack was still so shaken all he could do was nod.

"What the hell was going on here?"

"Just — just an accident."

"Didn't look like an accident. He had you pinned."

"I'm fine, Larry, thanks." The feeling was back in his legs. He shuffled to the door of the Audi and unlocked it.

"Did you know that driver?"

"No."

"I noticed he had a student sticker on his

vehicle."

"Please, let's just drop it, okay?" Jack slid in behind the wheel.

"I got a partial read on his plate number. Pennsylvania."

Shit. He would probably call it in. Jack needed to get out of here, fast.

He drove down the ramp, tires squealing, and pulled out of the garage. There was a parking space behind his campus building. He could warm up in his office, think over his next moves, and try calling Maggie again. Then he spotted the Boston PD patrol car parked near the entrance to his building, and instantly his plans changed. Instead, he drove past his building and kept going. Powered off his phone so it couldn't be tracked.

But where to?

Home. He was desperate to see Maggie, and that was where she would be.

He took a roundabout route, cutting through the back roads of Cambridge and Belmont. When he neared his house, he didn't slow down but kept driving past it, noting that the windows were dark and Maggie's Lexus was nowhere to be seen.

He spotted two unfamiliar vehicles parked on the street. Unmarked police cars?

As he drove away, he kept glancing in the

rearview mirror, expecting to see the head-lights of a car in pursuit. The street behind him remained dark.

He had to find Maggie. He had to make things right between them. If she wasn't home, there was only one other place she would be.

CHAPTER 44
FRANKIE

"Yeah, I'm absolutely sure the man was Professor Dorian. I've been working Buildings and Grounds for twenty-eight years now, so I know most of the professors. I know their cars too. I make it my business to keep an eye on everything that goes on around this campus."

Larry Walsh is the university's facilities supervisor, and judging by the excitement in his voice, this is the most thrilling thing that has happened on his watch in a long, long time. He has all the hallmarks of a wannabe cop: buzz-cut hair, boots planted in a wide stance, a tool belt sagging with keys, plus a walkie-talkie and a comically huge flashlight. In a spiral notebook, he's jotted down all the relevant details of "the incident," as he calls it, which he now proceeds to read to Frankie and Mac. "The vehicle was a black Toyota SUV, late model. Student-parking sticker on the windshield. I

397

didn't get a good look at the license number because the vehicle pulled away so fast, but I know it was a Pennsylvania plate, first letter *F,* then a two." He closes his notebook and looks at the two detectives as if expecting a gold star for his performance.

"You said it looked like an assault on Professor Dorian, not an accident?" says Frankie.

"Oh, it was absolutely an assault. Crazy kid had the professor pinned between two vehicles, like he was about to crush him. If I hadn't come around the curve just then, who knows what could've happened. Might've found his dead body lying here."

"Tell us about this kid," says Mac. "You said he was out of the vehicle when you got here?"

Larry nods. "As soon as I showed up, he jumped back into his SUV and took off. I don't know his name, but I've seen him around before. White male, on the hefty side. Dressed all in black except for a red baseball cap."

"What do you mean by hefty?"

Larry looks down at his own bulging belly and sighs. "Okay. *Fat.*"

Frankie and Mac exchange glances, both of them thinking the same thing.

"I'll check if Cody Atwood drives a black

SUV," says Mac, and he steps away to make the call.

"Why would a student attack him, Mr. Walsh?" Frankie asks. "Do you know what their fight was all about?"

"No idea. But you know, some of these students are spoiled rotten by their parents. They don't know how to deal with the real world or with real criticism. Give 'em a bad grade, hurt their widdle feelings, and they go nuclear. I wouldn't want to be a teacher these days, having to put up with these snowflakes. Poor Professor Dorian looked real shook up by the attack."

"Yet he didn't want to report it."

"Maybe he was embarrassed. Or he didn't want to get the kid in trouble. But I thought I should call it in anyway, and I have to say, I'm impressed by the response. Just a few minutes after I got off the phone with Boston PD, a cruiser came squealing up this ramp."

"I'm glad you did call it in, Mr. Walsh. As it turns out, we've been trying to locate Professor Dorian all afternoon."

"Why are you looking for him? He didn't do something wrong, did he?"

"That's what we're trying to establish." Certainly Jack Dorian is behaving like a guilty man. He isn't answering his phone, and now he's avoiding any contact with the police. Frankie looks around at the garage, picturing the events that Larry has just described to her. She imagines Dorian pinned between his vehicle and Cody Atwood's black SUV. She thinks of how easy it is to shatter bones and crush flesh with one stomp on the accelerator. Why did the boy attack him? Was this about Taryn Moore, a battle between someone who'd loved her and someone who'd wanted her dead?

"Frankie," Mac calls out, waving his cell phone. "You'll never guess who *just* walked into Schroeder Plaza and wants to talk to us."

"Jack Dorian?"

"No. His wife."

On a normal day Dr. Maggie Dorian would be considered a beautiful woman, but this is not that day. She sits slumped at the interview table, her red hair in disarray, her eyes hollowed out by anguish. Now approaching her forties, she no longer glows with the rosy flush of youth; how can she compete with the parade of eternally fresh-faced girls who pass through her husband's classroom? Frankie and Maggie belong to the same sisterhood whose husbands have betrayed them, so it is all too easy to identify with her pain, but sympathy could blind Frankie to the truth. As she pulls out a chair and sits down, Frankie keeps her face neutral, betraying no hint of that sympathy. Although Mac is next door, watching them through the one-way mirror, neither Frankie nor Maggie can see him. In this room there are only the two of them facing each other across the table, woman to woman.

"We've been trying to reach you all afternoon, Dr. Dorian," says Frankie.

"I know."

"Why didn't you return my calls?"

"I didn't want to talk to anyone. I needed time."

"Time for what?"

"To think. To decide what to do about my marriage."

Maggie's head droops, and Frankie notices streaks of gray in her auburn hair. This woman has devoted years to her marriage, to a man she trusted, and she has every reason to be angry. But instead of rage, what Frankie sees in the slumped shoulders and bowed head is grief.

"If he were my husband, I know what I'd want from him," says Frankie. "I'd want to know the truth."

"The truth?" Maggie raises her head and

looks at Frankie with haunted eyes.

"About his affair with Taryn Moore. Do you know about it?"

"Yes. He told me."

"When?"

"Today. He said you'd questioned him about the girl's death. He said it was all going to come out anyway, and he wanted to be the one to tell me."

"What else did he say?"

"That she'd gotten pregnant and . . ." Maggie pauses, holding back tears. "He might be the baby's father."

"That must have been painful to hear."

Maggie wipes a hand across her face. "Especially because we've been trying for years to have a baby. And then, a few weeks ago, we found out it was finally going to happen."

Frankie frowns. "You're pregnant?"

"Yes. And we were so happy. *I* was so happy." Maggie takes a deep breath. "But now . . ."

In the face of such misery, Frankie can scarcely bring herself to ask the next question, but it must be asked. "Did you have any idea your husband was having the affair?"

"No."

"Has he done this before? Been involved

with other women?"

"No."

"Are you sure about that?"

For a moment Maggie stares at her with tear-swollen eyes. *This is the point when it could get interesting,* thinks Frankie. Now the woman is questioning everything she thinks she knows about her husband. She is wondering if she's been blind to other secrets, other infidelities.

"Dr. Dorian?"

Maggie gives a sob. "I'm not sure of *anything* anymore!"

"So there might have been other affairs."

"He told me this was the only one."

"And do you believe that?"

"Maybe I'm crazy, but I do. I can even understand how this happened. Why it happened."

"The affair, you mean."

"Yes." Maggie wipes away another tear. "God, marriage is so complicated. I know how easy it is for things to get stale, monotonous. But even on our worst days, I never once believed that he stopped loving me. I know he still loves me. Yes, part of me wants to strangle him. But another part of me wants to forgive him."

"You'd forgive a murderer?"

Maggie stiffens. "You don't really think

403

Jack would kill anyone?"

"Let me present you with some facts, Dr. Dorian. We know that Taryn Moore was murdered. We know there was a struggle in her apartment and she fell and hit her head against a coffee table, fracturing her skull. The killer then dragged her out to the fifth-floor balcony and dropped her to the side-walk, discarding her body like a used-up piece of trash. And you can't decide whether to *forgive* him?"

Maggie shakes her head. "He couldn't have done that. It's not possible."

"Not only is it possible, it's likely."

"I know my husband."

"Yet you didn't know he was having an affair."

"That's different. Yes, he made a mistake. Yes, he was stupid. But *killing* a girl?" Again, she shakes her head, this time emphatically. "He'd never hurt anyone."

Frankie glances at the one-way mirror, wondering if Mac feels as frustrated as she does. It is time to strip the veil from her eyes and force the woman to confront the brutal truth about her husband.

"Dr. Dorian," Frankie says, "here's what we *can* prove. Your husband had an affair with his student, Taryn Moore. She became pregnant and was about to reveal the truth.

She was a threat to his reputation, his career, and his marriage. He would lose everything. I'd call that a pretty good motive for murder."

"It still doesn't mean he killed her."

"Friday night — the night she was killed — he went to her apartment."

"No, he didn't. He stayed home."

"Are you prepared to swear to that?"

"He told me —"

"Will you *swear* he was home with you that night, all night?"

Maggie sags back in her chair. "I can't," she says softly.

"Why not?"

"Because *I* wasn't home all night. I was called into the hospital around midnight to see a patient. When I got back home at four, Jack was still in bed, sound asleep. Just the way I left him."

"So there were four hours when you weren't at home. That's plenty of time for him to have slipped away to Taryn's apartment. He had both the motive and the opportunity to kill her."

"Where's your proof that he actually went to her apartment? Is there a witness? Surveillance video?"

"We have his text messages."

Maggie blinks. "What messages?"

"The ones he sent to his girlfriend," Frankie says and notes the way Maggie flinches at the word. *Girlfriend.* "Taryn's wireless carrier provided every text message she sent and received. Lo and behold, your husband's cell phone number shows up again and again. On the night she died, they'd made plans to meet at her apartment."

"But Jack stayed home that night. He *told* me he was home."

Frankie pulls out the printout of Taryn's text messages and shoves it toward her. "Then how do you explain *this*?"

Maggie stares at what her husband texted to his mistress. There it is, printed in black and white, the evidence that he lied to his wife.

Tonite, your place. Wait for me.

"He wrote that on Friday evening, the same night Taryn Moore died. While you were in the hospital, busting your butt as a doctor and saving lives, your hubby slipped out of bed — *your* bed. He drove to his girlfriend's apartment, the girlfriend who'd been causing him all that trouble, and he took care of the problem. He cleaned up the blood to make it look like a suicide, and then he went home. In time to be back in bed when you returned."

"No. This is all wrong."

"Where is your husband right now?"

"This can't possibly be —"

"Tell me where he is."

"He's probably at home."

"He's not there. We've been watching your house."

"Then he's at the university."

"He's not there either."

"Oh God, this isn't happening!" Clutching her head, Maggie stares down at the table. "I know my husband. I know what kind of man he is, and he can't even kill a fucking *spider.* How the hell could he . . ." She stops, her gaze fixed on the printout of text messages. "Maybe he didn't write this," she says softly.

"Oh, come on. You can see it was sent from *his* phone. Friday, six thirty-seven p.m."

"Friday," Maggie murmurs. For a moment she sits perfectly still, staring at the sheet of paper. "That's the night it rained so hard. The night we had dinner and . . ." Her head snaps up. She rises from the chair. "I think I know where Jack is."

"Dr. Dorian! Where are you going?"

Maggie doesn't even glance back as she

heads for the door. "I'm going to save my husband."

CHAPTER 45
JACK

It was nearly eleven when he arrived at Charlie's house. The only car in the driveway was Charlie's. No silver Lexus. And to his relief, no squad cars.

The bluish glow from the living room told him that the television was on, which meant Charlie was home. But where the hell was Maggie?

As he walked to the front door, he pulled out his cell phone, tempted to power it on and check if Maggie had messaged him. No, bad idea. If he turned it on, the police would be able to track his location. He started to slip it back into his pocket and suddenly paused, thinking. Remembering the evening when he'd received Taryn's text message: I'm pregnant. He remembered how he had gone downstairs to fold Charlie's laundry while Maggie had been upstairs in the kitchen, loading the dishwasher, grinding coffee, setting cups and saucers on the tray. How long was Charlie alone at the dinner table? Five minutes, ten?

Long enough.

For a moment he stood outside Charlie's front door, feeling as if the world had suddenly tilted off its axis. He should leave, now, except that he had nowhere else to go. The police were after him and his life was crumbling, but he had to know the truth.

He used his key and entered the living room. "Charlie?"

"In here," Charlie called out.

Jack made his way into the kitchen, where Charlie sat on a barstool at the island, drinking a glass of whiskey. He was dressed in pajama bottoms and a sweatshirt. The air was laced with the odor of disinfectant and the sour smell of a man full of cancer.

Charlie held up his glass. "Want to join me?"

"No, I'm fine." Jack stood on the other side of the island, facing him. He couldn't reconcile this dying man with the images that were now flashing through his head.

"Everything okay?" Charlie asked.

"Yeah."

"You don't look like it is. Sit down; take a load off your feet." Charlie nodded at an empty barstool.

Jack frowned at the scratches on Charlie's

face and the bruise over his left eye. "What happened to you?"

Charlie made a dismissive shrug. "Slipped in the shower."

"Even after we installed those grab bars?"

"I wasn't quick enough to catch myself."

"Actually, I think I'll have that drink." Jack lowered himself onto the barstool.

Charlie pushed himself to his feet. He hobbled over to the cabinet where he stored the liquor, then crossed to another cabinet near the stove to fetch a glass. Jack tensed as Charlie opened the cabinet door. On the top shelf of that cabinet was where Charlie kept his Smith & Wesson .45. But all Charlie removed was a glass.

"Ice?"

Jack allowed himself to breathe. "Straight up is fine."

Charlie poured whiskey and set the glass in front of him. "So what's up?"

"Have you seen Maggie? She hasn't been home."

"Did you try calling her?"

"She doesn't answer."

Charlie hobbled back to the counter and refilled his own glass.

"You're limping," Jack observed.

"I told you. I took a slip in the shower."

"Uh-huh."

Charlie turned to look at Jack. "Why're you staring at me like that?"

"You know that Commonwealth student who died last week? Taryn Moore?"

"Yeah, it's all over the news. Committed suicide, they say."

"The police have changed their minds. They think it might be murder."

"That right?" Charlie took another swallow of whiskey. "Based on what?"

"Based on a text that was sent from my cell phone."

"Come again?"

"The police think I killed Taryn Moore because of a text message sent from my phone. It said I'd meet her at her apartment that night. Funny thing is, I never sent that message. I never went to her place. And I certainly didn't murder her."

He gave Jack an impassive look. "Okay."

"But *you* did. Didn't you, Charlie?"

"How the hell do you figure that?"

"That Friday you were at our house for dinner. When I went downstairs to do your laundry, I left my phone on the windowsill in the dining room. Taryn must have texted me while you were sitting there, right next to my phone. You saw the message. You know my pass code is Maggie's birth date. *You're* the one who texted her back."

412

Charlie took another sip of whiskey, set down his glass, and wiped his mouth. He then gave Jack a look so poisonous that Jack shrank away. "I knew weeks ago that something was going on between you two. When Maggie said a girl came in to see her, I saw the way you reacted when she said the girl's name. Taryn Moore. I'm not blind. I have an instinct about these things, Jack, and I always have. I hoped I was wrong about you. About her. Then I looked up her Facebook page. I saw her photo." He shook his head in disgust. "You're not the first man to let a pretty face ruin his life. But I thought you were a better man than that."

"But I'm not the one who murdered her. I'm not the one who sent her that text. *You* went to her apartment to kill her, Charlie. *You* threw her off the balcony."

"Two out of three."

"Two out of three what?"

"Yes, I sent the text, then deleted it so you wouldn't know. And yes, I went to her apartment. Didn't even need to hunt down her address. There it was, right in your contacts. But I didn't go there to kill her."

"You sent that text to frame me."

"No. I did it to fix the fucking mess you made! I did it for *you,* goddamn it. And for my daughter and my grandchild. I did it to

413

save your family. But I most certainly did not go there to kill her."

"Then how the hell did she end up dead?"

"I went to apologize on *your* behalf. I told her I was sorry for all her problems, blah, blah, blah. Said I was willing to pay for an abortion. She refused." He stood up, went to the freezer, and dug around through the packages of frozen food. He took out an envelope and slapped it onto the counter where Jack was sitting.

"What's this?"

"Open it."

Jack opened the envelope, and a banded brick of cash fell out. He stared at the bundle of fifty-dollar bills lying on the counter.

"Five thousand dollars," Charlie said. "I keep it in the freezer for emergencies."

"You were going to give this to her? To pay her off?"

"She told me to go fuck myself. She didn't want my money. I told her I didn't know whose baby it was, and I didn't care. But I'd give her the benefit of the doubt that it was yours. I told her that I loved my daughter and didn't want your affair to destroy her marriage. Her happiness." There was nothing in Charlie's face that suggested he was lying, no involuntary flicker of his eye, no telltale twitch. Just that tired old face full of conviction.

"And?" Jack asked.

"The fool girl went ballistic. Said she didn't want my fucking hush money. That I couldn't buy her off, not with a million dollars. So I asked her what she wanted, and that's when she got ugly. She said she wanted to bring you down, to destroy you. And she didn't give a shit who else got hurt."

"And then what happened?"

"I slapped her. I couldn't help it. The way she was talking about my Maggie, as if she didn't matter. As if my grandchild was nothing but a nuisance. I slapped her across the face, and she came at me like a fucking lunatic. I tried to hold her off, but she reached for a statue on her bookshelf and swung at me."

"She *hit* you?"

"Would have cracked my skull if I hadn't swung back. She fell, slammed her head on the coffee table. When she didn't move, I thought she might be dead, but then I saw she was still breathing. Oh, I thought about calling nine-one-one. Then I thought about the consequences if she woke up and told everyone what I did. What you did. Most of all, I thought about Maggie and how that

415

— that cheap piece of *trash* could destroy Maggie's happiness. That girl was relentless. She'd never give up, so I had no choice. I had to finish it.

"I dragged her to the balcony. Figured the fall would mess her up enough to hide the fact she'd already slammed her head on the coffee table. I took care of your problem. And then I cleaned up all the blood."

"You *really* thought the truth wouldn't come out?"

"I was a cop, Jack. I know how hard they're worked. I figured they'd just call it a suicide, close the case, and walk away."

But Detective Frances Loomis hadn't. She was never going to walk away.

Jack shook his head, stunned by Charlie's confession. "She was still alive. And you *killed* her."

Charlie took a long wet breath, suddenly looking frail, as if he were standing on the edge of his own grave. "I haven't got much time left before I step off this bus, and I don't give a rosy-red shit about what happens to me. But I do care what happens to Maggie. I care about the baby and, by association, you. I had to do *something.*"

"But you pinned it on *me.*"

"I tried not to. I took her cell phone to hide those text messages. Smashed it so it couldn't be tracked. I really thought the police wouldn't bother to look for it."

"They got hold of the messages. They think I did it."

"Don't blame me for that. You're the one who got yourself into this mess." Those ice-blue eyes pinned Jack to his seat. "Did you love the girl?"

"No."

"Then why? Why risk losing everything just to fuck her?"

Jack flinched at the question. "It was a mistake," he said quietly. "If I could turn back the clock . . ."

"Does Maggie know?"

"Yes."

Charlie took several deep breaths, and Jack could hear the cancer gurgling in his chest. "Well, you made a clean sweep of your life. You fucked up your marriage. You fucked up that girl's life. And you'll never see the inside of another classroom. Way to go, Jackie boy."

A sound from the other room. The front door opening and closing. Jack jumped to his feet. "Maggie?" he called, relieved that she'd finally arrived.

But when he stepped into the living room, it wasn't Maggie standing there. He halted, staring at the intruder who loomed before him, eyes like burning coals in the shadow of the baseball cap.

"Cody," Jack said. "Why —"

"I loved her. And you didn't."

"You shouldn't have followed me. I'm calling the police." Jack reached for his cell phone, but it was still powered off. Frantic, he pushed the on switch.

"Now I'm going to finish it."

Only then did Jack focus on what Cody held in his hand: a crowbar. Even as Jack registered what Cody was about to do, even as Cody raised the weapon, Jack could not move, could not speak.

The crowbar came hurtling at his skull.

At the last instant, Jack dived to his right, flinging himself behind an armchair, and landed hard on his elbows. He heard wood splinter as the crowbar crashed onto the coffee table.

Cody pivoted toward him, moving faster than Jack had ever thought he could. Before Jack could scramble to his feet, Cody swung the crowbar like a baseball bat. It slammed against Jack's ribs, and he sprawled to the floor, stunned. As he lay there, trying to catch his breath, his chest screaming in pain from the blow, he heard Cody's heavy footsteps moving closer.

The footsteps halted, and Jack saw the

boy's shoes planted right by his head. In a telescoped moment he saw Cody raise the crowbar like a club over Jack's skull. And he thought: This *is how I die.* A fitting finale to all that he'd set in motion from the moment he'd let Taryn Moore enter his life.

"Drop it, or I'll blow your fucking head off." Charlie stood in the doorway, his .45 aimed at Cody.

Cody froze, still gripping his crowbar.

"I said drop it!"

Cody looked down at Jack, then at Charlie.

Jack dragged himself to his feet and staggered toward Charlie. "Don't hurt him," he said. "He's just a kid."

"A *kid?*" Cody's voice rose in fury. *"That's* what you think, you bastard? That I'm *just a kid?"*

Jack's back was turned to him, but he could feel the force of Cody's rage rushing toward him, as inescapable as death. He saw Charlie's gun wavering in the grip of unsteady hands, the barrel trembling toward Jack and away and back toward him.

The gun blast threw a punch to his chest. Jack stumbled backward against a wall. Looking down, he saw red seep through his shirt in an ever-spreading stain.

"Oh no," Charlie wailed. "God, no!"

In fury, Charlie wrenched the crowbar out of Cody's hands and whacked him in the back of the knees. The boy screamed and collapsed to the floor, whimpering.

The lights seemed to be flickering in and out. Jack's legs slid away beneath him. He heard Charlie's wet and rattling breaths as he leaned close.

"You're going to be okay, Jack," he muttered. "You have to be okay."

Jack tried to say something but could not draw in a breath. How had he ended up on the floor? Why couldn't he feel his own limbs? A chill spread through him, as if ice water were pumping through his veins.

In the distance he heard the crash of the door flying open. Haloed by the light was the one face he wanted to see, a face sent from heaven. *Maggie.*

"He's going to be all right!" Charlie insisted.

Jack heard cloth ripping, then felt Maggie's warm hands pressing against his chest, trying to hold back the blood that was spilling out of him.

"Jack, baby, hold on for me," she pleaded. She turned and yelled, "Detective Loomis! Tell them to have the cardiothoracic team standing by!"

He wanted to tell her he was sorry. That

he loved her. But his voice wouldn't work. And it was hard, so hard, just to draw in a breath. He looked at Maggie's bloodstained hand, pressed against his chest, and focused on her diamond ring. The ring he'd placed there twelve years ago. *I'd marry you again. Again and again and again.*

If only he could have said the words out loud. If only he could say so many things, but already the room was fading to black. The darkness descended, blotting out the face of the woman he loved.

CHAPTER 46
FRANKIE

Too many things are happening all at once: Cody, red faced and flailing as two officers wrestle him to the ground and handcuff him. Maggie kneeling beside her husband, who lies sprawled and unconscious in a widening pool of blood. The far-off wail of an approaching ambulance. And Maggie's father, Charlie, standing with his head bowed, his face as gray as a corpse's. The weapon he has handed to Frankie is still warm, and it carries the acrid stench of gunfire.

"I didn't mean to hurt him, Maggie," the old man moans. "I swear I didn't mean to hurt anyone."

"Stay with me, Jack," Maggie begs. "Please, stay with me!" She's pulled off her scarf, and as she presses it to her husband's wound, blood instantly transforms the beige cashmere into red. "Towels!" Maggie yells to her father. "I need towels!"

Charlie is too stunned to move. It's Mac who runs into the bathroom and comes back holding a bundle of hand towels. Maggie presses them to Jack's wound, trying to stanch the flow of blood. She is the only person in the room who might be able to save him, but already the battle seems lost. Jack's breaths, shallow and rapid, have the rattle of drowning lungs. Maggie looks up at Frankie. "I can't stop the bleeding."

"I didn't mean to shoot him," Charlie says again. Unsteady, he wobbles toward a chair and sinks down. "All I ever wanted was to make everything right. Make you happy, Maggie," he moans. No one is listening to him. In the chaos of the room, he is a forgotten old man, lost in his own grief.

Outside, the ambulance whoops to a stop, and two paramedics sweep into the house, adding yet more bodies to the pandemonium. They rip open bandages, insert IV lines, slap on an oxygen mask. The EKG beeps the frantic rhythm of a heart racing to stay alive. Frankie can only stand back and let other people work. Even Maggie is little more than a shell-shocked bystander. The paramedics are in charge, and she watches, numb and silent, as her husband's blood dries on her hands.

"Okay, we're ready to move him," the

paramedic says.

"Where?" asks Maggie.

"Mass General. Trauma team's already waiting."

Maggie grabs her purse. "I'll be right behind you."

"Dr. Dorian, wait," says Frankie.

"I'm going to the hospital."

"We need you here to —"

"Fuck that. I need to be with my *husband,"* Maggie snaps and follows the paramedics out the door.

Frankie lets her leave. She surveys the detritus the paramedics have left behind: torn packaging and stained gauze and a forgotten tourniquet, coiled like a snake swimming in the pool of blood. The blood of an innocent man.

A police officer has already led Cody Atwood out to the patrol car, but Maggie's father is still sitting in his chair, head bowed, shoulders drooping. He looks as frail as a sack of old bones. Maggie told them Charlie is dying of cancer, and Frankie can see it in the man's wasted temples, can smell it in this house where the air is sour with sickness.

She pulls over a chair and sits down so they can be face to face. "Mr. Lucas," she says. "I need to inform you of your rights."

"No need to. I know my rights. I was a cop. Cambridge PD."

Frankie glances up at Mac, who's already pulled out the handcuffs, and she shakes her head. The handcuffs can wait. This man is not going to fight them. Everything about him signals defeat, and she thinks they owe him some semblance of respect because, after all, he was once one of them.

"You killed Taryn Moore. Didn't you?"

"I had no choice. She brought it on herself."

"I don't understand."

"She attacked my family. She attacked *me.*" Charlie's head comes up, and he meets her gaze. As frail as he is, his eyes are coldly defiant. "You and I, we're both cops. You've seen the same things I have, so you understand. You know as well as I do that this world would be a much better place if certain people weren't in it."

"People like Taryn Moore."

He nods. "Girls like her, you can't talk sense to them. You can't reason with them. They're like wild animals who need to be reined in. Controlled."

Staring into Charlie's eyes, Frankie realizes he actually believes what he's just said, that the world would be better off without women like Taryn, women whose

425

turbulent emotions and desperate choices complicate the lives of men. She thinks of her own spirited daughters who so passionately embrace life and sometimes get into trouble for it. She thinks of the tragic heroines whom Taryn wrote about, the Medeas and the Queen Didos — women who loved too deeply and who suffered for it.

No, thinks Frankie. The world would *not* be better without such women.

"That girl had to be stopped," says Charlie. "My family needed to be protected. I just did what I needed to do."

"Now I'm going to do what I need to do." Frankie takes Mac's handcuffs and places them over Charlie's wrists.

They close with a deeply satisfying snap.

CHAPTER 47
FRANKIE

Maggie Dorian sits at her husband's bedside, her head bowed as though in prayer. Through the beeping monitors and the whoosh of the ventilator, she doesn't seem to hear Frankie enter the SICU cubicle. Only when Frankie stands facing her across the bed does Maggie at last look up at her.

"I can't believe you're still here," Frankie says.

"Where else would I be?"

"You should go home and get some sleep."

"No, I need to be here when he wakes up." Maggie reaches out to grasp her husband's hand and adds, in a whisper: "If he wakes up."

Frankie surveys the various tubes snaking into and out of the inert body and focuses on the EKG monitor, where the rhythm is rapid but steady. It is a miracle that he has any heartbeat at all. After all the blood he lost, all the devastation left by Charlie's bullet, Jack Dorian should be dead, and his wife should be planning his funeral.

Something that will probably come to pass.

Frankie pulls up a chair and sits down. For a long time, neither woman speaks, and the only sound is the wheeze of the ventilator cycling its twenty breaths per minute. What words of comfort can she offer to a woman whose life has so completely collapsed into ruins? Maggie's father, Charlie, will almost certainly die of cancer in prison. Her husband might never awaken, and she will be left to raise their child on her own. In all this tragedy, that was the one point of light: there is a baby on the way.

"How is my father?" The question is asked so softly Frankie almost misses it.

"Charlie is cooperating. Fully. He understands what will happen to him next, and he's prepared for it." Frankie pauses. "I promise I'll do everything I can to make sure he's kept comfortable till the end."

Maggie sighs, as if sorrow is squeezing the breath out of her. "I can't believe he actually did it. That's not the father I grew up with."

"He told us he never planned to kill the girl. He just wanted her to leave you and Jack alone. He went to her apartment hoping to buy her silence, but she became angry. She struck him, he defended himself, and there was a struggle. He let his rage get the best of him, and he lost control. After it was over, he tried to salvage the situation by making it look like suicide. That, at least, is what he told us. I don't know if all of that is true, but I *am* certain he was trying to protect you, Maggie. Trying to save your marriage."

"I know." Her hand tightens around her husband's inert hand. "And now I might lose both of them."

Frankie does not tell Maggie what else she's learned about Charlie Lucas, after a phone call to Cambridge PD Internal Affairs. She does not tell her about the prisoner whose skull he fractured or the cocaine he was suspected of planting during a drug raid. She does not tell Maggie that Charlie retired under a cloud of suspicion after he had taken his brand of justice too far. No, Maggie does not need to know any of this; she has more than enough heartbreak to deal with now.

"Please, Jack," Maggie whispers. "Come back to me."

Frankie stares at Maggie's fingers, twined around the hand of the man who was unfaithful to her, the man whose brief and

429

reckless fling led to so much pain and bloodshed. "And if he does wake up?" Frankie asks. "What happens then?"

"Would you forgive him? If he were your husband?"

"It's not my decision. It's yours."

Maggie stares at Jack and gently strokes back his hair. "After twelve years of marriage, sometimes it's hard to remember what made you fall in love in the first place. Why you ended up with *this* particular person. And for a while, maybe I did forget. And so did he. But last night, when he was lying on the floor, when I saw all that blood and I thought I was losing him . . ." Maggie looks up at her. "I remembered why I fell in love. I don't know if that's enough to make me forgive him. But I *do* remember."

A nurse enters the cubicle. "Excuse me, Detective? If you could step out for a moment, I need to check the patient's vital signs."

"I was about to leave anyway," says Frankie, and she rises to her feet. "Take care of yourself, Dr. Dorian," she says to Maggie. "Go home and get some rest."

"I will."

But when Frankie walks out of the cubicle and glances back through the window, she sees that Maggie hasn't moved. She is still at her husband's side, stroking his hair, waiting for him to wake up.

Frankie drives home through deserted streets, her vision blurred by a haze of fatigue. Even though it's now April, this night has turned clear and frosty, a step backward toward winter. She is tired of the cold, tired of wearing wool scarves and down jackets. Tired of shivering at death scenes.

She has vacation time coming up, two weeks during which she could drink piña coladas while lying on a beach somewhere, but she knows herself too well. This will not happen. Instead she will almost certainly spend her vacation at home with the girls.

While she still can.

When she walks into her apartment, she's glad to see that both her daughters' coats are hanging in the closet, relieved that her family is safely home for the night. Just to be certain, she peeks into their room, and yes, there they are, sound asleep in their beds after yet another night out. Though the beds are on opposite sides of the room, they lie facing each other, Gabby on her left, Sibyl on her right, as though reaching out to embrace each other, the way they did while sharing her womb. It makes Frankie happy, knowing her daughters have this bond. If marriages fall apart or husbands disappoint, at least the girls will have each other to lean on.

She closes their door and goes into the kitchen. She's exhausted, running on empty, but she knows she won't be able to sleep. Not yet. After tonight's events, she needs to sit quietly and take a few deep breaths. From the cupboard she grabs the scotch and, out of habit, checks the bottle to be sure the level hasn't dipped beneath the tiny black dot she last drew on it with permanent marker. The level is right where it should be, so she knows the girls haven't been sipping. Oh yes, Mama knows how to keep an eye on her babies. She pours out a generous glug, takes a deep swallow, and thinks about Taryn Moore and Charlie Lucas, about Jack and Maggie Dorian.

Most of all she thinks about Maggie, the woman who had everything until suddenly she didn't. But that is the nature of tragedy. You go through life never appreciating the joy of a normal day until the instant it's gone. All it takes is a knock on the door. A police officer standing outside to inform you that your husband is dead, found collapsed in a stranger's stairwell. You think you'll never know a normal day again.

You bury the body, pick up the pieces of

your life. You stumble forward, into the new normal. That's what Maggie Dorian will have to do, with or without her husband.

Frankie carries her empty whiskey glass to the sink, and as she stands there, stretching out the kinks in her neck, she hears her cell phone ring. Oh no, she thinks. Even as she pulls the phone out of her purse, she is steeling herself for the news. She looks at the caller's number.

It is the hospital.

CHAPTER 48
FRANKIE

Fourteen months later

Two granite gravestones lie side by side, each decorated with its own pot of geraniums. The flaming-red blossoms are too much of a temptation for any baby to resist, and Nicholas Charles Dorian, seven months old, crawls across the grass like the speediest of turtles, moving straight for the nearest plant. Just as he closes one chubby fist around a blossom, Maggie scoops up her son, and he lets out a wail of frustration.

"Oh, sweetie, let's find something else for you to play with. What's in our big bag here, hmmm? Look, a pretty pony!" She hands Nicky a stuffed animal, but he's not interested, and he flings the pony onto the grass.

"He really wants that geranium," observes Frankie.

"Isn't that just how it goes?" Maggie laughs. "They always want what they can't have."

434

"Here, let me take him. I'll walk him over to the pond."

Frankie takes the baby and carries him down to the cemetery's duck pond. She has never been to Mount Auburn Cemetery before, and she marvels at the beauty of the place on this warm June day. Across the water is the neoclassical rotunda that is the final resting place of Mary Baker Eddy. The trees have fully leafed out, sparrows chirp overhead, and the sky is a bright-blue dome with a pale crescent moon hovering just above the tree line. She inhales Nicky's scent of baby shampoo, and a flood of memories washes over her: Her twins splashing in their plastic bathtub. Their fat legs kicking as she changed their diapers. Those exhausting but exhilarating nights of their infancy. She misses those days, especially now, since both her daughters have left for college. How good it feels to be holding a baby in her arms again, to rub her cheek against a downy head.

The walk to the pond did the trick; Nicky has forgotten all about those tempting geraniums, and his attention is now focused on what is swimming in the water.

"Those are ducks," says Frankie, pointing to the mallards paddling by. "They go *quack, quack*. Can you say *quack, quack*?"

Nicky only squeals.

She tries to remember how old her twins were when they said their first words. A year? Older? It all seems so long ago. She is now old enough to be a grandmother, and during Maggie's pregnancy, that's the role Frankie was happy to step into, because she does not know how long it will be before she'll hold a grandchild of her own. In the seven months since Nicky was born, Frankie has brought baby clothes and blankets and a never-ending stream of advice. Maggie Dorian is like a daughter to her now, and Frankie has come to admire the woman's strength and optimism. Like Frankie, Maggie is a survivor.

As Frankie carries the baby back from the pond, Maggie spreads a blanket on the grass and unpacks their picnic. It's a simple affair: tuna sandwiches and potato chips, fruit salad and chocolate chip cookies. The cookies are Frankie's contribution, something she hasn't baked since her girls were children and her hips were a few sizes slimmer. All this food Maggie lays out only a few yards from the gravestones, which seems a sad place for a picnic, but Maggie says this is a Lucas family tradition. Every June, her father, Charlie, used to bring her here to picnic at her late mother's grave. It is a way to feel close to those who've passed, and now she is carrying on the tradition.

Maggie pours Lagavulin whiskey into a shot glass and kneels beside her father's gravestone. Six months ago, while in prison hospice, Charlie's cancer finally took him, but at least he lived long enough to lay eyes on his new grandson.

"Love you, Dad," Maggie says and pours the shot of whiskey onto his grave, letting the precious liquor soak into the grass. "Drink up."

Frankie hears a car engine and turns to see a blue Audi pull to a stop nearby. Out climbs Jack, moving slowly as he plants first one foot and then the other on the ground. Despite a year of physical therapy, his legs are still weak from the injury to his spine, and he grips a cane as he hobbles toward them.

"Sorry I'm late," he says, shaking his head. "I left my apartment right on time, but I didn't allow for weekend traffic. How's my big boy?"

"He's probably ready for a bottle now, if you want to feed him," says Maggie. She slides a folding chair toward Jack so he can sit. Frankie gives him the baby and hands him a bottle of formula.

"Lunch, Nicky boy!" Jack smiles as his

son hungrily gulps down the milk. "Wow, you feel like you've gained a pound in just a week!"

As Jack feeds his son, Frankie notes the new streaks of gray in his hair and how deeply the lines now etch his face. He has aged in the last year, but he seems calmer and resigned to his losses. Since he was fired from Commonwealth, the only class he teaches is a weekly literature course to inmates at the Massachusetts Correctional Institution at Concord. His days as a university professor are gone forever, and surely he must grieve the loss of his status and his paycheck, but at this moment it does not show. Certainly not now, as he lovingly cradles his son.

Maggie comes to stand beside Jack, and she rests her hand on his shoulder as they both smile down at the baby. Although they no longer share a home, these two will always share their son. And perhaps someday in the future, they will once again share their lives. But healing must come first, and on this fine summer day, they seem to be moving in the right direction.

In Frankie's line of work, there are no happy endings; there is only grief and loss and tragedy. For the rest of his life, Jack Dorian will surely be haunted by all three.

He has destroyed his job and his marriage. He will always bear the physical scars from the bullet. Worst of all, he will never escape his role in the death of a vibrant young woman. No, thinks Frankie, this cannot be called a happy ending.

But in this moment, it comes close enough.

ACKNOWLEDGMENTS

We would like to thank Mark Jannoni of Northeastern University for his guidance on university compliance with Title IX policies.

We also thank Linda Marrow for her editorial expertise and encouragement during the early stages of the manuscript.

For her insight and good humor, our deepest thanks to the ever-savvy Meg Ruley, who is any writer's dream agent. And a special thanks to our editor, Grace Doyle, whose wise guidance and positive spirit made this a better book. It was a pleasure working with her and the dedicated marketing-and-publicity team at Thomas & Mercer: Sarah Shaw, Lindsey Bragg, and Brittany Russell.

ABOUT THE AUTHORS

International bestselling author **Tess Gerritsen** took an unusual route to a writing career: it wasn't until she was on maternity leave from her job as a physician that she began to write. Since then, she's written twenty-eight suspense novels, with more than thirty million copies sold. Her books have been translated into forty languages, and her series featuring homicide detective Jane Rizzoli and medical examiner Maura Isles inspired the hit TNT television series *Rizzoli & Isles,* starring Angie Harmon and Sasha Alexander. Gerritsen now writes full time and lives in Maine.

Gary Braver — pen name of college professor Gary Goshgarian — is the bestselling author of eight critically acclaimed mysteries and thrillers, including *Gray Matter* and *Flashback,* the first thriller to win the Massachusetts Book Award. His work has been translated into several languages; two have been optioned for film, including *Elixir*. As Gary Goshgarian, he teaches science fiction, horror fiction, bestsellers, and fiction writing at Northeastern University. He lives with his family outside Boston. Learn more at www.garybraver.com.